SAVED
by the
MATCHMAKER

Books by Jody Hedlund

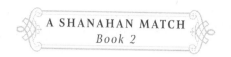

A SHANAHAN MATCH
Book 2

SAVED
by the
MATCHMAKER

Jody Hedlund

BETHANYHOUSE
a division of Baker Publishing Group
Minneapolis, Minnesota

© 2024 by Jody Hedlund

Published by Bethany House Publishers
Minneapolis, Minnesota
BethanyHouse.com

Bethany House Publishers is a division of
Baker Publishing Group, Grand Rapids, Michigan

Printed in the United States of America

Library of Congress Cataloging-in-Publication Data
Names: Hedlund, Jody, author.
Title: Saved by the matchmaker / Jody Hedlund.
Description: Minneapolis, Minnesota : Bethany House, a division of Baker
  Publishing Group, 2024. | Series: A Shanahan Match ; 2
Identifiers: LCCN 2023048236 | ISBN 9780764241970 (paper) | ISBN 9780764243110
  (casebound) | ISBN 9781493446506 (ebook)
Subjects: LCGFT: Christian fiction. | Romance fiction. | Novels.
Classification: LCC PS3608.E333 S28 2024 | DDC 813/.6—dc23/eng/20231013
LC record available at https://lccn.loc.gov/2023048236

Cover design by Jennifer Parker
Cover image of couple: Ildiko Neer / Trevillion Images
Cover image of steamboat railing: Arcangel Vintage Collection / Arcangel
Cover image of steamboat: Science History Images J Alamy Stock Photo
Cover images: Shutterstock

Baker Publishing Group publications use paper produced from sustainable forestry practices and postconsumer waste whenever possible.

24 25 26 27 28 29 30   7 6 5 4 3 2 1

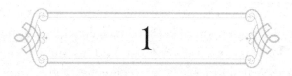

1

World's biggest fool.

The words felt engraved on Enya Shanahan's forehead. Not only did they feel engraved, but they were probably also blaring in bright colors that not even the darkness of the dreary Shrove Tuesday evening could hide.

No doubt her da and brother Kiernan, both sitting in the barouche on the seat across from her, could see the bold lettering as they spoke together, congratulating themselves on cleaning up the mess she'd made of her life.

She turned her face to the window, as if that could somehow transport her away from her shame and guilt—a shame and guilt that had been her constant companions in the two weeks since she'd returned home after her short-lived and failed marriage to Bryan Haynes.

Aye, she was the world's biggest fool, to be sure, for giving her heart and body to Bryan.

The knots in her chest yanked tighter. The lying scum.

The cowardly ratbag. The cheating hornswoggler. She hated him and hoped he'd drown in a river during his trek to the California goldfields. Well, maybe not drown. But at least that he wouldn't find a speck of gold, not even gold dust.

"I didn't doubt the archbishop would give us the annulment." Kiernan's voice held too much cockiness for his own good. He'd taken off his top hat, and his auburn hair was combed casually forward. It was much browner than Da's and hers, which happened to be a flaming red that rivaled a summer sunset. Kiernan also had blue eyes and not the green that Da and she also shared.

In his low-cut vest and tightly tailored frock coat, her older brother made a dashing picture as always. His high collar and cravat brushed against his smooth chin and cheeks, and his handsome features contained the distinct Shanahan heart-shaped face, wide cheekbones, and dimple in his chin.

Da was loosening his own cravat. "It was easy to prove the fellow never intended to have a permanent relationship with Enya." Her da's tone was gentler, but it held immeasurable relief.

Enya squeezed her eyes closed and fought back the hot tears that came all too easily over recent days.

He was relieved the marriage scandal was behind them, that he'd found a stipulation among those accepted by the Church that would allow for the annulment.

Little did he know the scandal had only just begun.

The carriage wheels hit a rut in the unpaved road and tossed Enya up and down several times. Her already queasy stomach lurched in protest, and she cupped her hand over her mouth to hold back the nausea.

She had to say something. But she also didn't want to ruin Da and Kiernan's good moods after so difficult a meeting with the archbishop and other church officiants. Da's wealth and prestige had likely moved the annulment proceedings along more swiftly and easily than usual. Even so, the process had been unnerving for all of them.

"I'd like to put the past behind us." Da leaned back against the leather seat as though trying to get comfortable, which was nearly impossible with all the jostling. The streets in St. Louis were notoriously bad, especially in February with the winter cold and snow.

Though the interior of the carriage was dark, the outside lantern attached to the front side of the conveyance illuminated enough to see Da smile warmly her way. "We'll leave the city tomorrow morn, so we will."

"Thank you, Da. That will be lovely." She couldn't muster a return smile, but she appreciated his efforts to soothe her nonetheless.

Kiernan's brow crinkled. "We discussed moving back home now that the spread of cholera is waning."

The dreaded and deadly cholera had arrived in St. Louis last month shortly after the new year started. Many families, including theirs, had panicked and left the city, expecting the illness to take a devastating toll the same way it had a decade earlier. But so far, it hadn't spread as the naysayers had predicted. Now many people were resuming life as normal.

"Aye," Da said. "It won't be hurting us to stay at Oakland a wee bit longer now, will it?"

Kiernan didn't respond, usually unable to oppose their da—unlike her. Of her brothers and sisters, she'd ended up getting most of the spitfire. She had enough to spread out among all five Shanahan children, with leftovers to distribute to a dozen more people.

"If Kiernan wants to linger in the city, I don't mind staying." Enya clutched the edge of the seat as the barouche bounced again over the uneven street.

Kiernan shot her a grateful look.

Her brother clearly didn't want to go back to their country home. Was he bored there? More likely he had a woman or two in the city he missed and wanted spend time with. And now that their oldest sister, Finola, was happily married, he was ready to enlist the services of the local matchmaker in forming his match.

Of course, with the start of Lent tomorrow, a wedding would have to wait for at least forty days since the Church frowned upon marriages during the holy weeks leading up to Easter.

"We'll be going to the country home." Da's words held the finality of a judge's gavel. "Mind you, it'll be for the best. Until the wagging tongues have nothing else to say."

Of course Da would be worried about what everyone was thinking. The Shanahan image was so gloriously important to him. More important than anything else. "Tongues will wag no matter what we do. So we may as well ignore them."

"We can be doing our best not to fuel them." This time her da's voice contained an edge.

"Do you think I want to fuel them?" An edge crept into her tone too. This was the problem. No matter how much she and Da tried to be civil to each other, they ended up arguing.

Kiernan's gaze bounced back and forth between Da and

her, and he opened his mouth as though he intended to jump into the conversation and intervene before full-scale fighting commenced.

But Da spoke again first. "Try, Enya." Da was sitting up tall on his seat now, his backbone as rigid as a lamppost. "That's all I expect."

"I have tried."

"If we live rightly, then we don't have to be worrying about the gossipmongers, now do we?" His voice rose a notch.

Hers did likewise. "I did live rightly. I wasn't living in sin."

"You ran off with a dirty, damp dog!"

"At least I got married!"

"You married the dog without my permission!"

"I don't need your permission for everything I do." Her declaration rang hollow. The one time she'd broken free of her parents' strict control—to choose her own marriage partner—the situation had ended in disaster.

"You're my daughter, and as long as you're living under my roof, you'll do as I say, that you will." Da's words now boomed in the small confines of the carriage. Even in the dim lighting, it was easy to see that his face had reddened, and his thick brows furrowed together above flashing eyes.

All the angst inside her swirled into an eddy that was quickly sucking her down. "Maybe I'll find another place to live." She tossed out the threat, even though she wouldn't be able to follow through on it, would never be able to live where she wanted, and wouldn't be able to support herself. Not as a single young woman.

"You'll live at Oakland until summer, so you will." Da sat back and dropped his voice a decibel. "Now, say no more about it."

She hated that her da could cut her off with such callousness, giving no merit to her opinions and ideas. But that's the way it had always been, not only with where to live and who to marry but how to spend her time, including the dreams she'd once had about composing music and becoming a concert pianist.

The heat of anger and helplessness roiling inside swelled, like a boiler about to explode.

"I'm pregnant." The words bubbled up and spilled over before she could stop them. The only person she'd told about her pregnancy was Finola. But now, ready or not, the news was out.

Her da's eyes rounded, shifted to her stomach, then returned to her face.

She jutted her chin and met his gaze, letting him see the truth. Because it was the truth. She'd known the day after she'd missed her courses last month. And now that she'd skipped a second month, there was no denying it.

He held himself rigidly only a moment longer before his shoulders slumped and the hard lines of his face melded into haggardness.

Of course. She'd disappointed him again. As usual.

"Sweet blessed mother, Enya," he whispered. "What am I to be doing with you now?"

"Nothing." She shot the word past the ache that pushed into her throat. "I'll take care of myself and my baby—"

"She'll get married, that's what." Kiernan knocked against the front of the carriage to get the attention of the coachman.

"I don't want to get married." At least not so soon after the disaster of a marriage with Bryan.

But Kiernan was already calling out instructions to the coachman and taking charge of the situation, which was something he was good at, a quality he'd inherited from their da.

Aye, she knew her da had worked hard over the years to build up the Shanahan name and reputation and that Kiernan was trying to build a name for himself too. But why couldn't he stop for a moment and acknowledge that she had a baby growing inside her and show some support instead of rushing to fix her again?

Kiernan twisted back around on his seat. "We'll try to find someone for Enya to marry."

Her da shook his head. "We're out of time. The wedding will have to wait until after Lent, and by then, it will be too late to attribute the child to the new husband."

Kiernan's jaw was set with determination, and he glanced at Enya's abdomen. "How far along are you?"

She settled a hand on her stomach. It was still flat. But her da was right. After Easter, she'd be almost four months pregnant. "If you hope to make some poor fellow believe my child is his, you're out of luck."

"Ach, no," her da said.

Kiernan recoiled. "Holy thundering mother, Enya. No. Of course not. We're not aiming to trick anyone."

"Then why does everyone need to believe the baby belongs to a new husband?" She already knew the answer, but she wanted to make her point—that they cared more about appearances than about her.

"Now that we have the annulment," Kieran said, his voice filled with sincerity, "we want to put your past behind you and give you a fresh start."

A fresh start, someplace away from her da's disappointment? Aye, she'd take it. And keeping her distance from Mam? Aye, she'd take that, too, because once Mam learned of the pregnancy, Da's disappointment would look like sheer joy in comparison. Maybe not quite. But Mam's judgment would be worse. Much worse.

Enya buried her face in her hands. She couldn't bear to face Mam. Not tomorrow. Not the next day. Not anytime soon.

If only there was a way to magically sail away someplace where no one knew about her or her family. . . .

"We'll find a nice Irish fellow and a good Catholic who will make a fine husband for you." Kiernan spoke smoothly and softly. He'd obviously learned well over the years that such a method worked better with her than Da's more direct approach.

Her da released an exasperated breath. "We don't have time, Kiernan."

"We didn't use up all the favors owed to us." The arrogance returned to Kiernan's tone. "I'm sure if we went to the archbishop next week or even the week after and asked him to make an exception for Enya, he probably would allow for a wedding."

Da shook his head. "Requesting a hasty annulment is one thing. But I can't push for more."

"You don't have to. I will."

The barouche rolled to a stop, but not in front of their home. Instead, they were still in the business district.

A group of strawboys singing boisterously swaggered past the carriage. They were wearing tall, conical-shaped hats made from straw that rested on their shoulders, concealing their identities. A few even had straw stuck into their clothes.

Ancient lore predicted that a newly married couple would be very lucky if strawboys showed up at their celebration, beating their great sticks against the door, hammering the floor, and joining in the festivities.

Enya scowled. Such joviality shouldn't be allowed. Not tonight. Not now. Not in front of her.

As the fellows passed, the sign on the nearby establishment was all too easy to read. The bright green calligraphy contrasted the white background. Oscar's Pub.

She didn't need anyone to tell her what they were doing here. She already knew. They were visiting the matchmaker.

2

*O*scar won't be here tonight." Her da paused outside the pub door.

Like half the Irish population of St. Louis, the owner of the pub and the local matchmaker, Oscar McKenna, was probably making his way to all the wedding parties, drinking and dancing and taking full advantage of the last night of revelry that would occur until after Easter.

Kiernan guided Enya, having tucked her hand into the crook of his arm. His touch was gentle, as though she were fragile glass that could break with the slightest pressure.

Maybe her brother hadn't exactly been enthusiastic about her news that she was pregnant. But at least he was treating her with extra tenderness and consideration now that he knew she was in the family way.

Her da and Kiernan had admonished her to wait in the barouche while they went inside the pub, since proper women didn't frequent such establishments. Kiernan had even reassured her that he only planned to invite the matchmaker to visit them at their house tomorrow.

But she had no intention of being left behind, not even for the initial contact with the matchmaker.

"We don't need Oscar." Kiernan twisted the doorknob. "Not when we're looking for Bellamy."

As the pub door swung open, Enya halted. "You want Bellamy to find me a husband?"

"Aye." Kiernan's lips rose into a grin. "If anyone is up to the challenge of finding you a husband, Bellamy will be."

Everyone speculated Oscar's youngest son would take over for him, not only in running the pub but also with the matchmaking role. Being the matchmaker was an important job, one Oscar had inherited from his father and grandfather. In fact, the matchmaker blood had been a part of the McKenna family as far back as the days of St. Patrick himself—at least according to Oscar.

Even if Bellamy had succeeded in helping Finola find her true love with Riley Rafferty, that didn't mean he would have success in matching anyone else. He was, after all, a young man of only twenty-two years of age, untried in the ways of love and marriage.

As Kiernan stepped with Enya into the pub, the stale odor of cigar smoke and beer assaulted her, turning her stomach. She sucked in a quick breath and blinked through the hazy, dimly lit room.

Spittoons sat in every corner, and a dozen or more square tables spread out over the establishment. Only two were occupied, and those by older men who weren't partaking in Shrove Tuesday festivities. They paused in their discussions, gawking at the newcomers.

Were they shocked that a lady was entering the pub? Or

were they surprised to see the Shanahans? Either way, Kiernan paid them no heed, and neither did Da.

She'd expected the pub to be busier, even on Shrove Tuesday. But Kiernan had likely known it would be deserted, or he wouldn't have stopped and chanced bringing more embarrassment upon the Shanahan name.

With dark wood paneling covering the walls, the only color in the gloomy barroom came from the lovely oil paintings, each a different setting of somewhere in Ireland, most of rural landscapes depicting the beauty of the old country.

Of course, Enya didn't know what the old country looked like, since she'd been born in St. Louis and had never traveled far beyond their country home, Oakland, just outside the city. But her parents were native-born Irish and had immigrated to America during their youth and ended up in St. Louis on the western frontier.

A lone old fellow with light red hair sat on a stool at a polished mahogany bar counter that ran the length of the room, with shelves lining the wall behind it. Rows of glasses and bottles of all colors and shapes filled the shelves. A tub of dirty dishes and a few mugs, empty except for dregs, littered the counter.

With a nearly untouched glass of amber liquid in front of him, the older patron at the bar swiveled on his stool and stared just like the others had. His face was pale from too much time spent inside the dark pub, and the tip of his nose was large and purplish from a lifetime of heavy drinking.

"Georgie McGuire, where is Bellamy?" Kiernan directed his question to the pale, old man.

"Where is Bellamy?" Georgie's lips curved into a crooked

smile, revealing only a few remaining teeth. "That's the question now. And I'd say it's a good one, to be sure."

Kiernan released Enya and gave her a stern frown, one that cautioned her to remain by the door. Then he stalked toward the bar, her da right on his heels. Their footsteps thudded ominously, so much so that Georgie's smile disappeared, and he picked up his mug and took a slurp, sloshing liquid over the edge.

Kiernan didn't halt at the bar but instead made his way around toward a door that led to the kitchen at the back of the pub. Before he was halfway there, Bellamy, with dark mussed hair, stepped out of the kitchen with a pencil and pad in one hand and a thick leather-bound journal in the other. He was wearing an apron that covered his trousers and vest, and his white dress shirt was rolled up at the sleeves, revealing muscular arms.

There once was a time when Enya had considered Bellamy incredibly attractive. With his tanned skin, well-built physique, and devastating dark brown eyes, he was the kind of man who easily turned the heads of women. But she wouldn't let that happen to her. Not anymore. She'd let one such handsome and charming man turn her head, and she'd learned her lesson.

"Bellamy McKenna." Kiernan approached the matchmaker, hand outstretched. "Just the man we're here to see."

Bellamy set the bulging book on the counter along with his paper and pencil before accepting Kiernan's handshake. "Kiernan Shanahan, what brings you out on a night like this?"

Bellamy's gaze flitted from Da to her to Kiernan and then back to her. He had a sharp gaze, one that seemed to see right past every facade.

Her black velvet cloak was open to reveal one of her best gowns—emerald with the low, V-shaped bodice that made her waist appear smaller and her bosom fuller. Her red hair was coiled in ringlets that were artfully arranged under a velvet cottage bonnet that matched her cloak.

She'd wanted to look her best for the meeting with the archbishop, and from the appreciative glances she'd received throughout the annulment proceedings, she'd succeeded in her efforts at maximizing her womanly allure.

But under Bellamy's scrutiny, her heart quaked. If she really went along with Kiernan's scheme, then she would be putting her fate into Bellamy's hands. What if he didn't like what he discovered about her? Worse yet, what if he didn't understand who she was and what she needed?

Bellamy and Kiernan rounded the bar, and Bellamy greeted Da and shook his hand.

"We need a favor, Bellamy," Da started.

Kiernan half perched on a stool a few down from Georgie. "We're here to discuss the possibility of enlisting your matchmaker services again."

"Are you now?"

"We are."

The few patrons in the place were hanging on to every word of the conversation, especially Georgie McGuire. He seemed to be eating it up as if it were the very food that nourished his body.

Bellamy quirked a brow in that devilishly handsome way of his and then leaned against the counter casually. "So this doesn't have to do with Finola and Riley?"

"Heavens, no." Kiernan released a scoffing laugh. "Those two are so in love it's sickening."

Was that jealousy in Kiernan's tone?

Whatever the case, he was right. Finola and Riley were most definitely in love, so much so that at times it *was* slightly nauseating. Da had told the newly married couple to live in the Shanahan mansion while the rest of the family was in the country, but on occasion when the family had to be in town—like for the meeting today—they were together under one roof with the newlyweds.

Enya was happy for her sister. She really was. But she couldn't deny that it was difficult to watch how much Riley adored Finola. He treated her so tenderly, selflessly, and sweetly. He couldn't seem to get enough of her, was always touching her and sneaking kisses.

It was so different from the way Bryan had interacted with her. Oh sure, he'd been solicitous and amorous right up until their wedding night. It was almost as if he'd been wooing her to get her into bed. And once he'd accomplished the challenge, he'd cast her aside like a half-used cigar no longer worth smoking.

So, aye, maybe she was jealous of Finola too. But she was also realistic enough now to know that what Finola had found with Riley was a rare treasure, one that many couples would never have. She didn't expect to find it for herself. Not anymore. The dreams of having a beautiful and loving marriage died the day Bryan told her good-bye and walked out of her life.

Bellamy was studying Kiernan's face. "I'm taking a wild gander you didn't come for yourself either."

Kiernan tilted his head toward Enya still standing by the door. "We came for Enya."

Finally all eyes in the pub turned upon her. She'd never

minded attention, and at times she rather liked it. But under these circumstances, a slow burn of anger simmered deep inside. Anger that she was in this situation at all and not happily married. Anger that she was carrying a child and had no husband. Anger that if she didn't want to cause her family shame and scandal, she would have no choice but to get married again.

If she could have her way, she'd raise her child by herself and never talk to another man as long as she lived. Yet no matter how many times she'd considered the option, the results never changed. She had no way to make a living and provide for herself and a child. Even if she could find the wherewithal to start composing again, she was an unknown in the world of piano composers and wouldn't be able to make a living off her music.

She'd considered the possibility of giving piano lessons. But how could she support herself and a child on the meager income of a piano teacher?

"Enya." Bellamy spoke her name as though she was a riddle he intended to solve. "Are you in agreement to me finding you a match?"

Had he just read her mind? "What do you think, Bellamy?"

Her da broke into the conversation. "The archbishop gave her an annulment today, so he did. And the best course now is for Enya to find a good match."

The best course for *him* so the Shanahan reputation didn't suffer.

Bellamy tapped at the leather-bound journal on the bar counter. He'd obviously been busy, and they'd interrupted him.

As if recognizing the same, Kiernan took a step back. "Come over to the house tomorrow morning. We'd like to meet with you before we return to our country home." Bellamy dropped his gaze to the paper he was still holding, and he seemed to read whatever he'd written there. Then he peered across the room at her again, his eyes narrowing and seeing all the way through her so that she felt entirely exposed, all her secrets laid bare.

She crossed her arms, hugging her cloak closed over her body, as if that would keep him from learning she was with child. But, of course, it wouldn't. Even if she wasn't showing, she sensed that he'd been able to deduce her condition. After all, what other reason would cause them to seek out his services so quickly after getting an annulment?

He would probably tell her to be on her way, that no decent, God-fearing man in St. Louis would want a ruined woman like her.

She didn't shift her gaze to the ground in shame the way she was tempted to. Instead, she forced herself to keep her chin up, even if he could read those words emblazed on her forehead—*world's greatest fool*. She took a step toward the door. "Let's go."

Bellamy shoved aside the leather-bound book. "I won't be coming tomorrow."

Kiernan's brow shot up. "Whyever not—"

"Because I'll be finding Enya a match tonight, that's why."

"Tonight?" Her question came out at the same time as Da's and Kiernan's.

Georgie McGuire was watching them with wide eyes again, and he was making a humming noise at the back of his throat. "Bellamy said he'll be finding Enya a match tonight."

"I heard Bellamy." Kiernan pinned a pointed look on the matchmaker. "But I guess I expected him to put more effort into making the match than—all of one minute."

Georgie pulled his pocket watch from his vest pocket and squinted down at it. "Actually, it's been at least two minutes."

"This is Enya's future we're deciding upon," Da interjected, "and we want her to be happy with this new choice."

Enya held back a snort. If Da was thinking about her happiness, then maybe he'd stop and consider what she wanted rather than pushing her immediately into marriage.

Bellamy turned and reached for a tall brown bottle on the shelf behind him. In the same motion, he swiped up two glasses and placed them on the bar counter. "Happiness doesn't always come easy. But with the right man, 'tis possible."

"Oh aye," Georgie piped in. "The right man is always deaf and blind . . . to his wife's faults."

"A wife's faults?" Bellamy uncorked the bottle. With practiced, fluid motions, he poured liquid into first one glass and then the next. "What faults?"

"True enough," Georgie chortled. "The right fellow always takes the blame for every argument."

"Good man, Georgie." Bellamy smiled as he slid one of the glasses across the counter toward Da and the next to Kiernan. "I can see you're learning well under my tutelage."

"I only learn from the best."

Kiernan wasn't smiling, and neither was Da. Obviously they weren't finding any humor in the situation.

Good. Because she was more than ready to leave. She grasped the door handle. "This is a waste of our time. Bellamy is clearly too young to make matches."

Georgie, in the middle of taking a sip, scowled. "Bellamy might look like a suckling babe on his mammy's lap, but he's no dozer."

Suckling babe on his mammy's lap? Bellamy with all his brawn and beauty was a far cry from that picture.

Rather than taking offense, Bellamy's lips quirked into a half smile. "I'm not the Almighty."

"He's not the Almighty." Georgie spoke over his shoulder, as if to clear up the confusion with everyone else in the pub.

"But I have just the man for Enya." This time Bellamy's gaze was serious, so much so that Enya's heart gave a traitorous kick against her ribs.

No, she wouldn't let herself believe Bellamy could work his magic matchmaking skills for her the same way he had for Finola, that maybe he'd found her someone like Riley.

Kiernan took in the patrons still quietly observing the interaction. Then he lowered his voice. "Let's go someplace private to finish the discussion."

Bellamy cocked his head toward the kitchen door. "There's an office at the back of the pub."

As her da and Kiernan made their way toward the kitchen, Bellamy paused and lifted a brow at her. "Nip along, now. We can't make plans for your future without your say in the matter."

She hesitated only a moment before starting across the room. Her da and Kiernan wouldn't be pleased to have her sitting in on their matrimonial discussions—traditionally known as "plucking the gander." But if Bellamy was inviting her to participate, she wouldn't turn him down.

As she passed by him into the kitchen, she noted that the

work area was empty, save a sink full of dishes that needed to be washed.

When Da and Kiernan disappeared into the office, she stopped and faced Bellamy, her hands on her hips. "Before we start, you need to be knowing one thing."

"You're with child." His gaze turned gentle.

She'd been right that he'd already figured out her condition. Even so, she couldn't keep the embarrassment from welling up inside.

"If you go into the match with your eyes wide open, Enya, you might eventually find love."

"My eyes are open, and I'm not looking for love." She'd thought she'd found love once, but she'd been wrong and had ruined her life in the process.

She wouldn't make that same mistake twice.

3

The cravat was choking him. Sullivan O'Brien yanked it from his neck and tossed it onto the bed of the spacious cabin he always reserved for himself on the texas deck of the *Morning Star*.

"Blast." He stared at himself in the gilded mirror mounted to the wall above the settee, which was bolted to the floor like all the furniture to prevent shifting during rough voyages.

The lantern was glowing brightly on the pedestal table beside the settee, illuminating his imposing figure—his broad shoulders, large torso, big hands, and towering legs. At six-feet-four inches, he'd always been too brawny.

His brown eyes peered back at him in his leathery face, tanned from hours, months, and years spent in the sunshine and on the river. The layer of scruff on his face and the over-long locks of his dark brown hair made him appear even more rugged.

He combed his fingers through his hair, pushing the strands off his forehead. Maybe he should have gotten a haircut and a shave to look his best for his wedding.

He tugged his high collar and tried to cover the splotch of puckered red on his neck. If only the spot wasn't so hard to conceal. At least the scars that stretched over his shoulder and down his back were easier to keep hidden.

Even without the burn marks that covered a third of his body, he'd never considered himself a particularly appealing man. He'd always struggled with feeling clumsy and awkward.

But since returning from the Mexican War half dead two years ago, he'd struggled even more with his inadequacies. He was the first to admit those insecurities had kept him from fulfilling his father's requirements to get married, until tonight. Until it was almost too late . . .

Of course, he'd never been without female attention, especially whenever he was at home in New Orleans. But that was because women knew he was the son of Commodore Callahan O'Brien, the wealthiest, most powerful steamboat magnate in Louisiana—maybe even in the entire United States. That status drew women to him like bees to pollen. And he could have chosen one of them to be his wife.

However, most of them were friends of the family. Or friends of friends. And that, therein, was the problem. He didn't want to marry a woman who knew what an oaf he was but was willing to marry him regardless because of his family's fortune.

He released a loud huff. What made him think that a woman in St. Louis would be any different? And what in the name of the holy mother was he thinking in trying to get married tonight?

He dropped onto the settee and bowed his head. Maybe he'd been a blathering idiot to have a conversation with the matchmaker tonight. He almost hadn't spoken to Bellamy McKenna, had almost left the pub without bringing up the need for help.

But somehow Bellamy had guessed why he'd been at Oscar's Pub. No doubt it was partly because he'd lingered longer than he usually did and partly the fact that on Shrove Tuesday he was one of the only single men in St. Louis who wasn't out celebrating his own marriage or that of a friend.

Whatever the case, Bellamy had questioned him about his need for a match. And the matchmaker hadn't even acted surprised upon the revelation that he had to be married by midnight on Shrove Tuesday. Instead, Bellamy had behaved as though men came into the pub every day and made such requests.

Of course, Bellamy had warned him that most eligible women were already matched by Shrove Tuesday. But he'd indicated that he'd do his best to find an unattached woman who was still wanting to get married.

What if there weren't any young women left? Especially one who met the qualifications on the short list he'd given Bellamy?

Sullivan hopped up from the settee and then paced to the other side of the room, to the curtained window that over-looked the promenade running the length of the starboard deck.

The silence and the stillness of the steamboat was always strange but peaceful after the noisy and crowded two-week trip up the Mississippi from New Orleans to St. Louis.

It wouldn't be peaceful for long. Tomorrow the steamboat staff would be busy loading cargo and guests for the return trip. Thankfully, the cholera epidemic that had ravaged New

Orleans city since late last year had slowed down. He hadn't had to stop so many times on the voyage up to St. Louis to bury immigrants dying of the painful disease.

He peeled back the curtain and peered out at the dark levee. At the late hour, the normally bustling waterfront was deserted, except for a few loafers and wharf rats. Only the massive piles of cargo remained, unloaded from the dozens upon dozens of steamboats that docked in St. Louis—lumber from the Great Lakes regions, bales of hemp from Missouri, barrels of brined pork from Kentucky, and more from every region that intersected the great Mississippi highway.

Most of the mounds were covered in tarps to protect them from the damp February weather. But the majority of goods that arrived every day on steamboats were taken directly into the warehouses that lined the levee, where more crates and barrels filled with countless merchandise awaited transport in horse-drawn drays to various places within the city.

Sullivan breathed in a deep lungful of the chilly air and tried to calm his racing pulse. He could do this. All he had to do was show up at the church, take his vows, and then he'd be a married man. Once that was done, his father would finally be happy.

"You're a meddling old man," Sullivan whispered as a fresh wave of frustration swelled within him.

His father believed the reason Sullivan hadn't yet taken a bride was because he was gone on the river too often and was married to his work overseeing their fleet of steamboats. And the Commodore was partly right. Sullivan loved his work. He'd devoted years—aside from the one that he'd been gone to war—helping to build the New Orleans Steamboat Packet Company into what it was.

But the main reason Sullivan needed his life on the river was because there he could keep busy and not have to think about all the ways he was inadequate. Out on the river, no one cared what he looked like or that he came across as gruff. Instead, crew, passengers, and even other steamboat captains respected him for his skill and his strength and his ability to keep everyone safe.

He and his father had been arguing for months about the topic of marriage. Finally, back in January, his father had given him an ultimatum. He had to get married by Shrove Tuesday. If not, the Commodore planned to ground him in New Orleans until he chose a wife.

Sullivan had considered letting his father pull him off the fleet and try to get by for a few weeks without him. No doubt without his leadership and ability to keep the steamboats running smoothly, the Commodore would let him return to the river before too long.

At the same time, Sullivan didn't want to disappoint his father. Nearing thirty years of age, Sullivan understood that he wasn't getting any younger. In order to have a family of his own, he needed to start working toward that end sometime soon.

Yet the Commodore didn't understand that not everyone could have the same kind of happy marriage he'd found. Sullivan had begun to close the door on that kind of marriage the day Imogen had rejected him for not being attractive enough. The door had slammed shut after the war when he was burned and she realized he was a monster.

He supposed that's why an arranged marriage held so much appeal, especially to a woman he didn't know, someone who was plain and didn't take stock in her own appearance.

Such a woman would be less likely to care about how he looked and more likely to enter the marriage for practical purposes.

He pulled out his pocket watch. He had thirty minutes until eleven, thirty minutes until he was scheduled to meet Bellamy and his new bride at the cathedral, thirty minutes until he was officially a married man.

He tugged the heavy curtain back into place, then turned to face the cabin, with its large bed occupying half the room. If Bellamy didn't find him a wife, this would likely be his last mission for an indefinite time.

He crossed to the cabin door and made sure it was securely locked. Then he knelt beside the plush rug that covered the floor between the bed and settee. He rolled it back to reveal a hatch in the floorboards. Lifting it only a few inches, he peered inside. There, in the dark closet between the decks, a young man of about fifteen sat with his back against the wall in tattered garments hardly worthy of being called clothing.

Sullivan wished he could offer the young man fresh garments. But if he started bringing strange clothing into his cabin, he'd raise questions he didn't want to answer, especially because no one else on any of his boats knew about his secret operation of transporting slaves to freedom. He'd purposefully kept it that way. Then, if he ever got caught, he'd be the only one to get in trouble and thrown in prison, and none of his crew would be at fault.

While he wasn't able to offer new garments to the runaway, Sullivan had provided for all the young man's other needs during the two-week trek. He'd kept the closet stocked with blankets for warmth and comfort. He'd made sure the lad always had plenty to eat and drink. And he'd even emptied the chamber pot into his every morning.

Now, the young man peered up at him, his gaze less frightened and belligerent than it had been during those first days of traveling. Instead, his expression was filled with curiosity, a little fear, and maybe even excitement. The end of the lad's journey was within sight. While slavery was legal in St. Louis and Missouri, the free state of Illinois was directly across from the St. Louis waterfront.

Tonight Sullivan's unknown contact among the Illinois abolitionists would row out under the cover of the blackest hour of night. He'd locate the glowing lantern in Sullivan's cabin window and know which steamboat to approach. At two o'clock, Sullivan would help the runaway climb over the deck down into the waiting rowboat. Then the nameless rescuer would slip away into the mist and row back across to Illinois.

Of course, runaways weren't automatically safe in Illinois either, not with the laws allowing owners to hunt down their runaway slaves even in free states. But Sullivan had heard that the abolitionists had formed what they were calling an underground railroad to help the slaves go even farther north, possibly even into Canada, where their former masters wouldn't be able to capture them.

"I'm leaving for a little bit." Sullivan kept his voice to a whisper, even though he was alone on the steamboat, save for a few of the crew and the pilot. He always erred on the side of caution. He couldn't do the slaves any good if he was incarcerated.

He also couldn't do them any good if he was stuck in New Orleans and unable to make the journey upriver. That was why, more than anything else, he'd gone to Oscar's Pub tonight and talked with Bellamy. He needed to get married, and not just to make his father happy. More importantly, he couldn't give up his mission to help as many slaves to freedom as he could. Even though transporting one each voyage didn't seem like much, over time, it had added up.

"I'll be back by two o'clock." Hopefully earlier. But he didn't know what exactly would be expected of him on his wedding night. "Stay here until I come for you."

The lad nodded. "Yessir."

Sullivan lowered the hatch, replaced the rug, then stood. He swiped up his cravat from the bed and wrestled it around his neck. He did a quick job of tying it before reaching for his flat-brimmed captain's hat from the end of the bed. He situated it over his hair, then tugged on the lapels of his coat before rubbing a sleeve over the double rows of large brass buttons that ran up his coat, polishing them as he went. He gave himself a final glance in the mirror, then took up the lantern.

Whether he wanted to or not, it was time for him to get married. And whether he wanted to or not, he had to hope Bellamy had found him a bride at the late notice.

4

A steamboat captain from New Orleans as her match? That was an interesting prospect.

Enya sat stiffly on a chair in the office at the back of Oscar's Pub. Her da rested on a stool Bellamy had dragged in. Kiernan stood, and Bellamy perched on the edge of a writing table, having shoved aside ledgers and papers of all sorts.

Another beautiful painting of an Irish landscape hung on the wall behind the writing table, but otherwise the tiny closet was dingy—the walls gray and in need of fresh paint and the floor littered with crumbs and sticky with beer residue. Several crates full of what appeared to be mugs and other supplies for the pub made the room even more crowded.

"I've heard Callahan O'Brien owns over fifty steamboats." Her da rubbed at his smooth-shaven jaw while staring at the wall. He was probably calculating the fortune Callahan O'Brien had amassed with his fifty steamboats and was ready to sign the papers to make the match official.

Kiernan's eyes held a calculated look too. "Late last year,

Captain Sullivan O'Brien inquired with our solicitor about the possibility of buying our iron to build a railroad in St. Louis. So, obviously, the O'Briens are considering expanding their empire. We could include that as part of the nuptial agreement."

Da nodded. "Aye, 'twould be a boon for production, so it would."

Bellamy swung one of his legs as though he didn't have a care in the world, while in fact he was brokering a major deal. "Captain O'Brien—Sullivan—is in St. Louis about once a month, usually only for a couple of days."

Enya couldn't keep quiet. She never could. "Exactly why is he seeking a bride in St. Louis instead of New Orleans?"

Bellamy shrugged. "He didn't say. But I have my suspicions."

"And what exactly are those suspicions?" she persisted. If she was going to agree to marry the man, she had to know a few basic details.

"Obviously, marrying a stranger provides fewer romantic entanglements." Bellamy held her gaze.

Fewer romantic entanglements. Did that mean Captain O'Brien saw the marriage as a business arrangement without aspirations for love and romance? If so, then she'd agree to marrying him right here and now.

Kiernan opened his mouth to add to Bellamy's statement, but she cut in with another question. "Why does he want to get married?"

"I suspect his father is pressuring him to settle down." Bellamy spoke frankly, which was one more thing she liked about him. He was a good and honest man.

The real question was whether she could trust Sullivan.

JODY HEDLUND

After Bryan, she wasn't sure she'd be able to trust another man ever again. "Where exactly does he plan to live? New Orleans or St. Louis?"

"I imagine he'll need to have ties to both."

"And does he intend to bring his wife on his travels?"

"Would his wife want to go on his travels with him?"

"Aye, I would." Oh aye, would she ever.

"Then I'll talk to him about it."

She would even if just for a month, until her mam had time to adjust to the news of the pregnancy. Then, once Mam had resigned herself, Enya could return and hopefully avoid the righteous indignation.

She tossed out the biggest and most pressing question. "How will he feel about raising another man's child?"

At her bluntness, both Da's and Kiernan's gazes sharpened upon Bellamy. Because that was the real issue, wasn't it?

They might as well stop dancing around it. Bellamy was good at this. He'd had no trouble figuring out the qualities that would make Sullivan O'Brien the perfect candidate to Da and Kiernan—his wealth, prestige, and the possibilities of future business partnerships. And Bellamy had obviously sensed that she would find Sullivan the perfect candidate because he wasn't expecting love, which she would never be able to give him.

Ultimately, no matter how perfect a candidate Sullivan O'Brien might seem, he had to be willing to marry a pregnant woman.

"Enya is with child," Kiernan said quietly with a glance toward the closed door.

Bellamy already knew. But Enya didn't say so. Instead, she watched him and waited for his answer.

35

He studied her in response, taking her in from her head to her toes. Even though his expression contained appreciation for her looks, she didn't get the impression he was enamored with her the way other men usually were.

When he met Kiernan's and Da's gazes, his lips quirked into a small smile. "I don't anticipate the news will make a difference to Captain O'Brien. But I'll make sure he knows."

At that, Da stood and began to put back on his coat. "Good. Then you'll come by the house with him tomorrow morn?"

"No." Bellamy glanced at his pocket watch, then hopped off the writing table. "We'll go meet him right now."

Da paused. "Now?"

Bellamy grabbed his great cloak from a nail sticking out the back of the door. "Oh aye. Right now. Captain O'Brien would like to make the decision tonight."

"We've had a long day," Kiernan cut in.

"And we're tired," Enya added.

With his coat only halfway on, Bellamy's movements grew idle, and the wide-eyed look he gave them seemed to say that rather than his statement being odd, they were out of line for questioning him about so hasty a meeting. "He'll be leaving soon, so he will. We can't tarry on the matter."

Enya pushed up from her chair. "I'd like to get to know the candidate a little before making the choice."

"I agree with Enya, so I do," Da said. "We are needing a wee bit of time to evaluate him. After all, we've already had to deal with one failed marriage, and I'd like to be preventing Enya from getting herself into any more nonsense."

Enya stiffened. Getting into nonsense? What was she? Twelve instead of twenty?

Bellamy stuffed an arm into his other sleeve. "'Tis tonight, right now, or never."

"Then find someone else." Even if she didn't particularly care who she married, she had her baby to think of and needed to make sure he would be a kind man.

"Now hold on." Kiernan's handsome features creased into a scowl. "We just discussed on the way here that the sooner Enya gets married, the easier things will go and the less gossip we'll have to contend with."

"Oh aye," she muttered. "We can't forget about maintaining the perfect Shanahan image."

Kiernan leveled his scowl on her. "We're doing this for you, Enya."

She knew she was being partly unfair to Kiernan and her da. She didn't want to cause problems for them, and she didn't want to embarrass her family any more than she already had. But at times, she despised that the family had to appear perfect on the outside when on the inside they were just human and made mistakes.

"We'll go." Da spoke with finality. "We'll meet Captain O'Brien, so we will. After that, we'll be deciding what to do."

What was the point in arguing with the men any further? She supposed it wouldn't hurt to visit with Sullivan tonight instead of tomorrow.

Within minutes, they were bundled up in the barouche. Bellamy took the spot on the seat beside her, and during the short drive, he gave them more information about Captain Sullivan O'Brien. He was the oldest child and only son of Callahan O'Brien and heir to the man's fortune. He'd captained a steamboat during the war against Mexico in 1846. During a battle, when another steamer had been hit, he'd jumped into the water and rescued all but a handful of men. He'd been badly injured and had almost died, but he'd survived and returned a war hero.

Not only was Sullivan known for his bravery and daring deeds during the war, but he was well known among the steamboat community for his fairness, loyalty, and generosity.

Bellamy relaxed casually against his seat. "Every one of his deckhands and cabin crew who come into the pub have nothing but good things to say about him. He's firm but kind."

Once again, Enya could see the strategy Bellamy was employing. He was selling Captain O'Brien to Da and Kiernan with what they needed to hear. And he was selling the captain to her with what she wanted to know.

The wily matchmaker's strategy was obviously working. By the time the carriage came to a halt, Da and Kiernan were nearly ready to marry Sullivan in her place.

As Bellamy opened the carriage door, the chilly, damp wind coming off the Mississippi greeted her. Had they come down to the waterfront to meet him at his steamboat? When Bellamy stepped out and reached a hand back to help her out, she took his offer and ducked through the doorway only to freeze.

There, only a dozen paces away, stood the Cathedral of St. Louis, the fast-flowing water of the Mississippi visible beyond. The towering building with its Greek Revival–style architecture and tall pillars was unmistakable, along with the large windows with transparent paintings covering them. The light greenish–blue steeple rose from a tower at the front with a gilded ball and cross at the top.

Bright moonlight revealed the Latin words engraved in gold over the entrance, "In honor of St. Louis. Dedicated to the One and Triune God. A.D. 1834."

The moonlight also revealed a clock on the tower that read eleven thirty.

"Bellamy?" Enya quickly found her voice. "What are we doing at the cathedral?"

"I think you know." He finished helping her down the step to the ground.

When her feet were firmly planted, she wrenched back. "He's here? Right now? Waiting to get married?"

"Aye."

"You've had this planned?"

"Oh aye."

"And if I hadn't come to the pub, who would you have picked for the captain?"

"I had a short list of possibilities."

Was that what had been on the sheet he'd been reviewing when they walked into the pub? She huffed. "Well, don't be throwing away your list yet."

"Too late. I already did. The second you walked into the pub, I knew you were the one for Sullivan."

She shoved Bellamy's arm. "You're sure of your abilities to make a match, aren't you?"

He grinned. "As the matchmaker lore goes: a man cannot control love; he can only try to guide it."

As he escorted her up the wide steps to the front doors of the cathedral, Da and Kiernan followed, still in discussion over Captain O'Brien and the many benefits of the union.

Bellamy started to open the door, then halted. "Would you wait here and give me a moment first with Captain Sullivan?"

He didn't allow them a chance to object and disappeared inside the cathedral.

Enya was half tempted to follow after him and take a peek at the man the matchmaker thought she ought to marry. But she held herself back and dragged her velvet cloak closer.

Kiernan wrapped an arm around her, shielding her from the wind. "If he's the right man, you'll marry him, won't you, Enya? You won't delay this, will you?"

"I'll try not to." The shame and guilt of all that had happened with Bryan and her failed marriage rushed in to taunt her. How could she have been so naïve to believe Bryan's declarations of devotion? How had she been so naïve to mistake lust for love? And how had she been so naïve that she hadn't been able to see his greed for her family's money in the days leading up to their hasty wedding?

Was she a poor judge of character? And if so, what would keep her from making another mistake this time? Or maybe her mistake had more to do with being rash and impetuous. But if so, then was she being rash and impetuous again?

Doubts swirled around her mind along with weariness. When Bellamy opened the door and waved them inside, Kiernan assisted her to the back pew, and she sank down.

One of the chandeliers emanated a low light in the narthex, revealing the rows of deserted pews flanked by columns that rose to the barrel-vaulted ceiling. A few candles in the chancel were lit, glowing over the communion rail, the beautiful mosaic tile floor, and the large painting of a crucifix behind the altar.

Captain Sullivan wasn't in sight. Had he decided not to come after all?

"He's here." Bellamy cocked his head toward the eastside

chapel off the chancel. "The men will discuss matters for a few minutes to confirm the deal. Then we'll be letting Enya meet Sullivan after that. Does that sound fair?"

Da gave a firm nod. "Fair enough."

As the men started down a side aisle toward the east chapel, Bellamy smiled over his shoulder at her, as though to reassure her that everything would be alright. But would anything be alright ever again?

5

*T*hen you're in agreement to the union?" Bellamy leaned against the wall nonchalantly, but Sullivan was learning that underneath the surface, the matchmaker was anything but nonchalant. He was calculated, shrewd, and incredibly perceptive.

Sullivan held himself stiffly and tried not to fidget. Already he was perspiring, and he'd only been talking to James and Kiernan Shanahan for less than ten minutes.

Yes, he'd been keeping track of the time. With twenty minutes left of Shrove Tuesday, he had to move the proceedings along. "I'm in agreement, Mr. Shanahan, sir, if you are."

In fact, Sullivan was more than agreeable. He couldn't believe his luck. Or maybe it was God intervening and smiling down on him. Either way, he hadn't expected one of St. Louis's most prominent and wealthy men to show up at the cathedral tonight and offer his daughter in marriage.

Sullivan had seen the broad-shouldered, thick-boned man

on occasion over the years during his short visits to St. Louis. With his head of bright red hair, he was hard to miss, even when he was wearing a hat.

Not only was James Shanahan prosperous from all his business dealings in St. Louis as well as his iron foundry, but he was also well-known for his generosity to immigrants, his forward-thinking ideas for the city's development, and his influence over governmental matters.

Who could say no to a union with a family like that? In fact, during their brief discussion, both James and Kiernan had mentioned the possibility of partnering on a railroad that would connect St. Louis to the east.

Kiernan stuck out his hand first. Of similar build to his father but with a red-brown color hair, Kiernan was imposing too. "We're in agreement, Captain O'Brien."

Sullivan clasped the fellow's hand.

James held out a hand for a shake as well, but something in the man's eyes made Sullivan hesitate as he shook hands, almost as if the man was hiding information. Critical information.

What was it?

Was something wrong with his daughter that he had to resort to a clandestine, late-night marriage on Shrove Tuesday?

Sullivan tossed out the only objection he could think she might have. "Will she be in agreement to traveling back to New Orleans with me? I must introduce her to my father. It's part of his stipulations."

"Oh aye." James exchanged a knowing look with Kiernan. "She'll go, so she will."

The matchmaker pushed away from the wall. "Time to let Enya have a chance to meet Sullivan."

In other words, time for Sullivan to see for himself what was wrong with the young lady he was agreeing to marry. Was she feebleminded? Impaired in some manner? Suffering from an ongoing affliction?

Or maybe she was unattractive? So much so that no man in St. Louis wanted her?

Blast. What in the name of the holy mother was he doing thinking about a woman in terms of her appearance? He knew what it was like to be judged for his blemishes, and he wouldn't do the same to someone else. In fact, maybe that's why Bellamy had chosen Enya Shanahan for him. After all, he had asked Bellamy to find a wife who didn't put stock in physical appearances.

Bellamy was guiding James and Kiernan from the chapel. "We'll write down all the conditions of the agreement and sign papers tomorrow."

When the three exited, Sullivan released a taut breath. What was he doing here? Did he really think any woman would want him? Even before his war scars, he'd been big and bumbling and brash.

Imogen, the one woman he'd ever allowed himself to care about and consider a future with, had seemed to like him when they'd first started to court in those years before he'd left for the war. But as time had gone on, she'd grown more distant, until she'd pulled away altogether. In the end, when she'd told him that she didn't want to court any longer, she'd said it was because she wasn't attracted to him. Her parting words were, "You're too sullen and serious for me."

What if Enya wasn't attracted to him either? And what if his scars made it even worse?

He crossed to the altar with several lit candles and bowed

his head. He hadn't been a praying man over recent years. He supposed the day Imogen had rejected him, he'd taken that as a rejection from God too. At the very least, he hadn't believed God cared all that much about him.

Why would God start caring now?

A soft throat cleared behind him. A woman's throat.

Yes. It was for the best if she was plain or had a blemish. That's the kind of wife he wanted and would be satisfied with.

Holding his breath, he pivoted.

She stood just inside the door. He didn't let himself look at her fully. Instead, he focused on her dainty boots peeking out from the hem of a dark green gown. He let his gaze travel slowly up the length of her. When he reached her slender waist and perfectly sculpted hips, his mouth went dry. As his eyes rose to her ribs and curvaceous bosom, his pulse started to race. When he took in the creamy skin of her chest that the bodice didn't conceal and then her long, slender neck, heat prickled along his spine.

His sights lifted only a tad to land upon her dimpled chin that was delicately rounded and above that, perfectly rosy lips. Her cheekbones and nose were as delicate as her chin.

As he surveyed her eyes and hair in the same sweeping gaze, his every bodily function seemed to cease, and all he could do was watch her in silent, reverent awe. Her eyes were wide and rimmed with long lashes. And the green was as bright as a bayou, made even more vibrant by the long red hair that was arranged in ringlets to frame her face.

Chill bumps rolled down his arms and then his legs.

Everything about this woman was beyond exquisite. In fact, she was quite honestly the most beautiful woman he'd ever laid eyes upon. If there were a contest to find the prettiest woman in the states that bordered the Mississippi River, she would win. In fact, no one would even come close. Not in all of North America. Maybe not even in the world.

He let himself look at her again, this time all at once. But doing so was a little bit like staring directly at the sun—too intense, too blinding, too overwhelming.

"Captain O'Brien?" Her question was clear and direct.

He gave a curt nod.

Her pretty lips seemed about ready to say something, but then she stalled, and confusion flitted through those luscious green eyes.

He almost smacked a hand to his forehead at his boorishness. He should have been the one to introduce himself first and make her feel comfortable. Instead, he was gawking like an awkward idiot.

"I'm he." His voice came out an octave too high. He cleared his throat. "I'm Captain—Captain Sullivan—Captain O'Brien—that is, Sullivan." He had to stop. He was making a mess of the introduction.

He needed to cross to her and properly kiss her hand like a gentleman would do. But if he took even the tiniest of steps, he'd trip and fall flat on his face. Because one moment with this woman was turning him into a toddler.

This wasn't going to work. He couldn't marry a woman this beautiful. It would only make him think about his inadequacies at every turn. Besides, he'd told Bellamy he wanted a woman who didn't put any consideration into appearances. And this woman clearly paid great attention to her looks. She was stylish and attired in the very best of everything, from her velvet hat down to her fancy boots.

She was taking in his appearance too. No doubt she was thinking about all the ways he was lacking.

A scowl creased his forehead.

As she lifted her gaze to study his face, she didn't back away at the sight of his frown. Instead, she jutted her chin. "I can see that you find me displeasing. What exactly about me don't you like?"

Could he tell her she was too beautiful? Or was that rude?

Before he could think of a half-intelligent response, Bellamy stepped into the chapel, his gaze bouncing between them. Had he been waiting outside the door, listening, ready to jump in and intervene if things didn't go well?

"He doesn't like me, Bellamy." Enya didn't take her eyes from Sullivan as she spoke the words, almost as if she wanted to see his reaction.

Bellamy leaned against the arched doorway, a grin creeping out. "Oh, Sullivan will adore you, so he will. Don't you be worrying about that."

Adore her? A low scoffing sound slipped past Sullivan's lips.

Her delicate brows narrowed, and she straightened to her full height of not more than five-feet-four inches. "This won't work."

"She's not the one for me," Sullivan said at the same moment.

Bellamy crossed his feet at his ankles as if getting more comfortable.

"I told you my qualifications," Sullivan persisted, "and she's none of those things."

"What qualifications?" Her tone turned brittle.

Bellamy answered first. "Sullivan thinks he wants a woman who is quiet, boring, and plain."

One of Enya's brows rose, and she seemed to be asking him to deny Bellamy's statement.

Maybe Bellamy hadn't exactly spoken the list of requirements in the most flattering of terms, but Sullivan couldn't deny that he wanted a simple wife. Not an outspoken, sociable, and completely ravishing woman.

His sights dropped again to her figure, to the perfection of every curve and the smoothness of her skin. Even if she was everything most men would dream of having, he wasn't like most men. He wasn't meant to have a woman like Enya.

"I know what I need, and she's not it." He tore his gaze from Enya's curves.

Bellamy was watching him with a smirk. "She's perfect for you, Captain O'Brien, and one day you'll realize it too."

Enya started to turn back to the door, but Bellamy straightened and blocked her exit.

"He's perfect for you too, Enya. It's about time you have a man who doesn't fall down and worship the ground you walk on."

She huffed. "No man has ever done that."

"Oh aye." Bellamy's eyes twinkled. "They do. Everywhere you go."

Sullivan had the image of Enya walking along a busy St. Louis street, her parasol in hand, and the men throwing themselves at her, laying their cloaks on the ground for her to walk on, asking to escort her, and paying her lavish compliments.

The reason he could picture others doing it was because he could see himself falling under her spell and doing the very same thing. Which meant he'd end up worshiping the ground she walked on too.

Enya pinched her lips together. Even pressed firmly, her lips were much too pretty. "I can't—"

"He's intending to take you to New Orleans to meet his family, so he is. That means you'll get to travel for a wee bit the way you wanted."

Bellamy's declaration brought Enya's argument to a standstill. Her hands were fisted, and she slowly began to unfurl her fingers.

Sullivan's heart thudded a strangely hard, erratic rhythm. What would she say? Would she agree to marry him?

Did he want her to agree?

She cast him a sideways glance, one that was decidedly cold. What did she think of him? From what he could tell so far, she hadn't seemed to concern herself over his appearance, hadn't bothered with more than a cursory look.

She certainly wouldn't be quiet, boring, or plain. What would she be like instead? Demanding? Flighty? Arrogant?

She clutched at her cloak. "What is your stance on using physical force on a woman or on a child?"

He nearly recoiled at the question.

She was watching him expectantly, her gaze serious.

Had a man once hurt her? "Rest assured, I believe it is abhorrent to harm a woman or a child in any way at all."

She examined his face as if testing the sincerity of his words. "Very well," she said. "I'll marry Captain O'Brien." Before he could question her further, she sidled past Bellamy out of the chapel and disappeared into the dimly lit nave.

Bellamy pinned Sullivan with questioning eyes.

"No." Sullivan shook his head at the matchmaker. "No. I refuse to consider her."

Bellamy tugged his watch from his pocket and glanced at it. "Ten minutes left until midnight. Ten minutes left to say your vows on Shrove Tuesday."

Sullivan took out his own watch. The matchmaker was right. He only had ten minutes to decide his fate.

The dark eyes of the runaway slave hidden in his cabin bore into Sullivan as if the lad were present. The dark eyes of the many slaves he saw on other steamboats. The dark eyes of slaves who labored hard on the docks. The dark eyes of the slaves who lived and worked on the plantations all along the river.

If he didn't marry Enya Shanahan right now, then his hands would be tied for as long as his father decided to keep him in the company office. He supposed he could get involved in helping runaway slaves some other way until he could get back on the river. But the Ol' Man River was the best road to freedom, and he was loath to be gone from it for any extended time.

Besides, how could he turn down what James and Kiernan Shanahan were offering him? They were interested in helping him invest in railroads. As much as he loved the river and the life of a steamboat captain, railroads were the way of the future. He could see it, and he'd be a fool to ignore the potential.

"Nine minutes." Bellamy was staring at his watch.

The muscles in Sullivan's chest tightened. This was too important of a decision to make on a whim. He shouldn't have waited until the evening of Shrove Tuesday to approach the matchmaker. He should have done it during his last visit a few weeks ago.

But here he was, with only minutes to spare, and his lone

option was the stunning Enya Shanahan, who was everything he didn't want in a woman.

He heaved a sigh. "Fine. Let's do it."

"Good choice." Bellamy started to turn, then stopped. "Mind you, one last wee thing you need to be knowing about Enya."

Crossing toward the door, Sullivan raised his brow.

"Her previous husband ran off and left her pregnant."

The words halted Sullivan so hastily that he tripped over his own feet. When he caught his balance, he somehow managed to close his mouth, which was likely dragging on the floor.

Enya had been married? And she was with child? She didn't appear to be, not with the way her bodice had hugged her hips and stomach. "How long ago?"

"It's her story to tell, but she was married in January and got the annulment today."

Everything fell into place in Sullivan's mind. This was why James Shanahan wanted his daughter to get married. This was why the most beautiful woman in the world was agreeing to wed a stranger. This was why they were in a hurry for a wedding.

Because they needed to avoid the disgrace that would come from Enya being pregnant and without a husband. In fact, the disgrace was probably already well entrenched from all that had happened, and perhaps they hoped to prevent more shame when word of the pregnancy began to spread.

A small part of his heart bottomed out. Poor woman. How devastated and hurt she must have been to be abandoned by her husband. And after so short a time. Then to find out she was carrying the man's child?

A low burn of anger fanned to life in Sullivan's gut. What

kind of man would do such a thing, especially to a woman like Enya? Had he also been guilty of using the physical force Enya had asked about? Sullivan didn't know the fellow but wanted to give him a thrashing he wouldn't soon forget.

Bellamy was studying his face, likely reading every one of his emotions. "She needs someone who will cherish her, so she does. And I have the feeling you can be that man."

Could he?

"Now, let's go"—Bellamy waved toward the nave—"before we're too late."

This time Sullivan didn't protest. Not a single muscle offered even the slightest resistance. He exited the chapel and started down the aisle toward the chancel. James and Kiernan were standing at the prayer rail beside Enya, and the priest was present with his prayer book open.

As Sullivan approached, all eyes fixed upon him, even Enya's. Though the shadows of the night shrouded the cathedral, he glimpsed vulnerability in her expression and the slight slump of her shoulders.

"Everything in order?" James Shanahan directed his question to Bellamy, who was striding beside Sullivan.

"Aye, so."

"You've appraised Captain O'Brien of . . . all matters?" James persisted.

Sullivan answered before Bellamy could. "Yes, Bellamy told me. And no need to worry, Mr. Shanahan. I'll marry your daughter."

James and Kiernan both nodded their gratitude. But somehow the relief on their faces frustrated Sullivan. He wasn't sure exactly why, except that part of his heart ached again for Enya. He supposed her family only wanted to protect her reputation as well as theirs. But he could only guess how this rushed wedding must be making her feel. Rejected? Unsupported? Maybe even unloved?

As he neared her, he caught her eyes. Though he could see no sign of tears, sadness darkened the green, a sadness that tugged at him and made him want to fix everything for her.

Bellamy's admonition from just moments ago echoed in his mind: *"She needs someone who will cherish her, so she does. And I have the feeling you can be that man."*

He hadn't wanted a wife with Enya's qualities—and he was still hesitant about a union with her. But he'd never been able to stand back and do nothing when someone needed help. His burned back was testament to that.

Even if he was throwing himself into a proverbial fire this time, he would jump in with both feet and do his best to save her. Maybe he'd even learn how to cherish her in a way that she clearly hadn't experienced from anyone recently, if ever.

"Six minutes." Bellamy tugged Sullivan into place beside Enya.

Sullivan let his gaze stay connected to Enya's, hoping to reassure her that he wasn't like everyone else.

But she shifted her focus to the priest and straightened her spine, her expression hardening. Everything about her stiff posture declared her resistance. She was only here because she had no other options. She was only marrying him because her family was forcing her into it. And she only intended to be married to him as part of a business arrangement and nothing more.

Her reasons mirrored his almost exactly. Except now that he knew the truth about her predicament, his reasons no longer seemed important. In fact, they seemed childish.

Could he eventually break past all her barriers and win her over? Did he even want to?

He lifted himself to his full height. Yes, he wanted to try. Even though winning Enya might be one of the most difficult tasks he'd ever attempt, he liked challenges.

Bellamy lifted a questioning brow at him.

Sullivan nodded. Yes, he was accepting the matchmaker's challenge. If it was the last thing he did, he intended to be the man who cherished Enya Shanahan.

6

"Have you come here freely and without reservation to give yourself to each other in marriage?" The priest's feather-soft question hit Enya with the force of a ton of quarried rocks.

Was she here freely and without reservation? No. But what choice did she have?

She stood at the prayer rail beside Captain O'Brien—Sullivan—and fought back a wave of tears that threatened to knock her to the ground.

"Yes." Sullivan responded first. Gone was the animosity she'd felt from him when she'd met him in the chapel moments ago. Instead, he seemed to have resigned himself to their marriage. She wasn't sure what had changed his mind, but Bellamy had clearly convinced the captain to marry her one way or another.

Even so, she didn't like that upon seeing her for the first time, he'd been immediately opposed to her. Why? Did it have to do with his list of qualifications for a wife? Had he really wanted someone quiet, boring, and plain? And was he really dissatisfied that she was none of those things?

After the way Bryan used to like showing off her beauty, especially around other men, maybe Sullivan's disinterest in her appearance would be a welcome change.

She hadn't paid heed to his appearance. In fact, she'd hardly given him a glance, only enough to see that he was brawny and muscular and to notice he had dark brown hair and brown eyes. He wasn't dashing or handsome like the men she'd been attracted to over recent years. Certainly not anything like Bryan, who'd been more dashing and handsome than most men.

Instead, Sullivan had a rugged hardness to his features, muscles from long hours of labor, and a swarthiness that came from spending hours in the sun. He towered above her with an imposing, tough aura. But at the same time, she sensed she had nothing to fear from the captain. When she'd asked her question about physical force, the abhorrence in his eyes had told her more than words that he wouldn't harm her or the baby.

The priest exchanged a look with Bellamy, then spoke again. "Miss Shanahan, have you come here freely and without reservation to give yourself to each other in marriage?"

Beside her, Bellamy squeezed her arm and gave her a reassuring nod.

"Aye." She spoke the word required of her, though her heart rebelled against it.

"Will you honor each other as man and wife for the rest of your lives?" The priest asked the next standard question.

"I will," Sullivan replied without missing a heartbeat.

All she could think about was the last time she'd taken

vows when she'd gone with Bryan to a little Protestant church in Hannibal north of St. Louis. Of course, the ceremony had been different than the traditional Catholic rite of marriage. But at the time she hadn't cared, had only been filled with excitement at the prospect of becoming Bryan's wife.

Again, Bellamy squeezed her arm.

"I will." Her answer came out softer than the last one.

"Will you accept children lovingly from God and bring them up according to the law of Christ and His Church?"

"I will." Sullivan's voice was deep and calm, almost soothing. Did his easy acquiescence mean he wasn't upset about her being pregnant? That he intended to raise her child as his own?

She nodded, and this time answered without Bellamy having to prompt her. "I will."

The priest turned the page in his book. "Then you may speak your vows."

Bellamy had obviously instructed the priest to make the ceremony as short as possible by having them state only what was absolutely necessary.

"Do you, Sullivan O'Brien, take Enya Shanahan to be your wedded wife, to have and to hold, from this day forward, for better, for worse, for richer, for poorer, in sickness, and in health, to love and cherish, till death parts you, according to God's holy ordinance?"

"I will."

Bryan's face floated to the front of her memory again. She'd loved the crooked grin he'd leveled at her while they were saying their vows, a grin that told her she was beautiful and desirable and wanted. In fact, he'd told her countless times in the days before their elopement just how much he wanted her.

It hadn't been until after they were married that she understood just how selfish his wanting had been.

She closed her eyes to block out the image of him on their wedding day and instead pictured his cold eyes on the morning he'd told her he was leaving along with his expressionless face when she'd pleaded with him to stay.

"Do you, Enya Shanahan, take Sullivan O'Brien to be your wedded husband, to have and to hold, from this day forward, for better, for worse, for richer, for poorer, in sickness, and in health, to love, cherish, and to obey, till death parts you, according to God's holy ordinance?"

Love? She didn't even know this man. Yet what difference did getting to know someone really make? She'd thought she'd known Bryan before they'd spoken their vows, but clearly she hadn't.

Besides, she didn't have any love left to give a man. Bryan had stolen it from her, and every ounce was gone.

Bellamy glanced at his watch.

"Enya?" the priest said.

She mustered up the last of her energy. "I will."

She could almost hear each of the men sigh in relief.

"Good." The priest made the genuflection of the cross. "Then I pronounce that you are man and wife. What God has joined together, let no one put asunder."

As the priest closed his book and took a step back, Bellamy grinned. "We did it with one minute to spare."

The men congratulated each another, and then the priest had them sign the marriage certificate. Once the deed was done, Enya sank onto the front pew, exhaustion overwhelming her.

She pressed a hand against her forehead. When she'd left

the house for the meeting with the archbishop, she'd never expected her day would turn out like this.

What in the name of all that was holy had she done? Had she really allowed Da and Kiernan to pressure her into marrying a man she didn't know? And what was wrong with her that she hadn't made more of an effort to oppose them? The old Enya would have.

She closed her eyes and fought back the tears. The truth was, the old Enya was gone. She'd been broken and crushed, and now only a ghost of herself remained.

Even so, her ghost should have taken a stand against the hasty marriage. What if she'd gotten herself into a worse situation than she'd been in with Bryan? What if Sullivan took advantage of her too? What would happen when he got tired of her? Would he leave her like Bryan?

She doubted a man like Sullivan would run off in the same manner Bryan had. As a captain, Sullivan had too much at stake, had a steamboat empire to run. But that didn't mean he wouldn't cast her aside when he'd had his fill and didn't find her desirable any longer.

At such a prospect in her future, a part of her wanted to simply give up. She could admit—albeit, ashamedly—she'd already contemplated walking down to the waterfront and throwing herself into the swollen river.

But every time she'd deliberated ending her life, she pressed her hand against her stomach and knew if she did so, she'd not only have to stand before God for murdering herself but also for murdering her child.

She didn't just have herself to consider any longer. She was responsible for the life of another human being. No matter how bleak her situation might be, she had to do her best for her child. Because the truth was, the baby wasn't at fault for her mistakes and messes, and the baby deserved a fair chance at having a good life.

Another wave of tiredness settled over Enya, and this time she didn't fight it. She simply gave in and let sleep claim her.

She wasn't sure how long she dozed before a tug awoke her. Weariness clouded her thoughts, and her body felt flat, as if the life had drained from her.

"Enya?" came a voice, one she didn't recognize.

She couldn't answer, didn't want to wake up from the dreamless sleep that had claimed her. Peace, even in sleep, was elusive.

Strong arms slipped underneath her.

She tried to turn away, but she was simply too tired to resist. In the next instant, she felt those arms lifting her up and situating her so that she was curled against a broad chest, her head resting on a shoulder.

"Where to?" The question was directed to someone else.

"Our driver and carriage are waiting for us." The answering voice belonged to Kiernan.

Enya didn't raise her head as she was carried. She didn't want to rely on others, not even for something as insignificant as walking to the carriage. But she couldn't gather any feistiness to protest. Besides, the arms holding her were incredibly strong and yet incredibly tender.

Several moments later, at the opening of the church door and the cool air slapping against her face, she shivered and pried her eyes open. She found herself tucked closely against a wide chest. The wool coat with its double rows of brass buttons belonged to only one person—Sullivan O'Brien.

The darkness of night surrounded them, broken only by

the pale light of the moon overhead. It was enough that she could see the outline of Sullivan's chiseled chin and jaw, the strong line of his cheek, and his broad temple.

As if sensing her eyes upon him, he cast a glance down at her face before staring straight ahead again.

He had nice eyes. Really nice. Long black lashes framed deep-set eyes. They weren't too large or too small, but well-proportioned in his weathered face.

"I can manage on my own now." The words didn't come out as forcefully as she'd intended.

He didn't respond, just kept walking.

"I don't need you to carry me."

"I realize that." His gaze flicked down to her again. "But we're almost there."

His tone said the matter was settled, and she didn't have the energy to insist on having her way.

A few seconds later as he reached the carriage, Sullivan stopped and waited for the coachman to open the door. She assumed he would put her down and let her enter on her own, and she was unprepared when he half climbed inside, still holding her, then gently lowered her onto the seat.

His presence was overpowering in the small space. And she expected him to delay, to take advantage of being close to her, to perhaps keep his hands on her. After all, they were married in the sight of God and man, and he had every right to linger.

In fact, in a short while, he'd crawl into bed with her and require her to fulfill her wifely duties. She wasn't naïve any longer about what the marriage bed was like. Although Bryan's kisses before they were married had seemed to promise secret passion and delights, that was far from what he'd delivered, and the wifely duties had been more like a distasteful chore that she'd had to endure.

However, if she'd endured the chore once, she could do so again.

Instead of lingering, Sullivan backed away until his large frame filled the doorway. The darkness of the interior cast a deep shadow over his face, preventing her from seeing his expression. He hesitated a moment, as if he wanted to say something.

Behind Sullivan, Da and Kiernan were talking with Bellamy, and they didn't seem in any hurry, not anymore. Not now that she was married and the Shanahan reputation was saved from further embarrassment.

Several more long seconds of awkward silence settled in the carriage. Normally, she was good at engaging in lively conversations and putting people at ease.

But tonight, she was too worn out to make small talk with the man she'd just married.

Finally, he gave a soft thump against the outside of the carriage and started to pull back. "I hope you sleep well tonight. I'll see you tomorrow."

Sleep well? And see you tomorrow? She sat up, confusion adding to the haze already in her head. "Where are you going?"

He cast a glance behind him toward the waterfront before facing her. "I'm heading back to my steamboat for the night."

"Oh." Didn't he expect her to come with him? Or, at the very least, didn't he want to return to her father's home and stay with her there?

"I'll be by sometime tomorrow."

That was strange. But she wouldn't complain. Their union had happened so quickly, they could benefit from getting to know one another before . . . everything else.

"Okay."

He hesitated again. "Good night."

"Good night."

As he moved away from the barouche, she was able to get a better view of him in the moonlight. This time she was struck by how solid and strong he looked. He held himself with authority, clearly accustomed to taking command of situations.

While part of her would always rebel against being controlled, tonight she only felt relief that someone else was making the decisions for her. She'd been floundering on her own for the past few weeks, trying to figure out how to survive. And it had been exhausting and frightening and unsettling.

Maybe now, she could finally begin to pick up the pieces of her shattered dreams and start to rebuild her life.

7

*S*ullivan eyed the wide doorway of the parlor. Where
was Enya?

He'd arrived at the Shanahans' home over an hour ago
with Bellamy, and he hadn't seen her once. Not that he was
thinking about her or eager to see her again.

No, he'd done well keeping his mind from drifting to her
too often since the wedding at the cathedral last night. He'd
been occupied helping the runaway slave into the rowboat
that had silently crept alongside the steamer at two in the
morning as planned. After that, he'd had to make arrangements for another captain to take over the *Morning Star*'s
voyage back to New Orleans.

This morning, he'd run several errands, including speaking with one of their family's attorneys about the accusations from smaller steamboat companies claiming that the
New Orleans Steamboat Packet Company's lower prices for
passenger fares were putting them out of business. Captain
Fitch of the Memphis Packet had been the most vocal, in-

sisting that eventually Sullivan and his father would have a monopoly.

Sullivan rationalized that there was enough room on the river for everyone. But the other truth was that he and his father ran a sound business with fair practices, and they shouldn't be penalized for their success by little companies who were still struggling.

Though the morning had been busy, now that he was at the Shanahan residence, he did hope to have the opportunity to speak with Enya. They hadn't had any time last night to converse because everything had been rushed and she'd been tired. But today, he wanted to get to know her better.

She wasn't the wife he'd anticipated. Regardless, he was trying to stifle a voice inside that told him he wasn't enough for her, that she wouldn't like him after she got to know him. And he'd decided he had to do whatever he could to prove himself a worthy husband.

Sullivan shifted on the settee, half tempted to rise and go seek her out. It probably wouldn't be difficult. The big home had a quiet, empty feel to it since apparently most of the Shanahan family had moved to the country.

One older daughter and her new husband were living in the home, but they'd been gone before Sullivan arrived, apparently taking food, clothing, and even medicinal supplies to the newly arrived immigrants who had so little and were often weak and sick.

Sullivan knew exactly how weak and sick the immigrants were. He transported them upriver from New Orleans after they arrived on steamboats from eastern cities or on ships that poured in directly from Europe.

Many of the immigrants had to stop over and work for a

short while in New Orleans before saving enough to afford passage into the heartland of the United States, where they hoped they would find cheap land, good jobs, clean air, and plenty of food.

Unfortunately, upon reaching St. Louis, most immigrants had to stop again to work and save. Eventually some went farther, either north to the Midwest or west on the Missouri River. But plenty stayed in St. Louis, lured by the demand for workers, not only on the levee but in the many factories and industries that populated the frontier city.

The Shanahans were clearly kind and generous people in their willingness to help the poor immigrants. His esteem of both James and Kiernan had risen throughout the past hour of conversing.

But he was done with talking. All he wanted to do now was see Enya.

As if sensing his growing unrest, Bellamy rose and lifted a brow at him while gathering up the papers they'd signed with all the details of the marriage arrangement. "'Tis time for me to be going."

Sullivan released a breath and pushed up to his feet. He'd groomed carefully earlier in the morning, had even called for a bath and asked for a shave. Not because he wanted to impress Enya in any way. But it had simply been a while, and he was due for one.

"We can't thank you enough." James Shanahan stood and shook Bellamy's hand. Kiernan did likewise.

"Ach, I'm happy I could help bring the two together."

"You're turning into a right fine matchmaker, that you are." James took a final drag on his Cuban cigar before he snuffed the tip in a green glass ashtray on the table beside his chair. The room was decorated in light green and gold with fancy gilded decorations, and Sullivan had felt right at home since his own family's residence in New Orleans was styled in much the same way.

"We'll be calling on you again soon, Bellamy." James cocked his head toward Kiernan. "Oh aye, Kiernan's getting the matrimonial itch himself."

"Is that a fact?" Bellamy held Kiernan's gaze, and Kiernan looked back almost defiantly. "I'll be ready to lend a hand if you need it."

"Soon. But not too soon." James grinned, revealing the same dimple in his chin that Enya had. "I'd like a wee bit of a breath between marriages."

Bellamy tucked the papers into his coat before he turned to Sullivan. "Remember, Captain. You're just the man Enya needs. If anyone can rise to the challenge of helping her, you can."

Sullivan nodded. He hoped with time and patience he could help her. He'd sensed her hurt and guessed it ran deep even though he still didn't know much about what had happened.

Bellamy gave him a final nod. "You know where to find me if you need a wee bit more advice."

"I'll be fine."

"Naturally."

James and Kiernan walked Bellamy to the door in the spacious entryway. As they did so, Sullivan eyed the curved marble stairway that led to the second floor. A chandelier with oil globes hung above it but was unlit since the morning sunshine streaming through the arched window above the door provided enough light.

He was tempted to barrel past the tall, silver-haired butler attired in a black suit who stood near the stairway, eyeing Sullivan warily.

Not only was Sullivan done with talking, but he was reaching his limits of being polite. He'd waited long enough to see Enya.

He started toward the stairway.

The butler intervened and moved to the center of the bottom step. "May I help you, sir?"

"No." He didn't hesitate in his stride and attempted to go around.

The tall man maneuvered himself quickly to block Sullivan's way. "No guests are allowed in the private chambers, sir."

"I'd like to visit with Enya." He sidestepped the man again.

The butler was more agile than Sullivan expected and moved with him, his eyes narrowing with censure. "I'll go speak with her and let her know of your request. Perhaps a meeting in the parlor, sir?"

Sullivan shifted once more, and the butler did the same. Finally Sullivan ceased his efforts, crossed his arms, and leveled a stern glare that usually got him what he wanted. Just to make sure the butler knew he was serious, he lowered his voice. "I'm going up to see my *wife*."

The hallway behind him had grown quiet.

Sullivan didn't bother to turn around and see the reaction of the other men. He had every right to visit with Enya anywhere he pleased.

In fact, he could have stayed the night in her room and in her bed if he'd chosen to. After he'd placed Enya in the carriage last night, James had been surprised about the decision to return to the steamboat. He'd expressed concern about the lack of consummation, as if without it the marriage wouldn't be real.

Sullivan had assured his new father-in-law that he would have a real marriage with Enya but that they both deserved the chance to get to know each other first. Although James had reluctantly relented to one night apart, he'd made it clear Sullivan needed to be with his new wife every night thereafter.

In some ways, Sullivan agreed. If they hoped to protect Enya from scandal, then he had to make people believe her baby was his. On the other hand, he didn't want to push Enya too quickly. He wasn't a brute. No matter how desirable she was—and there was no doubt on that score—he didn't intend to use her to satiate his needs.

"Thank you for your concern, Winston." James spoke from near the door. "But Captain O'Brien will be staying with Enya here at the house until they depart for New Orleans."

The butler eyed Sullivan from his hatless head to his shiny black shoes, and Sullivan was relieved he'd donned a freshly laundered and ironed day suit. It was one of his best, with a stylish frock coat, double-breasted vest, and a white shirt with a high collar sporting a cravat tied into a bow.

"If you must ascend," Winston said through pinched lips, "then I shall accompany you and announce your presence to Miss Shanahan."

"Mrs. O'Brien." Sullivan held the butler's gaze, refusing to look away.

After several tense seconds, the butler pivoted and began

to ascend the stairway. Sullivan followed. He could appreciate the butler's protective nature. In fact, he liked the man for it. But he wasn't in the practice of letting anyone intimidate him.

As he neared the top of the stairway, a low hum began to flow through his blood. He was on his way to be with Enya. His wife.

He still couldn't believe he was a married man. After putting marriage off for so long, he'd finally done it. Now that the wedding had come and gone, he was tempted to knock himself in the head to wake up from a dream.

He supposed that was part of the reason he was eager to see Enya again, to ascertain whether she was supportive of their union. After all, it was possible she'd been so exhausted last night that she hadn't known what she was doing. Maybe today she regretted her decision to be with him.

Or maybe the dimly lit cathedral had prevented her from seeing him. And now in the full daylight she'd view all his flaws and wish she hadn't married a giant like him.

Whatever the case, he needed to see her, and the need was mounting with each step he took. He didn't want to feel the need. He was a weakling for allowing it, especially now after keeping his emotions under solid lock and key for the past hours.

But the closer he drew to her, the faster his pulse pounded, until as he started down the carpeted hallway, he felt as though his heart were about to beat through his rib cage and out of his body.

He'd never had this sort of reaction or anticipation for any other woman. Why now with Enya?

He ought to muster the anger and frustration he'd felt initially upon meeting her yesterday. He didn't want so beautiful a woman in his life, one who would always make him feel insecure and aware of his own shortcomings. And he didn't want a woman who was stubborn and demanding so that he never had a moment of peace.

However, even if Enya was all those things and more, he wanted her anyway. He couldn't deny it. His heart betrayed him with desire for this woman that went beyond logical explanation.

Oh, he was trying to reduce the explanation down to the fact that she was in trouble and he planned to be there for her during the trial she'd fallen into. But deep inside, he couldn't fool himself. Even if she hadn't been in the family way and requiring his help, he would have been smitten with her just like every lovesick fool who ever saw her.

As Winston paused outside one of the doorways, he shot Sullivan a glare that warned him to stay back.

Sullivan halted and crossed his hands behind him, not sure what else to do with them.

Winston rapped his knuckles against the door lightly. "Miss Shanahan?"

"Mrs. O'Brien." Sullivan ground out the name.

"What is it?" she called.

At her soft answer, Sullivan's pulse pattered forward with a rush of fresh desire.

Winston opened her door a crack and peeked inside. "Captain O'Brien would like to see you. If you're agreeable."

Sullivan couldn't hear Enya's response.

"Very well." Winston closed the door, and with his hand still on the knob, as though guarding it, he leveled a haughty I-told-you-so glare at Sullivan. "She's having her hair styled, and indicated that when she's done, she'll come down to the parlor."

Sullivan had two younger sisters, and he'd seen them getting their hair styled by a maidservant a time or two in his life. There was nothing indecent about it, nothing that would be embarrassing or improper for him to witness, especially not as her husband.

No, Enya was offering the excuse to put him off. And the butler was too.

Well, she was about to learn—and so was this smug butler—that he didn't accept excuses.

Sullivan stepped forward so that he was only an inch from Winston.

The man didn't blink. Again, Sullivan had to give the fellow credit for his tenacity in defending Enya. Hopefully, he'd soon learn Sullivan was on his side and would do anything to defend Enya too.

But today, at this moment, he intended to see his wife. And he intended to show everyone that he was in charge, that no one and nothing would stop him from doing and having what he wanted when he wanted it.

He didn't have to exert much pressure on Winston's hand to remove it from the doorknob. All the while he held Winston's gaze, he turned the knob and tossed the door open wide. Then he stepped past the man into Enya's room.

With the draperies pulled back, sunlight flooded the spacious chamber, spilling over the unmade bed at the center. It was a decidedly feminine room, with everything a shade of pink—the wallpaper, chair cushions, decorative pillows, even the rugs.

Enya sat at a dressing table on a bench in front of an oval

mirror, a maidservant at her side using a hot iron to curl her hair, which hadn't yet been pulled up into a chignon and instead hung almost to her waist.

At the sight of him, both Enya and the maidservant froze. Enya's reflection in the mirror revealed that she was already attired in a dark blue gown, tighter than the one she'd worn to the wedding. Or maybe her corset was laced more firmly. All he knew was that a tantalizing amount of her bust showed above her neckline. And the tight bodice was off the shoulders, as was the style, leaving her neck and shoulders bare, showing miles of her smooth skin.

His mouth went dry, as it had last night. She was divine. No earthly words could come close to describing her. For a moment, he could only stare at her like a dumbfounded mortal at the appearance of a brilliant celestial being.

Her eyes were rounded and filled with surprise. She clearly hadn't expected him to barge past Winston and enter her chamber uninvited. But those wide green eyes added to her allure, making her too pretty for any man, especially for him.

What was he doing here? She'd take one look at him in the light of day and realize her mistake in marrying him. And if not today, then she would sometime.

He clenched his jaw, fighting against the urge to get out of their marriage first before she rejected him. After all, they hadn't consummated their union. They still had a chance to part ways, and no one would need to know.

Except that if he did so, he'd humiliate her and her family. Then she'd be back in the same position she was yesterday: pregnant and without a husband. Her father and brother would be forced to return to Bellamy. And Bellamy would have to find someone else for Enya. Who would he choose next?

Sullivan's mind played through all the possibilities of eligible bachelors around St. Louis. He didn't know many, but his gut cinched tight at the thought of another man standing in her room like this and getting to see her at her dressing table.

He didn't want any other man alive to lay his eyes upon her ever again. And touch her? The very thought of someone else approaching her and trailing his fingers across her smooth skin sent a hot burst of protest through his chest. Was it jealousy?

The undeniable truth was that now that Enya belonged to him, he didn't want to give her up.

Swallowing past his dry throat, he nodded at the maidservant. "You're dismissed."

The woman bobbed her head, then scurried from the room.

As soon as the door clicked shut behind him, he approached the vanity table.

Enya didn't move, had even seemed to stop breathing.

The long, thick auburn waves of her hair beckoned to him. He wanted to touch just one. The spot of her creamy shoulder also seemed to call him to graze her there.

But he wouldn't. She wasn't a possession he owned. She wasn't an object for satisfying his lust. And she wasn't a showpiece or prize he'd won.

She was a real person with real hurts and real needs, and she deserved someone she could trust and lean upon. Someone who would be there for her, who would stay solid, who would dive in and help save her after she'd been left to drown all alone.

Was he willing to dive in?

The puckered skin on his back twitched. The truth was, diving in was dangerous. He could end up badly burned. He could even end up losing a part of himself in the process.

But staying with her and learning to be a good husband was the right thing to do.

8

*E*nya's stomach roiled. She was going to be sick. In front of Captain O'Brien.

His dark eyes held hers in the mirror. Though she couldn't read his eyes, his expression was hard, almost daunting.

When she'd awoken a short while ago, she'd wondered if the midnight wedding at the cathedral had been a dream. Had she only imagined meeting the captain? Or had she really stood in front of the priest and spoken hasty marriage vows?

She'd wanted to believe none of it had happened.

Then she'd heard the captain's voice—and Bellamy's—when they'd arrived at the house. And she'd known she hadn't dreamed a single thing. She'd gotten married to Captain Sullivan O'Brien, a stranger.

She drew in a breath and tried to calm herself. After all, her da and Kiernan along with Bellamy all had confidence that Sullivan O'Brien was a good man and would make a worthy husband. Maybe someday she'd come to the same conclusion. But for now, she knew nothing about him.

Well she did know a few things. She knew he'd paid attention to her tiredness last night and carried her out to the barouche. She knew he was strong and yet gentle. And she knew he was honorable when he'd stepped away from the carriage and spoken parting words with her father and brother, turning down the invitation to spend the night with her.

He probably wouldn't stay away from her again, might even ask her to spend the day in bed with him. That was likely why he'd sent the servant away. But at least he'd shown restraint last night.

He stood behind her, his broad frame taking up most of the mirror. Without his captain's cap, she could see that his dark hair was thick and wavy. He was attired in a navy suit, and his face seemed to be freshly shaven, although his skin contained a faint shadow of scruff that was likely permanent.

His well-rounded face and jaw flexed in taut rigidness. What was he thinking? Did he regret their hasty marriage too? Maybe he'd come to tell her he was parting ways with her.

Before she could make sense of what he was doing, he lowered himself onto one knee next to her. She pivoted on the bench to face him. Even in his kneeling state, he was about eye level with her. He braced one arm on his upturned knee, and the rigid lines in his face seemed to soften just a little.

"We didn't get off to a very good start last night." His tone was much gentler than what he'd used for the servant. "And I apologize."

He was apologizing? When had a man ever admitted he'd made a mistake to her? Certainly not any of the men she'd ever known.

"I judged you on appearance alone, and that was unforgivable." His eyes were wide, and his brows drooped, giving him puppy-dog eyes and lending him a sincerity that was irresistible.

"Nothing is unforgivable, Captain O'Brien, to be sure. Making quick judgments is all too easy to do."

"I shouldn't have done it."

"And I shouldn't have rejected you so quickly in return."

"I feel certain you wouldn't have if I hadn't reacted as I did."

"Then let us be forgiving one another and putting our mistakes in the past."

"I would be grateful if you did."

"Very well. All is forgiven and in the past."

Though he didn't smile, his eyes crinkled just slightly at the corners. "Thank you."

"You didn't wake up this morning with regrets, Captain?"

"I cannot lie. The haste did leave me spinning. And you? Did you wake up with regrets?"

"I cannot lie either. When I woke up, I wondered if I'd dreamed the marriage ceremony or if 'twas truly real."

He fumbled inside his coat pocket. "I have something that may make it more real." As he slipped his hand out, he held up a ring with a large diamond in the middle surrounded by two circular rows of more diamonds.

It was breathtaking, so much so that she couldn't keep from pressing her hands to her lips.

"I stopped by Chaseman's Jewelry Store this morning on my way here . . ." His voice trailed off, and he stared at the ring, his brows furrowing as if perhaps he'd made a mistake.

Chaseman's was the finest jewelry store in St. Louis. "'Tis stunning."

"I asked Mr. Chaseman for the best ring he had, and this is the one he gave me."

"It certainly looks like the best. In fact, 'tis more than stunning. It is quite possibly the most beautiful ring I've ever seen."

"I'm only sorry I didn't have it last night to give to you at the wedding."

She shook her head and clutched her hands together in her lap. "Ach, it's too much, Captain O'Brien. I couldn't possibly accept such an exquisite ring."

He gently encircled her left wrist, giving her no choice but to extend her hand to him. "It's for you. If you'll wear it . . ."

Bryan hadn't given her a ring. Oh aye, he'd promised her one at their wedding ceremony. But he'd never meant to follow through. He probably hadn't thought of it again after that moment. Even though he'd pretended to be a wealthy man from a wealthy eastern family, he'd been little more than a pauper. She'd learned that truth when he'd demanded that she ask Da for money. When she'd refused, he'd slapped her.

"I won't force it upon you, Enya." Sullivan's eyes lifted to meet hers. The brown was flecked with amber, light and expectant and yet also reserved. For a man who carried himself with an intimidating fierceness, he was surprisingly gentle.

Although the doubts about her decision still warred within her, how could she refuse him, especially with him kneeling and apologizing and offering her a ring? She had to move forward with accepting this new marriage, no matter how difficult that would be and no matter how much she didn't want to be married again.

She peered down at her hand, his large fingers encircling her wrist. "You're not forcing me, Captain. I accept it and thank you for it."

"If you're sure?" He was kindly giving her the chance to tell him this wasn't what she wanted, that he wasn't what she wanted.

But she had no other option. Her father and Kiernan had made that very clear. She spread her fingers out and offered him the ring finger.

He hesitated but a moment longer, then slid the ring onto her finger, careful not to touch her needlessly. When he finished, he released his hold.

She could only stare down at the enormous ring of diamonds fit for a queen. Aye, she would have been drawn to it if she'd been the one shopping for the ring, although she never would have expected anyone to buy her something so extravagant.

So why had he done it? Most likely he was trying to win her over, soften her up, make her more willing to share the bed with him.

Regardless of his motivation, it was a generous gesture.

"Thank you, Captain O'Brien—"

"Sullivan." His tone was still soft. "Call me Sullivan."

She nodded, her eyes filling with tears and blurring the diamonds. "Thank you, Sullivan." Her voice cracked, and she quickly ducked her head, unwilling for him to see her emotion. She wasn't even sure why she was crying, except that the ache inside her chest swelled unbearably at times.

He didn't say anything, as though giving her a chance to compose herself.

She took a deep breath and blinked away the tears.

"I would like to spend some time with you today, Enya." He spoke hesitantly.

"Of course." She glanced to the bed. "I'll call for the maid-servant to help me take off my gown."

"Take off . . . ?" His brows rose, then he scrambled to his feet and stepped away from her. "*No*." He barked out the word forcefully, so much so that she shifted back on her bench, putting even more distance between them.

He towered above her, his jaw flexing with rigidness.

Had she mistaken his motives? "I assumed you joined me in my bedroom to consummate our marriage."

"No." He growled the word this time before pacing toward the door. He stopped, his rigid back facing her. He shoved his fingers into his hair and blew out a breath.

Was he leaving? She wasn't sure whether to feel relief or concern. He wasn't attracted to her the same way other men were. He'd made that clear from the very first meeting. Maybe it was her red hair. Some men didn't like red hair.

She pushed up from the bench. Usually around men she was so confident. She was able to read them well and even able to use her beauty to her advantage. But with Sullivan, not only couldn't she read him, but she suspected her womanly allure wouldn't hold any sway.

"You do want to consummate our marriage, do you not?" She tossed out the bold question. She'd never been afraid to talk directly about delicate subjects because she wasn't a delicate woman. He might as well learn that from the start. "And you're trying to make me more willing to do my wifely duties."

Sullivan's glare was out in full force. It was withering.

But she didn't cower.

"I gave you the ring," he said tersely, "because I wanted you to have the representation of my promise to you."

"What promise?"

"From our wedding vows."

"They were just words."

"They were more than words to me. They were a promise."

"Promises are easily broken."

"I never break mine."

She lifted her chin. "And I suppose you never lie either?"

"You're right. I don't lie."

She shook her head. She'd believed Bryan when he spoke his vow to love and cherish her, had believed he wanted to be with her forever, had trusted he was telling her the truth. But she'd learned that he'd said all the things she wanted to hear in the moment, and then when it came to following through, the words had meant little.

Sullivan's intense gaze narrowed in on her face. "What was his name?"

"Whose name?"

"The man who hurt you so badly."

The question sliced into her, and in the next instant all her defensiveness drained away. She felt suddenly weak and lowered herself back to the bench. Her hands trembled, and she quickly hid them in the folds of her skirt. She hoped he hadn't noticed, but his gaze was trained there.

She pressed her lips together. She didn't want to talk about Bryan—not with Sullivan, not with anyone.

Sullivan was silent for a long moment. Finally he met her gaze again, and the ire in his eyes was gone. "We will eventually consummate our marriage." His voice contained certainty. "But when we do, I want you to be in agreement."

"Have no fear. I'll agree to doing my duty."

He studied her face as if seeing deep inside to the truth about her physical relationship with Bryan and how disagreeable it had been. She wasn't a blushing person, but his scrutiny certainly made her want to blush.

"I'm a patient man."

"That's good to know." Her tone was sarcastic, and she wasn't being fair to him, but for some reason she couldn't stop herself.

Thankfully, her words seemed to bounce right off his broad, muscular chest, and he shrugged. "I'll wait until you no longer view it as your duty but instead it's something you want."

"That will never happen."

"I'll make sure it does." His voice dipped low. "In fact, I'll make sure you're the one who asks me for it."

"I won't." She'd had enough discomfort with Bryan and never wished for it again.

"In the meantime, I'll prove I'm nothing like him."

She didn't need Sullivan to clarify who he was referring to. She also already knew deep inside that Sullivan was different than Bryan. But that didn't mean she'd ever allow herself to care about him. No, she wouldn't let herself love another man. Never again.

Instead of answering, she merely lifted her chin another notch.

He turned and opened the door. He started to step through but paused and looked at her over his shoulder. "I want to spend time with you today. Have your maidservant finish your grooming, and then we'll go for a ride."

With that, he exited and closed the door behind him, not giving her the chance to protest.

And she did want to protest. She stared at the door, anger swirling inside. She didn't want to spend time with Sullivan. Not today. Not tomorrow. Not any day.

But he was her husband, and as she'd realized with Bryan, she had even less control and power with a husband than she'd had in her childhood home. As a wife, she'd lost her rights and felt completely helpless.

Unfortunately she needed Sullivan, needed his name, needed his protection, needed his help if she wanted to provide a good home for her baby.

She'd do what she had to for the baby's sake. But that was all. She'd married Sullivan for convenience, not for love. And she intended to keep it that way.

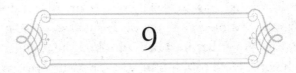

9

The silence in the carriage was stifling. Sullivan wanted to start a conversation with Enya, but he was terrible with idle chatter.

It didn't help that she hadn't made an effort to communicate with him. During the short drive, he'd asked her a few questions, but she'd replied with one-word answers, and she'd peered out the window the entire drive, as if the bleak, gray scenery of St. Louis was the most fascinating sight in the world.

As the carriage rolled to a stop in front of a three-story, red-brick house with a stucco front, he leaned toward the window to get a better view. It looked fine enough and was in a well-to-do neighborhood.

A moment later, the coachman opened the door. Sullivan exited first and then offered a hand toward Enya.

She eyed his hand as if he'd extended a snake that would bite her.

He bit back a sigh. He'd glimpsed vulnerability, maybe

even warmth, a short while ago when he'd gotten down on his knee and apologized to her and then given her the ring. She wasn't entirely frozen. But she did have thick walls of ice barricading her heart—walls she clearly had no intention of lowering.

As discouraged as he was by the nature of her accusations in the bedroom and how easily she'd assumed he was there only to get her into bed with him, he dragged in a deep breath. He'd told her he was a patient man, and he intended prove it.

There was no rush. He'd go slow and steady with her. And hopefully over time, he'd win her trust and affection.

But that didn't alleviate his growing frustration toward her previous husband. The fellow had obviously used Enya for his own needs and hadn't taken hers into consideration, especially when it came to the marriage bed.

Sullivan wasn't exactly an expert when it came to such matters. Although he'd had a period of rebellion in his earlier years and hadn't been chaste during that time, he knew enough that he didn't want his wife to just do her *duty*, as Enya had so boldly stated.

The truth was, he didn't want to possess her body without first possessing her heart. At the same time, he had no intention of letting her push him away every chance she got.

He extended his hand farther and grasped hers, giving her no choice but to allow him to aid her down from the carriage. Once her feet were on the ground, she started to tug away from him, but he held on and tucked her hand into the crook of his arm.

Thankfully, she didn't reject his polite offer and instead allowed him to lead her toward the front steps of the home.

He couldn't fault her in any way. Today, as with last night at the cathedral, she was every inch a lady in her style, mannerisms, and bearing.

Not only that, but she was just as stunning. From the moment he'd stepped into her bedroom and glimpsed her at the dressing table with her hair cascading around her, his chest hadn't stopped aching with awe.

The ache in his chest had only swelled as he watched her descend the marble stairway a short while after that. It was the same feeling he had when he was watching a sunset glisten on the river, reflecting the sky above. . . . He could never put into words just how beautiful it was, only that it took his breath away and made him want to savor the moment.

Even so, if he had any hope of chipping away at her ice walls, then he had to keep his focus off the physical, no matter how difficult that might be.

He could sense Enya's growing curiosity from the way she was taking in the home. She was trying to figure who they were visiting and why.

As they reached the stoop and paused in front of the door, he fished inside his coat pocket and retrieved the key his solicitor had given him. But before removing it, he waited a moment longer for her question.

It came a second later. "Who are we visiting?"

"No one."

Her brows furrowed just a little, enough that he knew he'd caught her off-guard. Something he liked doing.

He lifted the key and fit it into the keyhole.

"This is your home?"

"No." At least not yet.

He swung the door wide, then guided her inside.

She hesitated, glancing down the hallway and at the open doorways on either side as if she expected someone to rush out and chastise them for barging in uninvited. A large mirror hung near the door, conveniently placed for guests to check their appearance. Underneath it and on a tall stand was a silver bowl used for visitors' calling cards.

Without releasing her hand from the crook of his arm, he closed the door behind them, pocketed the key, and moved toward the front parlor.

"Shouldn't we wait?" she whispered, her steps hesitating. "We can't just walk into someone else's home."

"No, we have no need to wait." He didn't stop and instead guided her into the parlor. Everything in the room was decorated in bright red and gold. From the furniture to the drapes to the walls, the style was gaudy, especially with the elaborate gilt that outlined everything.

From the slight rounding of Enya's eyes, he could tell she thought the room was overdone too.

"You can redecorate in whatever style and colors suit you." He pretended to be interested in the enormous mirror above the fireplace. It, too, was embellished with gold.

"Redecorate?"

"My solicitor gave me the name of a designer who can help you." He reached into his pocket and this time pulled out a card. As he handed it to her, he started forward through the room toward a back pocket door, giving her little choice but to keep moving.

They entered what appeared to be a smaller parlor, a family parlor. It was less ostentatious but was still decorated in the bright red fabric.

"What color do you fancy?" Surely that was a safe topic, wasn't it?

This time, instead of answering, she tugged her arm from his hold and placed both hands on her perfectly curved hips. "What are we doing in this house, Captain?"

Her voice had a sassy note. And, for a reason he didn't understand, it gave him strange sense of satisfaction. "I'm considering purchasing it." Even if it was somewhat gaudy, he liked that it came furnished, that when the previous owners moved to California, they'd left everything behind with the home.

She didn't respond.

Finally, after the lengthening silence, he shifted and found her staring at him, her green eyes filled with uncertainty. "You don't like it? That's fine. I'll have my solicitor find us another place—"

"No!" Her voice held a note of eagerness.

He wanted to smile. Instead he raised a brow and tried to remain indifferent.

She glanced beyond the parlor into what appeared to be a dining room. "I do like it. Very much. But . . ."

"But what?"

"It's a lovely place—or will be after it's redecorated. But I can't—I don't want to—I couldn't impose . . ."

"Impose on whom?"

She peered around again as though trying to make sense of everything. Finally she released an exasperated huff. "Why are you doing this?"

"Doing what?"

"Being so nice."

"I'm not being nice."

"Aye, you are."

Apparently she wasn't used to men treating her kindly. Or at the very least, her last husband hadn't considered her needs.

After her insinuation about the wedding ring, he knew he had to be more cautious with his gifts. He didn't want her to think he was buying her love. Because he wasn't. He simply wanted her to have the best. In fact, someday he would build her the biggest and best house in St. Louis.

"I'm not being nice," he repeated. "I'm being practical. You and the baby will need a place to stay here in St. Louis."

"And you won't?"

He hadn't thought too much about the future. Only that he wanted her to have a home of her own so that maybe then she'd feel secure and cared for and valued.

"Will you be living in New Orleans?"

"I'll buy you a house there too." As soon as he spoke the words, he knew that's exactly what he intended to do.

She cocked her head. The dimple in her chin seemed to be begging for a gentle kiss. "That's too much. I don't expect that—"

"I want to do it." And he could easily afford it. Ever since he'd started working on the river, he'd saved and invested every dollar he'd made. Even though his father was one of the wealthiest men in the country, Sullivan wasn't far behind him, and he could afford to buy her a dozen houses if he wanted to.

She studied him, as though trying to discover for herself the true nature of his wealth. James Shanahan was also a prosperous man, and Enya had likely grown up always having everything she needed.

But she'd clearly never had a man who spoiled her beyond her wildest imagination. And he intended to be that man.

"We'll split our time between St. Louis and New Orleans, between your family and mine."

A thin crease formed between her eyebrows. Was she worried? About what?

He held out his hand. "Come. Let's tour the rest of the house."

She stared at his outstretched hand as she had when he'd helped her from the carriage. But this time, she wasn't recoiling. Instead, she placed her hand into his.

The moment he tightened his grip around her gloved fingers, his stomach flipped a dozen times. Even though the progress in getting her to trust him was miniscule, it was something. He almost intertwined their fingers together, but he didn't want to frighten her. So he did the safe thing—he tucked her hand back into the crook of his arm.

The rest of the time they explored the house, she didn't attempt to pull away. And he took that as a small victory as well. They strolled from one room to the next, and with each one, she grew more animated. By the time they reached the second floor and the bedrooms, she was busily sharing how she would decorate.

He didn't have much to add to her lively descriptions. In fact, even if he'd had ideas, he would have kept them to himself so he didn't have to interrupt her. He was surprised at how much he loved hearing her talk, especially with her growing enthusiasm.

Had Bellamy been right to choose a lively and spirited woman like Enya for him? Sullivan had thought he'd be happier with a quiet wife who fit into his more subdued lifestyle, thought he'd get annoyed with someone talkative. But he was anything but annoyed with Enya.

She'd released his arm and was walking around the perimeter, describing her vision for the baby's room.

"I think I'd like the walls a light yellow." She brushed her fingers along the chair rail. "The summery color will work for either a boy or a girl."

Her cheeks had a rosy hue, and her lips curved up into the beginning of a smile.

He leaned against the doorframe, content just to watch her. He wondered for just a second if he could quit being a steamboat captain and have the job of simply watching her every day, all day.

She paused in front of one of the two windows in the room and peered outside. "I can see the river from here."

"Probably not much."

"Actually, it's a grand view of the riverfront and many of the steamboats." She continued to take in the scene. "Which steamboat is yours?" Her voice had dropped a notch, almost as if she was embarrassed to ask and show any interest in him.

But that's what he wanted, or at least hoped for—that eventually she'd grow to accept him.

He pushed away from the doorframe and crossed to the window until he was standing directly behind her. The view *was* grand. While he couldn't see much of warehouses and bustling levee, he could see the steamboats forming a crowded line along the St. Louis waterfront.

There were side-wheelers whose paddle wheels were mounted on their flanks. Stern-wheelers had their enormous paddle wheels on their rears. Some were traders, and others, like his company's, were packet boats that made regular trips for both passengers and cargo.

No matter the size or type, the steamboats all shared the same black smokestacks that in some cases towered as high as seventy-five feet above the water. Made from iron, the chimneys rose from the furnace in the belly of the boat. Positioned in front of the pilothouse, most boats had double stacks topped with ornamental crowns. The belching smoke and heat from the furnaces poured from many of the steamboats and filled the skyline of the February day.

Though the vessels jockeyed for the lone patch of paved levee, he spotted several of the New Orleans Steamboat Packet Company boats.

He boxed Enya in on one side with his outstretched arm and pointed his finger at the riverfront. "The long side-wheel with the big American flag flapping in the breeze. That's the *Imperial*. She's three hundred feet long and has berths for three hundred passengers."

Enya didn't move away from him in such close quarters. Maybe she didn't even notice how near he was since she was squinting in the direction he'd indicated.

"The other superstructure, the *Morning Star*, she's down a little farther south but still along the paved portion of the causeway." He moved his finger in the direction of the other packet boat. "She's not quite as big as the *Imperial*, but she's still sturdy and fast."

"Which one are you the captain of?" Again, her question was hesitant.

"Whichever one I choose."

"How do you decide?"

"I usually pick the hardest one."

While he wasn't touching her back, he was close enough that he could lean in and catch the scent of her—some type of floral perfume that made him think of the flower garden behind his parents' home in New Orleans. He wanted to linger there and simply breathe her in.

But the plan was to woo her carefully and slowly, not to send her running from him scared.

He drew in a final breath, then forced himself to back up a step.

She remained where she was, focused on the steamboats, almost as if she were seeing them for the first time, which wasn't the case since she'd grown up in St. Louis and the boats were a staple of riverfront life.

Her cloak had slipped, revealing a stretch of her bare shoulders that drew his attention as quickly as dry wood drawing a flame. Her skin was flawless, and he could only dream of what it would feel like—probably more velvety than her cloak, velvety enough to stroke every day and never get enough.

"Why do you pick the hardest one?" She pivoted, as though she wanted to read his face when he gave his answer.

What should he tell her, that he'd witnessed too many disasters on the Mississippi, too many lost lives to captains who didn't attend to every single detail of the boat that needed to be cared for, repaired, and cleaned before starting a voyage? That he'd witnessed captains who didn't keep a lookout for snags and other dangers lurking beneath swollen waters that caused reckless crashes?

He could rattle off a dozen other answers to her question

about the financial risks, the inexperience of some of his pilots, the unpredictable weather conditions. The life of a steamboat captain was dangerous, and most steamboat owners were lucky if they could get five years out of their river steamboat. The New Orleans Steamboat Packet Company steamboats lasted longer than average, and it was because he took extra care with each vessel.

But Sullivan couldn't say any of that to her here and now. Instead, he crossed his arms over his broad chest—partly to keep from reaching for her hand again. "I pick the hardest one because I'm the best man for the job."

She dropped her attention to her gloved hands and the outline of her diamond wedding ring underneath.

His voice came out a little arrogant. Even if his statement was the truth, he didn't like to boast. "Mainly, I pick the hardest because I like the challenge."

After a moment, she lifted her chin and her eyes flashed with anger. "I'm not like your steamboats. I'm not another challenge for you to win."

With that, she slipped past him and out into the hallway. Her footsteps echoed on the wood floor as she hurried toward the stairway. She clomped down the steps and through the front entryway. A few seconds later the front door opened, then closed.

He stood frozen to his spot in the middle of the bedchamber, the one she'd said she wanted to turn into a nursery.

What had just happened here? He'd made some progress with her. She'd been more talkative and comfortable with him. So what had he done to send her running?

He released a tight exhalation. Maybe for as many steps

forward that he made, he had to expect some steps back. Perhaps many.

Whatever the case, he couldn't allow himself to get discouraged, and he had to keep trying. But what if even after everything, he could never measure up or be enough?

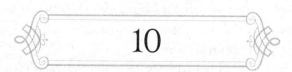

10

*E*nya paced across her bedroom floor. A small lantern on the bedside table cast a glow over the bed, its covers turned down by one of the servants.

In her nightgown and thick robe with her hair unplaited and hanging loose, Enya was ready for bed, but she'd been waiting for Sullivan. Even though he'd said he wouldn't share the marriage bed until she invited him, she wasn't sure what to believe.

He hadn't done anything that had given her cause to think he was lusting after her. He'd kept a respectable distance all day, had only assisted her the way any gentleman would, and had hardly even looked at her most of the time.

But he was, after all, still a man. And his valise and garments had been delivered to the house and brought to her room, which meant he was staying with her, whether either of them wanted the close quarters or not.

He'd been polite to her ever since their return from visiting the house he was considering purchasing. But the camaraderie she'd felt with him there had disappeared the moment she'd realized that he saw her as a challenge—one he was determined to win.

She'd been a challenge to Bryan too. He'd done all he could to win her over in those few weeks before they'd gotten married. He'd told her how beautiful she was, wooed her with promises of their future together, charmed her with his humor and teasing and wit.

Sullivan certainly had no humor, teasing, or wit. But was he trying to gain her affection by giving her the ring and buying her a house? She didn't want to have him work hard at winning her heart only to trample it under his feet once he got what he wanted.

She paused in the middle of the room. She wasn't being fair to Sullivan. Just because he said he liked challenges didn't mean he would use and hurt her the same way Bryan had. In her head, she knew that was true. But her shattered heart refused to believe any man could truly care without wanting something in return.

Even so, she needed to apologize for running out on him and being cold the rest of the day. He didn't deserve that from her. She could find a way to live with him cordially, couldn't she? At the very least, she had to make an effort to be polite.

She also had to make him understand that she didn't like his proposal to wait to sleep with her until she wanted it and asked him for it. His plan felt too much like another contest. And she didn't want him doing nice things for her so she'd invite him into her bed.

At the heavy tread of footsteps in the hallway, she drew in a breath and hugged her arms to her chest.

She wasn't familiar enough with him to know how his footsteps sounded, but it was likely him. Who else would it be? Especially since Riley and Finola had excused themselves from the parlor after supper and had disappeared into their bedroom. She'd made her escape a short while later, and Da, Kiernan, and Sullivan had hardly seemed to notice her leaving.

As the purposeful and determined footsteps slowed outside her room, her muscles tightened.

It was Sullivan.

He paused for several seconds, then cracked open the door and slipped inside, his large frame and powerful presence immediately filling the room. While he carefully closed the door behind him, she didn't budge from her spot.

As he pivoted, his attention jumped to the bed first and then swept over the room before landing upon her. In the dimness, his expression remained shadowed. But even if he'd stood in full daylight, his face would have been stoic. She was learning that he rarely gave away his emotions. Unless it was frustration.

In fact, rather than asking her what she was doing awake and standing in the middle of the room, he leaned back against the door and crossed his arms. With his gaze trained upon her, he waited.

His cravat was untied and hung loosely around his starched high collar. His vest was unbuttoned, revealing more of his wide chest. And his cuffs were rolled up so that his muscular forearms showed with all his prominent veins. An intensity radiated from him that told her he was anything but cavalier about the moment at hand.

Maybe she should have been in bed the way he'd expected. And maybe she should have pretended to be asleep. Why couldn't she push issues aside the way Finola did? Why did she always feel the need to be so direct?

She hugged her arms closer to her body. "I apologize for being rude to you at the house earlier today."

He studied her face, his brown eyes almost black.

"I'll try to be more careful about comparing you to—" She didn't want to speak Bryan's name, didn't want any questions, didn't want to have to share any of the sordid details of her failed marriage.

Thankfully, he remained silent.

"I don't want to be causing tension between us and will do better to be more agreeable."

He still didn't reply.

Was he angry with her?

She'd only let Bryan slap her twice. The third time he'd tried to hit her, she'd left the hotel room before he could lay another hand on her. She'd told herself she wouldn't let any man push her around like that ever again. And Sullivan had indicated that he'd never use physical force.

Even so, she couldn't stop the tremble in her hands and hoped he wouldn't see.

But, of course, he never seemed to miss anything, and his attention shifted to her hands.

His dark brows furrowed together, and he pushed away from the door and started toward her.

She stiffened her backbone. "Well?"

He stopped a foot away and lifted a hand toward her face. Or maybe her arm.

She couldn't stop herself from flinching.

He halted, and his scowl turned fiercer. "Do you think I intend to hit you?"

"No, I suppose not."

"Blast." The murmured curse contained an entire moun-

JODY HEDLUND

tain of frustration. He rubbed a palm across his forehead and then over his eyes. He seemed to be gathering his thoughts and his momentum to answer her. When he dropped his hand, he met her gaze directly, his brows still puckered. "Did he hit you?"

"'Tis none of your business."

Sullivan shook his head and narrowed his eyes. "He deserves to be hunted down and tarred and feathered."

"Aye." She wholeheartedly agreed with Sullivan. In fact, she could imagine a lot of worse fates for Bryan—already had imagined them.

"If he ever comes near you again, will you promise to tell me?"

"He's gone west to California, and hopefully I'll never have to see him again." Besides, before parting, he'd made it clear enough that he didn't want her anymore, that she wasn't good enough for him or any man.

"Once he realizes his chasing of gold is a fool's dream, he'll be back."

"Then you think that everyone heading to California to mine for gold is chasing a fool's dream?" She was finished talking about Bryan.

As if realizing her tactic, Sullivan stalked to the bed. He took the blanket from the end and snatched up a pillow. "I never approve of any efforts to get rich quickly. Very rarely does that work out."

"If the tales from California are true, then it has worked for some, to be sure."

"If a man wants to succeed in life, then the best way is to roll up his sleeves, get to work, and put the time and effort in to making dreams come true."

101

"Is that what you've done?"

"It's what my father did and what he taught me to do. Nothing can take the place of determination and hard work."

It's what her da had done too. His father had been a well-to-do silk manufacturer in Ireland, so after moving to America, Da hadn't been as destitute as the immigrants currently arriving in St. Louis. But still, he'd made his own way and had used the little capital he'd had to start sawmills. Later, he'd used his profits to invest in real estate and eventually sold the mills to build his ironworks.

Sullivan crossed to the fireplace with its low coal flames and dropped the blanket and pillow. Was he intending to sleep there?

Even though she didn't relish the prospect of sharing her bed with another man, she would rather get the consummating over sooner rather than later.

She untied the belt wrapping her robe closed and slipped it off. She let it puddle on the floor, then stepped over it and crawled onto the bed. What should she do? Sit back and try to look seductive? Lay down and beckon him over?

Her nightgown was one of her thicker winter wool gowns and covered her from her feet to her neck. There was nothing enticing about it, unlike the nightgown she'd worn with Bryan. Regardless, she was sitting in bed waiting for him.

She didn't usually embarrass easily, but heat warmed her cheeks at the thought of being so brazen. No, she couldn't make herself entice him. After all that had transpired with Bryan, the prospect was not only mortifying but repulsive. In fact, the whole idea of sharing the bed and offering her body to another man was the last thing she wanted to do.

But she was married, and it was expected of her. Besides,

she couldn't let Sullivan pursue her as a challenge to be won. "You must share the bed with me, Captain."

In the middle of spreading out his blanket, he paused. His eyes locked on her for several seconds with searing intensity before he resumed his task, although much more slowly. "I intend to wait until you ask."

"I am asking—"

"And I told you that I want you to be willing and no longer view it as your duty."

"Aye, I am willing."

He released a soft scoff. "We both know you're not willing."

She shook her head, her unbound hair swishing around her. "I don't want you to be doing and saying the right things to get me to like you and win my body only to discard me once you have the prize you've sought."

He straightened, his back suddenly rigid, his jaw taut, his gaze hard. She didn't have to wonder what he was feeling this time. His anger was clear in every single line of his face and body.

She drew her knees up. Had she pressed him too far?

"Let me see if I'm hearing you correctly." His voice was filled with condescension. "You'd rather I use you right from the start because you're afraid that eventually I'll use you anyway?"

Was that what she was saying? Maybe she was. At least if he used her right away, he wouldn't make promises of love and happiness. And she wouldn't have to face such heartache and disappointment when he didn't carry through with his promises.

"You have a jaded view of marriage if you think me capable of either using you now or later."

"I do have a jaded view. If you must know, I had no desire to get married again and only did so because my da made me."

"I gathered that's the only reason you agreed to a union with a man like me." He practically growled the words.

Man like him? What did he mean by that? Because he was a steamboat captain? Or because he was quiet and serious and almost severe at times?

"Regardless," he continued, "I refuse to use you now or in the future. In fact, I would rather have a celibate marriage based on friendship and companionship than a consummated marriage based on selfish passions."

His words had a noble ring. What if he was being honest? What if he meant what he said? On the other hand, what if he was simply saying what he thought she wanted to hear and manipulating her into caring about him?

He opened the stove, tossed in a shovelful of coal, and stoked the fire, getting it ready for the cold night ahead. Then, before she knew what he was doing, he crossed to the bed.

Was he planning to join her after all?

As he towered above her, her stomach quivered, and she tugged the blanket up over her body to her chin. But he wasn't looking at her, was instead staring at a spot on the wall.

In the next instant, he bent and blew out the lantern on the bedside table. Darkness descended over the room except for a low glow from the stove.

She remained motionless, waiting for the bed to bow and squeak as he climbed in. But his footsteps thudded against the carpet and took him back across the room. She couldn't see much except for his outline as he shed his garments down to his drawers and undershirt. Then he lowered himself to the floor and covered himself with the blanket.

Only then did she release the tense breath she hadn't realized she'd been holding. As she sank against her pillow and the mattress, she closed her eyes and let relief flow through her.

She hadn't necessarily set out to test his resolve. But maybe all along that's what she'd been doing, forcing him to prove he was a man of his word, that he'd honor what he said.

Whatever the case, she allowed herself the tiniest sliver of admiration for Captain Sullivan O'Brien.

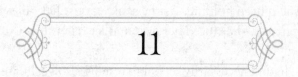

11

$\mathscr{S}$ullivan stood on the texas deck at the ornate white railing beside Enya as the steamboat prepared to leave the St. Louis waterfront.

Huddled beneath her black velvet cloak, she shivered in the cold gray of the early morning.

He was tempted to wrap his arm around her and lend her some of his warmth, but he didn't want to upset the fragile peace that had settled between them since the first night he'd slept on the floor in her room.

He'd bedded there for a total of three nights in a row. And he would have stayed longer, but at dinner last night, she'd learned that her mother and the rest of her siblings were returning to the city, and later she'd privately asked him if they could depart for New Orleans.

She hadn't spoken of her reason for wanting to go. But the urgency in her tone and in her expression had told him all he'd needed to know—she didn't want to face her mother. Was it because her mother would condemn her for the pregnancy? For the hasty marriage? Or for both?

He'd granted her request without a moment of hesitation. Not that he hadn't enjoyed his time in St. Louis. He'd kept busy over the past few days in meetings with investors as well as working out more details with James and Kiernan for future railroad plans.

He'd also taken Enya to visit two other homes, but in the end, she'd liked the first one they'd visited the best. So he'd purchased it for her and had accompanied her to the initial meeting with the decorator, not because he cared how she designed the home, but so she would know he wanted her to have her way with anything her heart desired.

In the evenings during dinners with her family, she seemed to participate more in the discussion. And each night when he came to her room, she talked more with him too, particularly about their home and all the plans she was making. Her beautiful face came to life as she spoke animatedly about her dreams for the house, and he loved sitting in the chair by the stove while she sat under the covers on the bed and shared about it all.

He couldn't deny the difficulty in bedding down on the floor with her only a dozen feet away in bed . . . in her night-gown . . . and with her hair falling around her in tousled abandon. The first night had been torturous, especially after rejecting her offer to join her in the bed. All he'd been able to think about was sliding in next to her and holding her.

But he'd resisted his urges and forced himself to walk away, snuffing out the lantern before shedding his garments so she wouldn't have to see how hideous his scars really were.

He'd needed to prove to her and to himself that he'd meant what he said—that he'd rather be celibate and have friendship than have passion and no relationship.

"Can you see our house from here?" She peered over the St. Louis skyline.

Our house. He loved that she was referring to the home as theirs.

He analyzed the various buildings and structures beyond the levee, mostly row town houses, a few colonial-structured homes from the city's early days, and even the flounder homes with their high front facades and roofs that slanted down to the lower back wall.

Among the hundreds of buildings, he couldn't pinpoint the fine home he'd just purchased. "I don't see it."

"Maybe I'll have to hang a flag from the roof or paint something special in one of the upstairs windows so that every time we return to St. Louis, we can spot it easily."

"I like that idea." He shifted closer to the rail to make room for a porter hurrying past carrying two valises as an older woman trailed behind. From what Sullivan could tell, the steamboat crew were all going about their business as they should and didn't need his supervision.

Although he'd come aboard the steamboat before dawn to make sure everything was in order for the upcoming voyage, he'd decided to ride as a passenger this time rather than assume the role as captain. The *Belle* already had one of the best captains of their fleet and didn't need his leadership.

Besides, he didn't want to be so busy with captain duties that he had little time left to spend with Enya. The captain work was demanding and required overseeing nearly every aspect of the boat and the crew. And the truth was, he wanted the time to get to know Enya and continue to show her that he was different from the cad she'd been married to before.

"I admit." She shivered again. "I've never been to New Orleans. What is it like?"

He slipped out of his greatcoat and draped it over her shoulders. "It's warmer there. You won't need a coat."

She hesitated a moment, as though she intended to thrust the coat back toward him, but then she drew it tighter. "Thank you, Sullivan." Her tone held tension—a tension that was always present but grew tighter whenever he did something nice for her.

She was obviously attempting to remain polite, but he sensed her mistrust of his motivations.

"Maybe I should have packed my summer gowns."

"If you need new gowns, we'll call upon my mother's seamstress to make some for you."

"Ach, that won't be necessary. I'm sure I'll be able to get by."

At the pumping of the *Belle*'s steam whistle, one long blast that signaled a moored vessel was departing, Sullivan swept his gaze over the entire boat in a final check. The landing stage was pulled up, the deckhands were below with the cargo, the pilot was at the wheel in the pilothouse, and the engineer was overseeing the running of the steam engines.

As the vessel started moving, the motion threw Enya off-balance, and she grabbed on to his arm before she quickly released him, taking hold of the railing instead. He wanted to tuck her hand into the crook of his arm as he had from time to time over the past few days. But he'd already pushed her into accepting his coat, and he had to keep moving slowly and being patient with her.

Three more short blasts echoed in the air, this time indicating that the steamboat was backing into the river. Not all steamboats had adopted steam whistles as a mode of communication. Many of the smaller vessels still relied upon shouting and hand-rung bells, which, in his opinion, weren't loud enough. He hoped eventually all the steamboats would be required to use a central form of communication to make river navigation safer. But at least his fleet had the whistles.

Enya clutched her hat to keep it from blowing off and swayed again.

This time he gave her no choice. He placed a hand against her back to protect her.

He stared straight ahead, careful to keep his expression neutral. He didn't want her to know just how much the slight touch affected him, because it always did. The merest brush against her made his insides flip just like the paddle wheel, turning over and over, with just how attracted he was to her.

As he stared out at the levee with the dockworkers and stevedores and others that stood on the shore watching the *Belle* pulling away, he suspected that every one of their gazes was trained upon Enya. Even though her womanly figure was concealed beneath her cloak and now his coat, there was no hiding her lovely face and radiant hair.

In fact, every time he'd taken her out in public over the past few days, she'd drawn admiring glances, so much so that he'd had a difficult time resisting placing his arm around her or touching her arm to warn off men and let them know she was his.

Of course, they were probably wondering what a man like him was doing with such an incredible woman. And he still wondered that at times too. How had he ended up married to her? Why had God intervened in his life to bring him together with Enya?

He certainly hadn't deserved a woman so beautiful, and all he could think was that he was meant to help her heal.

"What will your family say when you show up with a wife?" As usual, she didn't notice the admiration directed her way. Instead, she'd shifted to take in his expression and gauge his reaction to her question.

"They'll be thrilled I'm finally married." That was likely an understatement, at least when it came to his father.

Sullivan had sent a letter with the *Morning Star* earlier in the week. He'd instructed the captain to make sure the Commodore received the note soon after docking. That way his father would learn of his marriage to Enya Shanahan and the deals he'd brokered as part of the nuptial arrangements.

His father would be surprised at the news, especially after their last parting when he'd made it clear he'd lost faith in Sullivan's ability to find a woman. Sullivan didn't blame his father for doubting him. He never would have been able to get married if not for the matchmaker's insight and ability to push him into it.

Bellamy McKenna was truly gifted at bringing people together.

Now Sullivan wanted to show his father that not only had he gotten married, but his wife was the most beautiful woman to ever walk the face of the earth. He relished the prospect of watching his father's expression when he introduced Enya. His father was expressive and emotional—different from Sullivan in just about every way. Sullivan had no doubt his father would gush over Enya and make his usual brash comments.

Enya was still watching him. "Will they find it odd that

you married a woman from St. Louis rather than someone from among your family's social circles?"

"My father stipulated that I needed to get married by Shrove Tuesday, but he gave me no other requirements."

She grew silent and returned her attention to the growing distance between the steamboat and the waterfront and the murky water churning into a foam in their wake.

As another smaller packet began to depart from the levee, it seemed to be moving directly backward toward the *Belle*.

Sullivan narrowed his eyes on the stern-wheeler with its bright red paddle wheel as well as the stripe of red paint along the hurricane deck. He didn't need to see the name painted on the side to know it was the *Ida May*. A Memphis Packet Company boat. The one that Captain Fitch often commanded.

The vessel was sliding through the river rapidly. And the pilot didn't appear to be paying attention to the *Belle* directly in its path.

Sullivan grabbed on to the rail in front of him, a sudden urgent pressure forming in his chest—a pressure he'd never felt before, even though he'd been in plenty of dangerous, even life-threatening situations on the river.

At a shout of alarm from a deckhand below, as well as calls from the clerk and possibly the mate above near the pilothouse, Sullivan knew the danger had been spotted. In the next instant, the pilot was attempting to maneuver the *Belle* out of the way of the coming disaster.

The *Belle*'s whistle echoed in the quiet of the morning, a drawn-out screaming blast of warning.

But the *Ida May* didn't slow down.

The shouts of more crew filled the air, the commands to

fire the engines and force the *Belle* to move faster to avert the danger barreling their way. No doubt the pilot was communicating with the engineer via the hollow speaking tube that ran down to the boiler deck. And the clanging of the bells below meant the pilot had also pulled on the bell ropes to signal the need to add more fuel.

But Sullivan had captained and even piloted enough of the superstructures to know that steering them was difficult, and heating the engines and gaining speed took time. Unless the *Ida May* veered course, they wouldn't be able to get out of the way quickly enough to avert disaster.

Another blast of the *Belle*'s whistle charged the air, longer and shriller than before.

All around, the passengers at the railings were beginning to murmur their concern. Even Enya stiffened and sidled closer to him.

A dozen scenarios raced through Sullivan's mind. Should he climb up the railing to the pilothouse and take over the steering? Or should he climb down and head to the boiler rooms? Climbing the steamboat's railing was faster than taking the steps, and he could do it effortlessly enough.

But even if he attempted to gain control of the situation above or below, he'd be too late to help. Should he start getting passengers to safety, if that were even possible? From the angle that the *Ida May* was heading toward them, she'd crash into the port side near the center of the boat. They'd be lucky if the collision didn't cause a boiler explosion that would send the whole boat up in flames and kill anyone nearby.

The better alternative would be that the *Belle*'s guard and hull cracked and began to take on water. A slow sink would hopefully allow for most passengers to be picked up by nearby boats. Even then, the Mississippi was running high from melting snow and recent rain. And the temperature was frigid. If anyone ended up in the river, they'd risk freezing to death.

Enya's eyes were widening with every foot closer the *Ida May* came. "Is that steamboat planning to stop?"

Sullivan didn't know how to answer. All he knew was that he had to keep her—and everyone else—safe. Somehow. He tugged her away from the railing and shouted out, "Everyone move away from the center of the boat. Go to the stern!"

On the promenade right below theirs, he could hear the crew echo his command.

Any other time, he would have stayed at the center and made sure passengers were moving out of danger. He wouldn't have cared he was putting his own life in jeopardy as a result. But this time, he didn't wait. An urgency drove him to protect Enya. His wife. He had to get her far away from the crash site.

Pulling her against his side, he draped his arm around her in an attempt to shield her body, intending to take the brunt of the hit if necessary. As he hurried her toward the stern and away from the dangerous engines, he kept one eye on the *Ida May* still on a collision course.

What was the pilot thinking?

Sullivan knew the fellow Captain Fitch normally put at the wheel, and he was a decent pilot who would never make the huge mistake of running into another steamboat right off the St. Louis levee.

Screams and shouts filled the air, followed by another blast of the *Belle*'s whistle, one that implored the *Ida May* to stop, to switch directions, to do anything but continue straight ahead.

With the impact only seconds away, Sullivan dragged Enya fully against him, wrapping her up as tightly as he could, hoping his body would shield her and the baby from whatever damage would erupt.

But just as he braced for the hit, the *Ida May* veered rapidly, using the *Belle*'s wake to turn south. The smaller steamboat was close enough that the landing stage—if lowered—could span the distance.

A swell of relief pulsed through him with such force, he couldn't keep from sagging against Enya, who remained in his embrace, for once not resisting his proximity. Clearly she understood that he'd been trying to shelter her from the danger.

He glared up at the *Ida May*'s pilothouse. The pilot needed to be fired. Immediately.

But instead of the usual pilot, the familiar face of Captain Fitch peered back at him. With scraggly whiskers and slick hair along with a thin, pointed nose, Fitch had always reminded Sullivan of a river otter.

Captain Finch tipped his flatcap at Sullivan before rotating his wheel and steering the *Ida May* farther away from the *Belle*.

Sullivan's gut churned faster. Had Captain Fitch purposefully driven the *Ida May* close to the *Belle*?

If the captain had witnessed Sullivan embarking on the *Belle* earlier, maybe he was trying to scare him, especially if he'd heard about the marriage and partnership with the Shanahan family. The news might have stirred up more animosity.

Sullivan released a short, taut breath and held back a slew of curses he wanted to spew at the captain.

What did the fellow think he'd accomplish with this stunt? He wouldn't get them to change their business practices, not when they weren't doing anything wrong.

If only Sullivan could report Captain Fitch to the authorities for nearly running into them. But Sullivan had no proof the fellow did it purposefully. Accidents happened all the time, and no one would be able to tell the difference, especially since there hadn't been any damage or injuries.

Enya was peering past him to the *Ida May* chugging downriver past them. "That was too close."

It *had* been too close. Had he made a mistake in bringing her aboard?

He'd been on hundreds of journeys up and down the Mississippi through all kinds of weather and conditions. And he'd never once lost a vessel. He had a remarkable record, one most captains envied, mainly because he was so experienced and savvy on the water.

But today, he'd almost brought disaster to a ship. Worst of all, he'd almost brought it to Enya.

As though she finally recognized that he was still cradling her tightly in his arms, she pushed away from him. He didn't want to let go, wanted to hang on and keep holding her for the rest of the day. But as her muscles strained in her efforts to free herself, he loosened his grip.

She stepped back and didn't meet his gaze, almost as if she was embarrassed that she'd clung to him.

He wanted to tell her she could cling to him anytime, and he'd never tire of it. But he turned away from her and surveyed the rest of the passengers and crew, hoping to hide the desire that was emerging all too easily whenever he was with her.

◆ ◆ ◆ ◆ ◆ ◆ ◆

She was the most beautiful woman in the dining saloon. Not only was she stunning in her fashionable evening gown, but she was vivacious and animated and talkative with the other guests at their table.

Sitting next to her, Sullivan felt like the oaf he was—big, bumbling, and boring.

He couldn't carry on conversations with anyone, usually couldn't think of anything to say beyond one- or two-word answers that came out sounding abrupt. He didn't laugh whenever everyone else did because he rarely found anything funny. And he never had witty retorts.

He was the complete opposite of Enya. That had become increasingly clear during the evening meal in a way he hadn't noticed during the few days together in St. Louis when she'd been at home with her family and had been reserved.

Here, in the grand saloon, amidst the other guests, she'd come to life like a flower that had been wilting and was now starting to revive. It was almost as if getting away from her family and the ghosts that had haunted her in St. Louis had brought her new vitality.

Even throughout the day, he'd noticed her blossoming as he'd given her a tour of the steamboat, taking her to every deck, even showing her the engines and how they were powered by steam. He introduced her to all the crew, including the pilot, and let her take a turn holding on to the enormous wheel that directed the boat.

There had still been times when she withdrew, grew quiet, and seemed to get lost in her past. She'd wanted to rest for most of the afternoon. And she'd been silent on their walk to the saloon.

But now that he'd glimpsed her true temperament—what she would be like again once she had the chance to heal from her broken heart—he was afraid he'd made a mistake in agreeing to their union.

He laid his linen napkin over his empty plate, then reached for his glass of port. He should have insisted that Bellamy stick with what he'd asked for in a wife—someone plain and simple and quiet. Because eventually Enya would tire of how plain and simple and quiet he was. And then she'd regret marrying him.

She was laughing at something one of the other gentlemen was saying. The glow of the chandelier positioned over the table seemed to highlight her stunning hair, flushed cheeks, and sparkling green eyes.

"Enya Shanahan?" A woman passing by their table halted behind Enya's chair.

Enya shifted to take in the guest, her smile faltering.

"I thought that was you." The middle-aged woman stood beside another passenger who appeared to be her sister, at least from the similarities in their fleshy faces and large eyes.

"Mrs. Townsend." Enya's smile disappeared altogether, and wariness filled her expression.

"I do admit, I'm surprised to see you here." The woman— Mrs. Townsend—glanced around the table at the other finely dressed guests. "I heard you'd run away with a young man and that your dear father located you and brought you home."

Enya's face turned pale, and her lips stalled around a response as if she didn't quite know what to say.

Even though the music from the piano and chatter from other diners wafted around them, the guests at their table had grown silent and were watching Enya with interest.

Indignation ignited in Sullivan's gut. He didn't know Mrs. Townsend. But he'd encountered many people like her over the years, people who tried to elevate themselves by lowering the esteem of others. He wouldn't let anyone do that to Enya. Not tonight. Not for the rest of the voyage. Not ever.

He stood and pulled himself to his fullest height. "I'm Captain Sullivan O'Brien, and I'm Enya's husband." He didn't care that his voice was solemn and stern or that he probably frightened the women.

Enya started to stand, and he quickly took her elbow and assisted her to her feet.

Mrs. Townsend's hand fluttered to her chest, and her eyes rounded even more. "I didn't know. I wasn't aware—"

"My wife, Mrs. O'Brien, is well taken care of." Sullivan leveled a glare at Mrs. Townsend and her traveling companion. "You'd do well to abstain from spreading needless gossip."

"Of course." Mrs. Townsend had the grace to flush. "I beg your pardon. I assure you I had no idea."

Enya's eyes practically begged him to take her away from the room and the people staring at her.

Without another word, he steered her through the maze of tables. A steward quickly gathered Enya's wrap and brought it to them. When they stepped outside into the darkness of the evening, Enya finally sagged. It was almost as if she was wilting again.

"I'm tired." Her voice was low and wobbly. "I think I'd like to retire for the evening."

He nodded, wishing he knew what to say to make her feel better, to ease the sting of what had just happened. But as usual, he couldn't find any words. Instead, he situated her hand in the crook of his arm and guided her toward their stateroom.

"I don't think I'll eat in the saloon anymore," she said as they approached the room. "I'll take my meals privately."

"I'll arrange it."

She paused at the door and expelled a tired sigh. "Thank you."

Maybe he couldn't speak eloquently and wasn't entertaining, but he could take care of her and make sure she had whatever she wanted. He just hoped that would be enough for her—that *he* would be enough.

12

*E*nya took a deep breath and tried to stifle the queasiness inside.

"Better?" Sullivan's voice rumbled low, his presence steady and strong at her side.

She nodded and lifted her face to the sun, letting the warmth bathe her skin. Closing her eyes, she inhaled, the air laden with warmth and the scent of the early blooming azaleas.

She was embarrassed to have to cling to Sullivan. And she hated that he'd witnessed her nearly getting sick to her stomach a moment ago while sitting in the fancy restaurant he'd taken her to tonight during their stopover in Natchez.

"I'm sorry, Sullivan." The commotion of the main thoroughfare resounded around them—the passing of wagons, the bustle of pedestrians, and the businesses still trying to sell their wares. Fine brick buildings mingled with the older clapboard, attesting to the development of the town—although it couldn't begin to compare with the growth of St. Louis.

The biggest difference with St. Louis was that the dull

grays and browns had been replaced by color and growth. Surrounding Natchez and all along the river, the lush green was stunning—the oak, beech, and cypress trees already in full blossom. The full array of beautiful flowers loaded the fruit trees—peach, apricot, mulberry, and quince. The air was laden with their sweet scents.

She could admit she was relishing every moment on solid ground. After the past ten days of traveling downriver on the *Belle*, she was learning to take advantage of each extended stop in the port towns, including the chance to attend mass on the past Sabbath.

Sullivan had offered to find a room in a hotel for the night since they wouldn't be leaving until the next morning. But she didn't want the hassle of moving, not when their berth was the best and biggest on the steamer. It was a lovely room, and she was more than comfortable in it, especially because Sullivan catered to her every whim.

If she hinted their room was too dark, he'd have the chambermaid bring another lantern. If she mentioned that she was cold, she'd soon have extra blankets. He'd even made arrangements for them to eat in a private dining room away from all the other passengers so she wouldn't have to worry about anyone else like Mrs. Townsend embarrassing her.

No one had ever treated her the way Sullivan did. As a middle child in her family, she'd always felt overlooked, even insignificant. She supposed in some ways that had made her bolder and more expressive because she'd had to speak up more forcefully to let her voice rise above the clamor. Even then, she'd never felt truly understood.

But Sullivan saw her every need, sometimes even before she did. He listened to each word she spoke, even though he didn't always respond. And he seemed to make her comfort and happiness his priority.

"You should go back inside and finish your meal." She opened her eyes and nodded toward the establishment behind them, the waft of food again making her stomach lurch.

"I'll dine with you or not at all." His statement came out harsh. But after being with him night and day for the almost two weeks they'd been married, she was learning that though he might be gruff on the outside, he was sensitive underneath.

Tonight he was attired in one of his best suits, and she could admit he was a fine-looking man with his dark hair smoothed back with pomade, his jaw lined with scruff, and his tight coat and trousers hugging all his muscles. He always wore his collar pulled up high with his cravat covering his neck and hiding the bright scars there.

He rarely smiled. But neither did she, so she couldn't complain about his lack of jesting or humor. In fact, as far as she was concerned, the more serious he was the better because then he didn't resemble Bryan, who'd loved to banter.

"What would you like to do?" He took her hand and situated it in the crook of his arm. "Perhaps take a walk along the river?"

She extricated her hand and stepped back from him. "I want you to go eat. You're hungry. And just because I can't stomach the food doesn't mean you shouldn't enjoy the meal." Although she hadn't experienced much queasiness as her pregnancy progressed, sometimes the nausea came on unexpectedly.

Thankfully, the bouts were infrequent, and instead she struggled with being perpetually tired. She was ready for bed early every night and slept late. Some days she even took naps. She was slightly embarrassed by the amount of sleep she was getting, but Sullivan never seemed to mind.

"I'll eat later." His tone held a finality that told her he wouldn't be swayed. Never intimidated by her, he reached for her arm again and placed it back through his. "When we get back on board, I'll have the cook make us the baked chicken you like."

How had he known she liked the baked chicken? They'd had it for dinner one night. Aye, she'd enjoyed it more than some of the other fare that had been served, all of which had actually been pleasant for a steamboat. But she hadn't said anything about her preferences to Sullivan.

She quirked an eyebrow at him.

He ignored her silent question and started down the plank walkway that led toward the waterfront. Not only was he never intimidated by her the way other men were, but he also had no trouble taking command of her when the occasion warranted it—even sometimes when it didn't, like now.

She simply didn't know what to make of Captain Sullivan O'Brien. He was unlike any other man she'd ever known.

Although she'd done her best to keep her resolve to be polite with him, she still struggled with the fear that he'd turn into another man altogether, like Bryan had, and start treating her with contempt. What if he was being considerate because their marriage was still so new?

So far, other than the near crash the day they'd left St. Louis, their voyage had been uneventful. When she wasn't resting, they strolled on the decks, and they sat in the chairs outside their cabin and watched the passing scenery.

Because Sullivan had been traveling the Mississippi River

since he was an infant, he knew everything about the mighty river, including the history, the people who lived there, the vegetation and wildlife, and more. He faithfully and patiently answered each of her questions.

During the few times when she was queasy and in bed, he'd pulled up a chair and read to her from one of his volumes of old books, mostly from *Pilgrim's Progress* since it held her interest more than his well-worn copy of Augustine's *Confessions* or *The Imitation of Christ*.

Even though he claimed he wasn't working, he still spent a large amount of time overseeing the operations of the boat, mostly when she was sleeping. He was always gone when she awoke in the mornings, and he came in after she was asleep at night. Sometimes she wondered if he'd even been there at all. Only the clothes draped over the chair from the previous day proved that he'd come and gone.

Guilt nagged her that she was sleeping on the bed while he bedded down on the floor. But when she'd brought up the sleeping arrangements one morning, he'd insisted he didn't mind, that he'd gotten used to sleeping on the floor when he'd been younger and done all manner of work on the steamboat.

She drew in another steadying breath, the scent of the azaleas wafting stronger as they neared the waterfront.

A dozen other steamboats were tied up along the wharf, and the dockworkers were still busy unloading the heavy cargo. From what she'd witnessed already at the other ports, the steamboat would be loaded up again with more goods. Sullivan had described it as an endless effort of shuffling necessary items from one city to the next for consumers.

A worn path meandered along the riverbank. It was edged

with long grass and dotted with wildflowers she'd never seen in St. Louis, not even at her family's country home.

The evening sun seemed to paint everything with a golden hue, and it glistened on the river, turning the lapping waves iridescent.

"'Tis beautiful," she murmured, pausing and hungrily taking it all in.

"It is." He stood beside her quietly.

With her hand still tucked into his arm, she sneaked a peek at him, half expecting him to be watching her and admiring her instead of the scenery. She'd had boys and men lavish her with those kinds of silly compliments before.

But not Sullivan. He was appreciating the scenery, totally focused on it, and wasn't thinking about her at all—or at least that she could tell. Not that she wanted him to be thinking about her. But it was strange not to be the center of attention.

Why didn't he ever look at her? Didn't he find her beautiful?

"Sullivan?" What was she doing? Her heart trembled.

"Yes?" He kept his gaze on the river.

Why did she care what Sullivan thought? She didn't. She really didn't.

She stared at his strong profile—his chiseled cheek, his well-rounded chin, the hardness of his jaw. She'd learned so little about him, about who he really was.

Like that scar on his neck. She didn't know anything about it. Or his past. She only knew what he'd told her about growing up on a steamboat and little else beyond that.

She hadn't paid attention to anything about Sullivan the same way he had with her. She didn't know what his favorite meal was or what he liked to do or what brought him happiness. And the reason she didn't know anything about him was because she'd been so focused on herself, her own pain, and her own future, that she hadn't stopped to think about how he felt about everything.

A part of her wanted to understand more about this kind man she'd pledged to spend her life with. But another part of her wanted to stay oblivious. She was safer not knowing, safer with an emotional distance, safer keeping her defenses high.

He finally slid her a sideways glance. In the low light of the setting sun, his eyes were a warm bronze. For two heartbeats he seemed to give himself permission to stare at her face, and as he did so, his eyes darkened and filled with heat. Was that desire?

As his gaze met hers, she was left with no doubt. Oh aye. It was desire.

He dropped his attention to the grass in front of them.

A bubble of panic began to form in her chest. Even though she might have thought she wanted him to notice her beauty and flatter her the way other men always had, she didn't want anything to change.

She slipped her hand from his arm and started back down the path toward the steamboats. She lengthened her stride, not wanting him to follow her, reach for her, and try to convince her to give their relationship a chance to grow.

She needed to keep things the way they'd been so far since getting married—simple, at the surface, and without sharing more than they had to.

As she reached the wharf area, she didn't wait for him and continued toward the *Belle*, which sat like a stately queen among her ladies-in-waiting.

At the landing stage, she finally halted. Several deckhands were in the process of rolling barrels down the ramp toward the shore, and she stood aside to allow them room. The main deck was half-empty, the usual crowded storage area now deserted of the poor passengers who rode and slept wherever they could find a free spot among the cargo.

The steamboat beside the *Belle* was unloaded as well. Her gaze snagged upon a group of men still sitting in a huddle near the front of the deck. Though the area was shadowed and devoid of the evening rays, she had no trouble distinguishing the black color of their skin, the chains binding them to a post, and the tattered clothing that hung from their bodies. Clearly these men were slaves.

She gave a curt shake of her head at the atrocity. Even though Missouri had joined the United States as a slave state, her family didn't agree with the owning of one human being by another. Her da was a supporter of the growing abolitionist movement, and he'd taught them to loathe slavery.

Was Sullivan for slavery or against it? She hadn't thought to ask him before now. He wasn't transporting slaves on the *Belle*, but that didn't mean he opposed slavery. She couldn't be happy—maybe not even friends—with a husband who believed it was acceptable to treat other human beings with such contempt.

As Sullivan meandered closer, her ire at the sight of the poor men huddled together belowdecks only grew. If she could have her way, she'd stomp over and set them all free, regardless of the consequences to herself. But she wasn't naïve and knew that if she tried such a thing so openly, she'd never succeed and would only bring more hardship to the slaves.

The previous autumn she'd secretly attended an abolitionist meeting and learned what she could do that would truly make a difference. Of course, she'd neglected the meetings over recent months since her life had fallen apart.

When she returned to St. Louis, she would have to get involved in the meetings again. Maybe now that she had a home of her own, she could provide a secret refuge to runaway slaves as they traveled toward the free states.

"Well, if it isn't Captain O'Brien himself," said a fellow overseeing the unloading of cargo from the steamboat beside the *Belle*.

Sullivan stopped next to Enya, and his body stiffened.

"That your wife?" the fellow called. He wore a captain's cap and coat and had a scraggly beard. "Heard she's a Shanahan."

Sullivan didn't respond, but she could feel the tension radiating from him.

"Reckon you think you'll have even more control on the waterway now that you married her." The other captain didn't seem to mind having a one-sided conversation with Sullivan. "I'm already onto you, O'Brien, and it won't be long now before I ruin you."

Before Enya could think to halt Sullivan, he was already striding across the riverfront, past the dockworkers who were watching the interaction, toward the other captain.

At Sullivan's imposing size and presence, the captain took a rapid step away, but before he could escape, Sullivan snaked out a fist, caught a handful of the man's shirt and vest, and dragged him back.

"I don't care what you do to me, Fitch." Sullivan's voice was low and hard in the quiet that had descended over the riverfront. "But don't put my wife in danger ever again."

The captain released a scoff. "I've never even spoken to her—"

"You almost hit the *Belle* with the *Ida May*."

Was this Captain Fitch? After the near accident in St. Louis, Sullivan had briefly mentioned the conflict with the captain. He'd also explained that he'd known Captain Fitch since boyhood since their fathers had started out as captains working for the same company. But, of course, Mr. O'Brien had gone on to build an empire while Captain Fitch's father had never risen above the position of captain.

Sullivan held on to Captain Fitch's clothing for a moment longer, his other fist balled as though he intended to start a brawl.

Beneath the unruly facial hair, Captain Fitch's pale skin was turning red, and he shoved at Sullivan.

"Stay far away from her." With the low warning echoing in the air, Sullivan released Captain Fitch, spun on his heels, and stalked back toward Enya. He glowered at the dockhands who were watching, and they all quickly picked up their loads and continued their duties.

As Sullivan reached her, he gently tucked her hand against his arm and proceeded up the gangplank by her side. She wanted to pull away from him again, just as she had moments ago during their stroll. The attraction in his eyes before and now his defense of her with Captain Fitch . . . was he developing deeper feelings for her already?

When they stepped onto the deck, she couldn't keep her gaze from finding the slaves again on the other steamer. "I've neglected to ask you your stance on slavery."

He followed her gaze. "I don't transport slaves like that."

"But you do transport them?"

He hesitated. "No."

She had the feeling he wasn't telling her everything. "So do you or do you not support slavery?"

"I do not." Again, his voice held a strange hesitancy.

"If so, then you have surely considered using your fleet of steamboats as a way to help slaves escape to freedom."

He glanced around, as if embarrassed to be having the conversation. "It would be very difficult to do."

"The river is likely the easiest way."

He just shook his head. "As a steamboat captain, I can be sued by slave owners if their slaves board my steamer and I don't stop to question if they're bond or free. I can even be sued if a slave shows me a forged pass that says he's free and I inadvertently help him."

"Isn't being sued worth the price of freedom?"

"Did you know that the minimum sentence in Missouri for aiding a runaway is seven years in the penitentiary?"

"You would lose seven years of your freedom. But they have lost a lifetime of theirs." She was being unfair to him, but she couldn't seem to help herself.

She spun and started across the deck, her footsteps slapping with growing frustration. Maybe he didn't support slavery, but he clearly wasn't as passionately against it as she was.

His footsteps followed, and in the next instant, he had a hold of her arm and stopped her. He turned her so she had no choice but to face him. He towered over her, but his height didn't intimidate her and neither did the thunderclouds darkening his countenance.

"You're upset with me," he stated. "But this doesn't have anything to do with slavery."

"Yes it does—"

"No."

"I'm upset at your passivity on the matter." She tried to jerk her arm loose, but his grasp was unyielding.

"You're trying to cause a fight."

"I'm bringing up a perfectly legitimate issue."

"You want to push me away."

"You're ridiculous." She backed up a step, and this time, he let her go. She spun and rushed toward the stairs, needing to get away from him, needing to protect herself, but from what she didn't know.

13

*A*ngst swirled through Sullivan. He leaned against the rail of the deck and breathed in the familiar scent of the Mississippi—a mixture of muddy water, fish, and wet grass. The river was moving lazily along the bank, and the clear surface reflected the brilliant display of stars overhead.

Normally he enjoyed this time of the night, when the vessel was mostly silent and the pressure of keeping everyone safe fell away. He loved the untamed beauty all along the Mississippi, and now that they'd reached the south, the warmer temperatures and the greener scenery made him feel at home.

But not tonight. He hadn't enjoyed anything. Not since his fight a few hours ago with Enya.

Oh, he had no doubt she despised slavery. He'd learned from the first morning with the Shanahans that they were unabashedly against slavery. He'd been relieved to hear it. But he certainly hadn't been at liberty to reveal his role in helping runaway slaves.

He still wasn't. It was already dangerous enough that he was involved, and he didn't want to bring that danger upon Enya. Keeping her ignorant, just like he did with his crew, was for the best.

So far he'd remained fairly quiet about his antislavery opinions so he didn't draw suspicion from officials and slave owners who boarded steamers and searched for runaways. And so far, his strategy had worked. No one suspected what he was doing. He'd been able to travel smoothly from New Orleans to St. Louis without a single altercation or search of his steamer.

Even though Enya loathed slavery—and rightly so—he couldn't shake the feeling that the argument was her effort to put as many obstacles between them as she could, the same as when she'd run from him while on their walk along the river.

Had she sensed his attraction?

He'd been trying hard to keep his desires in check. He'd done his best to dig a hole and stuff those longings down so deep they'd never find their way to the top. But when she'd said his name out there on the river walk, he thought he'd heard something soft, maybe even inviting. That's all it had taken to break the lock and set that desire free.

Blast. He shouldn't have looked at her. Should have kept his gaze on the river. Maybe then she wouldn't have seen just how much his attraction was growing.

But it was too late to try to change his reaction. In one glance, he'd knocked down the fragile foundation he'd been building. All he could do now was start over in his efforts to prove he was a man of honor and integrity and would never purposefully hurt or use her.

He tossed another glance toward the cabin door. The lamp was extinguished, which meant she was already in bed.

He'd made sure the cook delivered her chicken dinner. And he even asked the cook to bake a tart that she liked. But he'd decided to forgo eating with her. He wasn't sure why, except that he'd felt more discouraged than usual about the setback in their relationship. And he'd wanted time to bolster his resolve before seeing her again.

Was his resolve strengthened?

He studied the faint outline of his reflection in the water below. Although he couldn't see his face clearly, he guessed his brows were drawn and his expression serious, making him appear older than his years.

He'd hoped with enough effort that maybe eventually she'd see past all his flaws. But maybe he was hoping for the impossible. What made him think she'd accept him when Imogen and no other woman ever had?

He straightened and headed to the door. Nights were particularly difficult, sleeping so close to her and yet feeling leagues away. But what choice did he have? For now, he had to keep on being patient and earning her trust.

But what if after weeks, months, maybe years, she still didn't trust him? Still held herself back? What would he do then?

He'd keep on fulfilling his marriage vows, that's what he'd do. Because marriage vows didn't come with a time limit or an end date. They were forever. And he'd spend that forever trying to win her.

As soundlessly as he could, he opened the door and stepped inside the cabin. He stopped short at the sight of the empty bed.

She was always in bed and deeply asleep when he came in at night, especially this late.

Where was she tonight?

His pulse lurched as though it had hit a snag, and his mind raced with the possibilities. Had she somehow managed to go ashore before the landing stage was pulled up for the night? If she had, surely he would have noticed her leaving. But what if she'd waited until he was preoccupied and had slipped off? What if she'd had enough of living with him and of their marriage?

With his blood pumping faster with every passing second, he made his way to the hurricane deck and started down the deserted passageway. Maybe she'd gone to the saloon, hoping to find staff who would get her something to eat. His sisters had often spoken of cravings and being hungrier during their pregnancies, so maybe that was the case with her.

As he reached the door of the saloon, he paused. It was open a crack.

He whispered a silent prayer that she was inside and then pushed the door open a foot. Through the darkness of the room, he scanned the tables and chairs and even the cushioned benches beneath the windows.

She wasn't present.

He started to back out, but at the sound of a sniffle, he paused. He glanced around for a lantern, but the room had nothing but the chandelier globes hanging from the ceiling, and he didn't have the means to light those.

Opening the door wider to allow in the star and moonlight, he surveyed the saloon again. This time, his gaze landed upon a slumped figure sitting on the bench in front of the piano. The light, though faint, illuminated her hair—

the striking red muted in the darkness, but long and loose and flowing down her back.

The sight of her hair free from the restraints of style and pins never failed to send his stomach diving deep, making him unable to come up for air. Most mornings when he awoke, her hair was like that, spread out around her on the bed. And he had to force himself to rush through his dressing so he wouldn't stop and stare.

What was she doing here? With her hair unbound? And in her nightgown?

He peered at her more closely, the white difficult to miss. Yes, indeed, she was in her night clothing, thankfully also in her robe.

If she was sniffling, did that mean she was crying? Was she upset about something?

He didn't want to disturb her if she'd come to the saloon for privacy. But at the same time, if she was despondent, he couldn't walk away from her without at least letting her know he cared. He had to offer her a measure of comfort— although he wasn't sure what she would accept, especially after how they'd parted ways earlier.

With a silent tread on the carpeted floor, he approached until he stood behind her. Should he whisper her name? Or maybe just touch her shoulder?

Before he could figure out how best to announce his presence, she slid over on the bench, making room beside her.

Had she done it for him?

He hesitated, didn't want to assume—

She patted the spot.

He lowered himself, his bulky frame hardly fitting and half of it hanging off. But she'd invited him to sit beside her, and he intended to do it no matter how uncomfortable he was.

Her face was buried in her arm on the closed piano cover.

He didn't feel the need to fill the silence. But his fingers twitched with the urge to sweep back her hair, to caress her back, and to soothe away whatever was causing her turmoil. Instead, he clasped his hands together in his lap.

"Do you know what I did?" came her muffled voice. It was filled with pain and heartache.

He knew she wasn't expecting an answer, so he waited for her to continue.

A moment later, she lifted her head and sat up. She peered unseeingly ahead. Though the darkness shadowed her face, he could still see the tears glistening on her cheeks.

"I ran away from home to marry him." Enya released a soft, mirthless laugh. "I ignored everyone who warned me about him. And I ran off with him anyway."

The censure in her voice told him she realized her mistake and didn't need him or anyone else pointing it out.

"You married a fool, Sullivan." More tears coursed down her cheeks. "I'm such a fool." The regret in her voice weighed a thousand tons and was heavy enough to sink a steamboat.

If she was walking around with so heavy a burden, then no wonder she was sad and withdrawn. If he could, he'd take the load from her and carry it on his own back. But he didn't know how to do that. The least he could do was offer to bear it with her.

"Your *choice* to ignore advice was foolish"—he kept his tone soft—"but that doesn't mean *you* are a fool."

"But I was so stupid to believe . . . everything he said . . . to fall for his charm."

Sullivan searched again for the right thing to say. "You're young and innocent, and it sounds like he took advantage of that."

Her chin dropped, and she stared down at the piano. "He wanted me to write to my da and plead with him to send me money."

Disgust for the man swelled inside Sullivan.

"But I refused. And after I told him I'd rather die than ask my da for money, he left me."

The disgust morphed into rage—burning-hot rage.

"I didn't tell my da that Bryan wanted a share of our family wealth. I was too embarrassed."

Bryan. The previous husband now had a name, and that made him seem all the more real. And everything Enya had gone through more devastating.

"But I think Da knew. His investigators learned that Bryan had been married before to another rich heiress and that her family paid him to go away."

"Then he's a swindler."

"Aye." Her response dropped low, filled with self-loathing. "And I let him turn my head and swindle me."

"Swindlers are good at what they do."

"I should have seen the signs."

No matter how much Sullivan despised Bryan for taking advantage of Enya, that didn't mean she had no fault. He wouldn't coddle her and absolve her from her responsibility in all that had happened. "Moving forward, you must not let your passion alone guide you; rather you must use sound reason as well as the advice of those who care about you."

She didn't respond but simply clutched at the closed piano lid.

Was she contemplating what he'd said? Had he earned a right to offer her instruction? Or had he overstepped himself?

He didn't want to offend her, not when she'd finally opened up to him about her past and her hurts. But he wasn't sorry for speaking the truth.

After several long minutes of tense silence, she smoothed a hand over the lid. "I haven't played since the day I ran away."

"Played?"

She trailed her fingers back and forth over the lid.

Ah, she played the piano. The very image of her doing so seemed to fit her. He sensed that she felt things deeply, and perhaps making music was one way she expressed herself.

If she hadn't played since she ran away, then she'd never played for Bryan. Maybe she'd never trusted him enough to let him in to this part of her. Or maybe she'd offered, and he'd never been interested in hearing her.

Should he ask her? He wanted to hear her—needed to hear her. The need shot through him so powerfully he was almost weak with the longing.

She pulled her hands back and then started to rise from the bench.

Before she could go far, he flipped up the lid with a clatter. "Play for me."

14

$\mathcal{E}$nya stared at the black and white keys that spread out before her.

"Play for me." Sullivan's request echoed in her head. Not just the words, but the reverence in his tone, as though he wanted to hear her play the piano more than he wanted anything else.

But she wasn't sure if she could play. As she'd tossed and turned on her bed a short while ago, her restlessness had prodded her up, and the need for solace had driven her to the piano. Except that she hadn't taken solace in music once during all that had happened over the past months.

It was almost as if she'd been punishing herself for what she'd done by depriving herself of something that had always brought her so much joy and comfort. Perhaps subconsciously she'd been telling herself that she didn't deserve any more happiness. Or maybe since she'd lost her innocence and a piece of herself, she'd lost her will to make music too.

Whatever the case, she'd put to death her desire to play the piano. And she hadn't planned to resurrect it.

But something stirred inside her, something sweet and warm and beautiful. It was only a thin wisp. But it was more than she'd felt in a long time, perhaps even before Bryan.

Was it possible this kindhearted man beside her was slowly helping to revive her?

She wasn't sure how he was breathing life into her, but being around him was waking her to the possibility that her life wasn't over, that she could learn to live again, that maybe she had more in her future than she'd imagined.

He wasn't afraid to challenge her. She needed only to think back to earlier in the evening when she'd tried to argue with him about slavery. He'd sensed her divisiveness and had chosen to address it.

Just now, his words rattled through her regarding her responsibility in her failed marriage: *"Moving forward, you must not let your passion alone guide you; rather you must use sound reason as well as the advice of those who care about you."*

They were hard, humbling words to hear. But they were wise.

He was wise. And he wanted to hear her play the piano.

She lowered herself back to the bench but couldn't make herself lift her hands.

He scooted off and stood. Then he turned and began to walk away.

Was he leaving?

A strange need nudged her. She wanted to play for him, wanted to communicate what she couldn't say aloud—that she appreciated his goodness to her.

She lifted her fingers to the keys. The ivory was cool and smooth to the touch. Somehow, as if her fingers had a mind of their own, they pressed the keys for the sonata she'd composed before she'd met Bryan—the last one she'd created during those days before her world had turned upside down.

From the corner of her eye, she glimpsed Sullivan setting down a chair beside the piano and lowering himself into it. And then she knew. He hadn't been leaving. He'd merely gone after a chair so he could give her the room she needed on the bench.

Of course. Because that's the type of considerate and caring man Sullivan was.

Her fingers easily found the rhythm of the first movement, which was fast and lively and filled with all the zest for life she'd once had. The innocence and naivety, the unquestioning trust in everyone she met, the blissful and fairy-tale-like view of the future.

As she finished the first movement and started into the second, the tempo slowed, the notes slipped into D minor, and the mood plummeted into melancholy. All she could think about was how it represented her time with Bryan—full of disappointment and hurt and broken dreams.

By the time she reached the third movement, her fingers had slowed, and she couldn't make them pick up the tempo again. The maturity of the notes, the deeper chords, the fulfillment of the new lighthearted F major—she couldn't go there yet. And her fingers stalled.

Would she ever be able to move forward into a new life? Would there be a day when she wasn't filled with remorse and guilt and sadness?

Silence settled over the saloon.

Only when she sniffled did she realize that tears were trickling down her cheeks.

She swiped at the tears, then slid her hands onto the bench on either side of her. A moment later, a large hand covered hers, tentatively, gently. Sullivan's. The touch seemed to communicate that he understood she wasn't ready to finish the sonata yet, that she still needed more time, and that he would be here by her side while she worked through the next movement.

He pressed her fingers more firmly and then began to lift away.

Before he released her completely, she grasped his hand and held it tightly. For a reason she didn't understand, she wasn't ready for him to let go of her, wanted his comfort, wanted him to hold her hand just a wee bit longer.

His muscles tensed, then he seemed to give himself permission to continue the contact because his large fingers wrapped around hers more securely, enveloping her hand and making her feel suddenly safe.

Safe. Was she safe with Sullivan?

She wasn't sure if she'd ever be safe from hurt with any man. Regardless, she drew strength from Sullivan's solid, steady hold of her hand.

He was leaning forward on his knees, her hand clasped in his. He didn't rush her or push her to talk. He didn't turn the moment into a sensual one. And neither did he make any apologies for touching her.

He was such a good man. Why hadn't some smart woman snatched him up and married him yet? Why was he still single?

"Sullivan?" His name came out a trembling whisper. She'd wanted to ask him personal questions on their walk earlier and hadn't been able to make herself do it. Could she gather the courage to find out more about him now? As one friend to another?

Aye, just as friends.

He didn't lift his head to look at her. He kept it bowed. But she could feel that he was waiting for her to continue, that he was giving her all the time she needed.

"I don't know much about you—that is, I haven't been good at . . ." She was botching her efforts and sounded like a young girl speaking to a boy for the first time.

His fingers pressed against hers reassuringly.

She breathed out a tense puff of air. "I'm sorry I've been so consumed with myself that I haven't taken the time to ask you questions and learn more about you."

"I admit, I am reserved." He spoke the words as if he was revealing a part of himself that she didn't already know.

She almost smiled. "Oh my. That does come as a great shock. Please do tell me more of your deep, dark secrets."

At her words—perhaps more at the playful tone of them—he glanced up. Even in the darkness of the saloon, she could see his eyes widening.

She'd surprised herself too. When was the last time she'd been playful? She couldn't keep from teasing him again. "I suppose next you'd like to reveal that you're not very talkative."

He studied her face intently. "No, I was going to reveal that I have no sense of humor."

His tone was so solemn that for a moment she almost believed he was serious. But at the twitch of his lips into the barest semblance of a smile, her own smile broke free. "You're funny."

"No, really I'm not."

"Aye. You may have everyone else fooled, to be sure. But not me."

His lips curled a wee bit higher.

Had she seen his smile come out completely yet? She couldn't remember him smiling or laughing. And that was a shame. He probably had a dazzling smile and a hearty laugh.

"What would you like to know about me?" Leaned over with his elbows still braced on his knees, he didn't let go of her hand.

A dozen questions all floated to the top of her mind. But since he was reticent, she needed to start with something non-threatening, topics that weren't overly personal, subjects that wouldn't send him into a full retreat into himself. Not that he'd retreat. That was probably her tactic more so than his.

"How many siblings do you have, and what are their ages?"

"If I answer your question, will you promise to answer it for yourself?"

She tapped her lips with her free hand and pretended to mull over his stipulation. "You drive a hard bargain. But aye, I will."

She wasn't sure why she felt more lighthearted and carefree than she had in a long time, but as he began to tell her the ages of his two younger sisters—both married with children—the tension eased from her body, and she found herself enjoying the conversation with him in a way she hadn't yet experienced.

She shared more about her family, that in addition to Finola and Kiernan, who were both older, she had three younger siblings—Zaira, who was nineteen, Madigan sixteen, and Quinlan thirteen. And she told him about each, what they were like, and how much she adored them.

Of course, next she asked him about his parents and what kind of relationship he had with them. She liked that he shared honestly and described that, although he loved them, he'd felt stifled and pressured, so much so that he preferred to be away from home much of the time.

When she had to answer the same question, she admitted that she had a similar relationship with her parents—they loved each other, but conflict often occurred between them.

They talked of how their parents met and what life was like growing up. They spoke of their childhood antics, favorite pets, and hobbies. They discussed their faith, and she admitted she was struggling with feeling far from God, and he confessed that he'd experienced that at times too. And when she couldn't hold back a loud yawn, he finally stood, tugging her up with him.

His hand still surrounded hers, solid and companionable. He'd done nothing that she could even remotely construe as sensual, not even to graze his thumb across her skin. And, as earlier, she felt entirely safe with him.

"Time for you and the baby to go to bed." His voice dropped to a whisper, likely so if any of his crew were listening, they wouldn't discover she was already pregnant only two weeks after being married.

She nodded and fought back another yawn. After the emotionally draining night, she swayed, exhaustion moving in and clouding her head.

He released her hand, and if she hadn't been so tired, she would have scrambled to grab his back into her grasp, not ready to let him go. But in the next instant, he lifted her off her feet and into his arms.

A part of her knew she needed to protest. She was a strong

woman and didn't need him to pick her up. But she liked that he'd noticed how tired she'd grown and that he was concerned enough to carry her back to their cabin.

As he settled her against his chest and started through the saloon, she snuggled in. Her head fit perfectly at his shoulder, tucked lightly against his chin. And her body melded into his arms and chest.

"Thank you, Sullivan." Her eyelids fell, and for the first time in a long time, as sleep claimed her, she had the feeling that maybe—just maybe—she'd find a way through to the other side of her heartache.

15

*T*ime for the reckoning with his father.

Sullivan tensed as the hackney carriage came to a halt under the sprawling cypress tree in front of his family home in New Orleans' Garden District.

Even if his father had received the letter ahead of their arrival, the Commodore would want proof of the marriage. In fact, the Commodore would probably require solid evidence, might even accuse Sullivan of fabricating a union, especially when he noted the date and time on the marriage certificate.

"Are you nervous?" Enya sat beside him, donned in her finest and most fashionable garment—a lovely pale blue gown that showed her every curve to perfection. Maybe even to too much perfection, if the constant heat in his low gut was any indicator.

Her matching blue bonnet was adorned in tiny roses and showcased her exquisite features. Her cheeks were flushed from the warmth of the day and the green of her eyes as bright as the palm trees that lined the ornate black wrought-iron fence that surrounded the mansion and the sprawling gardens beyond.

Her gloved hands rested in her lap, and he had the sudden urge to reach for her hand and hang on to her, just as he had that night in the saloon over a week ago when she'd played the piano for him.

Even though he'd refrained from holding her hand or touching her every day since, their relationship had been different. He couldn't put his finger on exactly what had changed. Only that she hadn't seemed angry at him anymore, as if she'd finally started to accept that he wasn't Bryan. And her despondency was lifting too. He'd sensed the shift in her mood, that perhaps she was making peace with all that had happened.

She hadn't played the piano again, but she'd taught him her favorite card game, and they'd played almost every evening in their private dining room. She'd also purchased a novel at one of their stops and had insisted they take turns reading to each other.

There were still times when he saw tears on her cheeks. And there were still times when she pulled away from him and retreated behind her walls. Yet, in spite of the setbacks, she'd made more of an effort to get to know him, and he could almost believe they were on their way to becoming friends.

Enya gazed upon the mansion several dozen feet back from the street. The Greek Revival and Italianate style building was designed with a curved balcony across the second floor and a curved portico as well, with prominent white columns and graceful, tall windows. It was one of the largest and finest homes in the district.

As the coachman opened the door, Sullivan started to

stand, but then he sat back down and faced Enya. He needed to be honest with her about his father so she wasn't shocked by how obnoxious the Commodore could be at times.

As much as he loved and respected his father, the Commodore's loud, unrestrained, and often brash communication was hard to take and had been part of the reason why he'd always loved being on the river, had even been part of the reason why he hadn't wanted to be taken off the river and forced to work in the office in New Orleans.

Sullivan cast a glance around to make sure his father wasn't anywhere nearby. "It is my duty to warn you."

"Warn me?" Her eyes widened, her long lashes fanning out and making her impossibly beautiful.

"My father is loud and overbearing. And he may be somewhat pushy when it comes to marriage."

"I don't understand."

"He's physically affectionate with my mother. Very much so. And he expects everyone else to be the same way."

Enya continued to stare at him, unblinking. Finally she seemed to process what he'd left unsaid, and although she didn't seem to embarrass easily, she focused her attention on her hands folded in her lap. "We'll tell him the truth, that we're waiting."

Sullivan cast another glance around. "If he discovers that we haven't consummated, he'll call into question the authenticity of my marriage."

"And then what will he do?" This time pink bloomed in her cheeks.

"He'll likely carry through with his initial threat to force me off the fleet and into the home office." He wouldn't let the Commodore push him into consummating his marriage before Enya was ready and willing. Nothing would shake his resolve on that score. "Have no fear, I won't pressure you. I am standing by my word regarding the issue."

She folded then unfolded her hands before clasping them tightly together again. She'd discussed the matter freely when they'd first been married, but now, after getting to know him, was she put off by the prospect of sleeping with him? Even if they were slowly becoming friends, that didn't mean she was attracted to him. He still hadn't shown her his scars, and once she saw them, she'd never find him appealing, would probably be repulsed.

Regardless, he had to figure out how to handle his father. "The best way to appease my father—and not draw his attention—is to make sure that I am showing you some physical affection."

"Oh." The word came out quietly.

Frustration pummeled through him. "I'm sorry, Enya. Please forgive me for even suggesting it. It's selfish of me. I'll find a way to explain our situation to my father—"

"No." Her hand shot out and covered his.

His father had forced him into marriage with the ultimatum. Now that Sullivan had done as his father had required, he couldn't let the Commodore command how he interacted with Enya. "I've already given him too much control over my life. I won't do it again—"

"Sullivan, stop."

He let his runaway thoughts halt and dropped his gaze to her hand upon his.

"We both made a bargain when we entered this marriage. I needed a home and a father for my baby. And you needed a way to appease your father."

"Yes, but our agreement came before we knew each other, before I understood just how difficult your previous marriage was."

"Along with all the hurt and regret that I bear?" Her voice carried a note of bitterness.

He gently slid his fingers around hers, hoping to reassure her. "I'm glad I can help you."

Every day he was thankful that he was her husband and not another man who might not be sensitive or patient or considerate of her needs. And he prayed he'd never do anything to hurt her.

She wiggled her hand against his, letting her fingers wrap around his more securely. Then she met his gaze levelly. "If you're glad that you get to do your part of the bargain, then let me do mine. Let me do this for you."

He hesitated. He'd already had setbacks with her and didn't want her to get upset with him again. He most certainly didn't want her to have any regrets.

"I'm sure it won't be too terrible," she said.

Too terrible? To show him physical affection? Sullivan bit back a sigh.

"I'll be performing just a wee bit. I've always had a knack for theatrics."

Performing? Theatrics? That was an even worse insult. He wanted to shoot straight up from his seat, hop out of the carriage, and stalk away. He did have a measure of pride, after all.

"I'll help you placate your father, and then we'll return to normal once we're on our way back to St. Louis."

But the truth was, he didn't want *normal* with her. He'd never intended that they remain only friends. In fact, the longer he was with her, the more he wanted a marriage where he had her whole heart, soul, and body.

He tugged free of her hold and stared at the quiet neighborhood and the other stately homes. His muscles were rigid, and his jaw flexed with the need to tell her he didn't want her physical affection if it wasn't genuine. That's why he'd been waiting to consummate and why he was being so careful not to touch her. Because he didn't want her to pretend or perform or simply go through the motions.

"Sullivan?" came a booming voice from the front portico, a voice that had always been loud enough to project over the roar of the steamboat engines, the slapping of the paddle wheel, and the rushing of the river.

"Your father?" Enya's eyes lit up. With mischief? Anticipation?

At least she wasn't dreading what was to come.

"What should we do first?" She sat back against the seat and studied him, her features livening with an animation that made her all the more alluring.

Even if she seemed to be rising to the occasion and willing to help make his father happy, they didn't need to go overboard with the playacting. "We don't need to do anything at the moment—"

"Aye, we do, and I know exactly what." She glanced out the door as if gauging where his father was. Then she clasped her hands around each of his biceps. "Ready?"

"For what?"

"Hug me."

A hug was innocent enough, wasn't it? He hesitated, even as the pressure on his arms went straight through his coat and shirt and seared his flesh.

Her gaze darted beyond him, widened, then she sat forward and threw herself upon him, wrapping her arms around his torso and burying herself against him.

At the feel of her body and the way her arms tightened against his ribs and her hands splayed at the center of his back, he couldn't think and couldn't move.

Even though he'd felt her body against his on the couple occasions that he'd carried her, it had been nothing like this. Her curves and her warmth and her vitality pressed into him, causing every inch of him to flare to life.

She lifted her head and shifted up so that her mouth was near his ear. "He's almost here. Hurry and put your arms around me."

Sullivan tried to comprehend her words through the loud humming in his blood.

"Sullivan. Now." Her urgent whisper against his ear was warm and only scattered his thoughts even more, like an early morning mist over the Mississippi.

Somehow, though, he managed to lift his arms and slide them around her, drawing her against him more firmly. The moment his arms encircled her slender length and luscious curves, his heart tumbled end over end, sucked into a rushing current, one he didn't want to escape, even if he drowned there.

With her face still close to his and her mouth near his ear, he could hear her soft intakes and exhalations.

He angled his head closer to her, and his nose bumped her cheek, then her ear. Her skin was softer than the finest silk.

He dragged in a deep breath, trying to stay rational. But as her floral perfume filled his nostrils, he lost all ability to reason. He lived only in that moment, with only her, with only the two of them existing outside of time and space.

"Sullivan?" His father's loud voice nearby dragged at him, but Sullivan couldn't make himself release her or back away. Instead, he was ready to move into this space with her permanently and never leave.

He tilted in just a little farther, and this time his nose grazed her neck. The graceful, slender length he'd tried not to notice over the past few weeks. He'd resisted. He'd forced himself to stay far away by sheer willpower. But now . . . he couldn't live without just one more touch.

He brushed his nose along that stretch, this time purposefully, slowly, letting himself blaze a trail from her jaw down to her collarbone. It was a trail he wanted to travel again and again.

But before he could inch his way back up to her jaw, his father's boisterous laughter resounded behind him and filled the carriage. "Well, well, well. Never thought I'd see the day. But zounds. You've fallen hard, boy!"

Enya was the first to pull away, releasing a gasp and pressing her hands to her mouth as if she was surprised they'd been caught in an indecent situation.

Sullivan, on the other hand, couldn't find the strength he needed to let go of her. In fact, his hands flexed against her back—in that elegant curve just above her waistline—and he wasn't sure he'd ever be able to move them.

"Whoo-ee! Looks like you can't keep your hands or mouth off your wife!" The Commodore's voice echoed loudly enough that not only did it jerk Sullivan out of his haze, but he guessed the entire Garden District of New Orleans had heard the proclamation.

With heat crawling up his neck and starting to strangle him, Sullivan slipped his hands out from around Enya. He'd known one way or another his father would embarrass him. He always did. Sullivan could only pray that since the Commodore had observed the hug and desire, he'd accept the marriage as authentic and wouldn't make any more issues about physical affection.

"That's my boy!" the Commodore continued. "Enjoying the bliss of marriage just the way I taught you!"

"Blast!" Sullivan mumbled, scooting away from Enya. "We need to get out, or he'll keep carrying on."

Enya had her hand cupped over her mouth still, but he could see the smile she was trying to hide. Did she find their predicament preposterous? Or was she amused by the Commodore?

Either way, thankfully she'd not been overwhelmed or undone by their embrace the way he feared. Instead, he'd been the one overwhelmed and undone. He was still in half a haze, unable to think clearly and aching to hold her again.

With stiff movements, he managed to descend the carriage's step and land on the ground beside his father. The Commodore was the same towering height as Sullivan, with similar broad shoulders and stocky girth. But his hair was much lighter, and his face filled with a full beard and mustache.

And a grin. His father was wearing a grin that was as wide as the Gulf of Mexico. "When I got your letter, I had my doubts. But you really did it."

"Good afternoon, Commodore." Sullivan reached out to shake his father's hand.

His father clasped his hand and then pulled him in for an

embrace as usual. The back thumping had ceased after the war when the burn scars had still been painful to the touch. But now, instead of the thunderous back slapping, his father took a step back and socked him hard in the arm.

Sullivan didn't flinch. "I'd like to introduce you to my wife." He shifted, expecting to find Enya in the carriage door, waiting to descend. But she'd scooted back out of sight.

He leaned in and extended his hand toward her.

She rested casually against the plush seat and was smiling, mirth dancing in her eyes. Although he wanted to be offended by her cavalier attitude toward the hug, he couldn't muster any irritation. Not at the sight of her smile. She smiled so rarely that the beauty of it now stopped his heart and lungs.

She laid her hand in his and allowed him to help her to her feet. As she bent forward into the door, the Commodore's grin fell away, and his mouth dropped open.

This time, Sullivan could hardly contain his smile. He'd been anticipating this exact moment, when his father got his first glimpse of Enya and saw how stunning she was.

From the way Enya paused, lifted her lashes, and curved her lips just slightly, he could tell she was most definitely putting on a show for his father, and she seemed to enjoy doing so.

Sullivan assisted her to the ground, then smoothed a hand over her skirt and straightened her shawl, both movements drawing attention to her womanly figure. Of course, his mind went back to a few moments ago when he'd held that womanly figure against his body. His dreams from now until eternity would be filled with the sensations of that lush form pressed to his.

Enya glanced first from Sullivan to his father, then back.

She quirked one of her delicate brows as though to prompt him.

But as he let his sights wander over her features, his gaze dropped again to her neck, to the pulse throbbing near her collarbone. What would it be like to skim over it, not with his nose, but with his lips?

She squeezed his hand that was still holding hers from assisting her down. And she tilted her head toward the Commodore.

"Oh yes." How had one hug turned him into such an ungainly idiot around her? "Father, may I present Mrs. Enya O'Brien, my wife." He hadn't said her full name before, and he loved the sound of it together, especially with the words *my wife*.

Enya offered a hand to his father.

With his mouth still gaping and his eyes bugging, he glanced down at her hand and then back at her face before clumsily grasping her hand, lifting it to his mouth, and kissing her knuckles.

"It's a pleasure to meet you, sir." Enya spoke in a breathy voice, one that turned up the temperature of the spring afternoon so that sweat popped out at the back of Sullivan's neck.

His father released Enya, then smiled tenderly. "The pleasure is mine."

Enya slipped her hand into the crook of Sullivan's arm, as had become their habit. But instead of their usual simple hold, she wrapped her arm through deeper, so her shoulder pressed against his arm, and met his gaze, a conspiratorial look in her eyes.

His father released a happy-sounding chuckle. "It's no wonder Sullivan is nearly out of his mind over you."

Sullivan bit back a sigh at his father's insufferable comment.

"Sullivan is a good husband, Mr. O'Brien."

"I'm called Commodore, my dear." His father's smile was creeping back.

"Your son is one of the kindest and most considerate men I've ever met." Enya was laying on the charm and was clearly enjoying herself.

Sullivan wasn't sure if she meant what she said. At the moment, it didn't really matter. She was happy and vivacious and showing a side of herself that he'd seen so little since meeting her.

All he wanted was for her to be truly happy again. If this pretending with the Commodore was what it took to bring her fully out of her despair, then so be it.

16

*E*nya stifled a yawn. She couldn't be tired yet. They'd only finished dining an hour ago. The night was still young.

On the settee in the O'Brien's parlor, she lifted her fan and pumped air against her face, hoping that would wake her up.

"Are you warm?" Mrs. O'Brien's kindly face creased with concern as she leaned forward on the settee beside Enya.

The lantern light from the pedestal table fell over Enya in the growing darkness of the evening. "Not overly so, thank you."

It had quickly become clear after meeting Mrs. O'Brien that Sullivan took after his mother. She was a dark-haired beauty with a calm and quiet demeanor, unlike her husband, who was every bit as loud and overbearing as Sullivan had warned.

Even now, the Commodore's voice carried across the parlor from where the men—including both of Sullivan's brothers-in-law—were sitting at a round table playing a game of cards, Irish whiskey filling their glasses and cigar smoke curling in the air.

They'd been discussing the steamboats' near accident with the *Belle* and *Ida May* in St. Louis. Apparently the Memphis Packet Company was the O'Brien's biggest competitor on the Mississippi, and the incident wasn't the first time Sullivan had been threatened by Captain Fitch.

The fellow had already trumped up charges in the past regarding fraudulent merchant certificates, embezzling government funds for private purposes, and avoiding custom taxes. But none of the indictments ever amounted to anything because they simply weren't true. Sullivan and the Commodore ran an exemplary company and tried to be above reproach in everything.

They'd also talked about the latest news, how the SS *California* had voyaged from New York to California in less than five months around the tip of South America. With the successful journey, the men had argued about whether regular steamboat travel could now happen between the east and the west.

The Commodore was of a mind to invest in building their own steamboats that could weather such a trip, especially with so many people eager to travel to California now that gold had been found, and Sullivan agreed that such a venture could be profitable.

Enya sat with the women in the cluster of settees across from the men, close enough that she could catch some of their conversation when she wasn't making small talk with the ladies, who were eager to learn more about her and her family and to hear of news from St. Louis.

All the while she'd been conversing and sipping tea, she'd had a direct view of Sullivan. He wasn't smoking or drinking like the other fellows, but he was more relaxed tonight than she'd ever seen him. He leaned back in his chair, the top button on his vest undone, his long legs spread out, and his hair mussed.

Most of all, the normally hard lines of his face were soft in the amber glow of the setting sun outside the windows. And without the scowl or the intensity, his features were markedly handsome.

Oh aye, he was a good-looking man. There had never been any question about that. But somehow tonight, in his home and around his family, he carried himself in a way that drew her attention.

Mrs. O'Brien took a drink of tea and watched Enya over the rim of her cup. "You can't keep your eyes off of Sullivan."

It was all in pretense, but Enya couldn't explain that.

The other two ladies smiled and nodded, both lovely and polite. Sullivan's sister, Neala, was with child and quite far along, due in less than a month. When the ladies weren't asking Enya questions, the conversation invariably came back to the baby and the delivery and what it was like to have a newborn.

Enya tensed every time. She wasn't sure how to participate in the discussion without giving away her own pregnancy. Revealing it would be an utter disaster after the way the O'Briens had so warmly welcomed her into their home and family the same way Sullivan had welcomed her into his life. What would they think if they knew the truth—that she was pregnant with another man's child?

The Commodore would realize Sullivan's marriage was one of convenience and would be furious at them for trying to dupe him into believing they had more affection for each other than was really there. So far no one had questioned

Sullivan's explanation that they'd met during one of his visits to St. Louis and had gotten married on Shrove Tuesday.

They hadn't needed to do much more convincing since their display in the carriage earlier. That little bit of affection had seemed to mostly satisfy the Commodore, although he'd motioned for Sullivan to put his arm around her once dinner was over.

Sullivan had quickly obliged, and when he started to offer her an apologetic look, she reached for his other hand and squeezed it, hoping to reassure him that she was fine.

Because she had been fine. She hadn't minded the hug in the carriage, not even when he'd lingered a little bit and bent in to make a bigger display by grazing her neck. She could admit, she'd liked being in his arms, and the caress against her neck had been pleasant.

She didn't want it to be pleasant, though, did she? What if the physical contact made things awkward between them? And what if they lost the easy camaraderie they'd had since the night she'd played the piano in the saloon and opened up about Bryan.

Maybe the pretending had been a bad idea. In the carriage when she'd made the suggestion, it had seemed innocent enough. But now that she'd spent the evening with his family, had an elaborate supper, and was ensconced in their intimate gathering, guilt reared its head.

Especially with Mrs. O'Brien's comment hanging in the air, unanswered. Enya glanced again at Sullivan, glad he wasn't aware of her attention upon him. He was too engrossed in the card game and hadn't looked at her once, at least that she'd seen.

Not that she'd been hoping he'd look at her.

"Oh aye." Enya spoke carefully, not wanting to overdo her adoration. The more she could stick with the truth, the better. "I rarely see Sullivan sitting and enjoying himself. And he should be doing so more often."

"He works too hard." Mrs. O'Brien's tone was soothing, just like Sullivan's.

At that moment, a footman approached with a serving tray. "More tea, madam?" He directed his question first at Mrs. O'Brien, then at Enya. Another footman entered the room, this one carrying a tray that had a distinctly fishy smell.

As he drew near the men at the table, the scent grew stronger. Enya hadn't been overly bothered by the smells or tastes of foods so far during her pregnancy. But once in a while, like the time she'd had to leave the restaurant in Natchez, the nausea came swiftly and unexpectedly.

"The alligator bites you requested, sir." The footman held out the tray to the Commodore. "And the Cajun crab cakes."

The talk over the meal had been all about the various foods unique to New Orleans. And the Commodore had requested that the cook make a couple of his favorites to serve as appetizers in the evening.

Enya had been interested in giving the new food a try, her sense of adventure growing stronger, as it had been doing more every day on the trip with Sullivan. But now at the waft of the food, the roiling in her stomach pushed up swiftly.

She stood abruptly and pressed a hand over her mouth.

At her rise, all the men seated around the table also scooted back and stood.

"Are you alright?" Mrs. O'Brien was on her feet in an instant and steadying her with a gentle touch.

Sullivan was already shoving his way around the table, tipping glasses as he passed, his dark eyes locked on her. He dodged the footman and reached her side before she could decide whether to run to the nearest window or find a container to retch into.

With a furrowed brow, he didn't hesitate. He scooped her off her feet and carried her out of the room.

He didn't stop in the spacious hallway. Instead he crossed into the conservatory and made a direct line to a set of double doors. He swung them open and stepped out onto a covered terrace. The fresh evening air greeted her, and she rapidly gulped it in, trying to push down the nausea.

His gaze hadn't moved from her face, and his jaw was rigid.

She breathed in again, and the queasiness began to subside.

The sky was turning lavender with a mixture of rose from the setting sun, and only a few stars were out. The balmy warmth from the day had faded into cooler temperatures.

The spacious garden spread out before them, as lovely now as it had been earlier when the Commodore gave her a tour of the home. The sweet scent of honeysuckle and peach blossoms greeted her again.

She took another deep lungful, then rested her head against Sullivan's shoulder.

"Better?" His low voice rumbled near her cheek.

"Aye." Wrapped against the crevice of Sullivan's body, she felt as safe and warm as she always did whenever he carried her. "Thank you for your help. If not for your quick thinking and rescue, I might have dumped the contents of my stomach into one of your mother's vases."

"Then it was the scent of the food that upset your stomach?" His expression was grave.

"I'm sorry." She pushed against him, intending to force him to put her down. "I feel bad that I've torn you away from time with your family."

"You didn't tear me. I chose to help you."

"So you did. But I still don't want to interrupt your card game and conversation."

"Your well-being is more important."

"Your family will be wondering what is wrong with me."

"We'll tell them the truth, that the food didn't agree with you."

She nodded. Would they suspect she was pregnant? Surely at least his sister Neala would.

"And we'll tell them you're tired and that you need to go to bed."

"I am tired."

"I know."

"How?" She let her gaze linger over his scruffy jaw and broad chin, before working her way up his cheeks to his nose and then meeting his eyes. His bottomless, dark eyes. "You didn't glance my way the entire time we were in the parlor."

"I saw you."

She shook her head, but she supposed that explained why he'd crossed to her so quickly. His consideration was always more than she deserved. "You can put me down now, Sullivan. I'm feeling better."

"I'll carry you up to the room."

"No, I've been enough of a bother and don't want to take you away from your family any longer."

He was already turning and entering through the double

doors. Though the conservatory was mostly dark, her attention fixed directly on the piano in one half of the room. A part of her longed to sit down and give voice to the melody that had been formulating in her head over the past few days.

But another part of her was scared to take that next huge step.

"We'll go say good night." His tone was commanding, and although she wanted to argue with him, she was learning he was stubborn when he wanted to be.

As Sullivan stepped through the wide parlor door, he paused. All eyes swung to them, mostly to her, and the faces wore curiosity.

"Good night." Sullivan was still holding her as effortlessly as earlier. "We're retiring for the evening."

"Retiring?" The Commodore was leaning back in his chair, his cigar poised in one hand, and his eyes crinkled with his smile. "Sure you are."

Was the man hinting that Sullivan was making an excuse to be alone with her? To take her to bed?

She didn't embarrass easily, but at the moment she wanted to bury her face and hide. Or to at least retort with a scathing comment. Before she could think of something, Sullivan replied first. "You're jealous. That's all."

The Commodore barked out a laugh, and the other two men guffawed.

Sullivan didn't smile, but his eyes took on a sparkle, almost as if he was enjoying the bantering.

Thankfully no one mentioned her queasiness. And thankfully, as they finished excusing themselves, no one insinuated anything else.

As Sullivan carried her up the stairway to their room, she

made a halfhearted effort to get him to put her down, but he refused. So she settled in without protesting any further.

Once behind the closed doors of the spacious room Sullivan occupied whenever he was in New Orleans, they fell into the easy way of relating that had become comfortable while rooming together on the steamer. He stepped into the hallway and gave her the privacy she needed to change into her nightgown. Only after she was securely buried beneath the covers did he reenter.

He pulled a chair beside the bed and read aloud from *Pilgrim's Progress* until she couldn't keep her eyes open any longer.

The next time she stirred, he was engrossed in reading Augustine's *Confessions*. She wasn't sure how much time had elapsed again when a rapping against the door awoke her.

Sullivan was in the process of laying out a bed on the floor as he usually did. He paused, glanced at the door, and then grabbed up all the blankets and stood. He scanned the perimeter of the room frantically, then crossed to the wardrobe on the opposite side of the bed, opened it, and stuffed the covers inside.

"Sullivan?" The voice on the other side of the door belonged to the Commodore.

"Sir?" Sullivan responded calmly.

What was the Commodore doing at their bedroom door? Had he come to check on them? To make sure they were sleeping together the way a real married couple would? Maybe this was one of the things Sullivan had been trying to warn her about.

Sullivan had already shed most of his clothes and wore

only underdrawers and a linen shirt that hugged every rounded muscle in his chest and arms.

She'd never seen him unclothed, had only ever been around him when he was fully attired. Now, at the sight of his thickly muscled bare legs as well as the veins running up and down his arms, her pulse stumbled and fell before picking itself back up and taking off at a strange, racing pace.

She pushed up to her elbows, the blanket falling away from her shoulders.

At her movement, his gaze swung to her. His eyes widened and filled with panic, almost as if he didn't want her to see him in his indecent state of attire. But why? Surely he wasn't embarrassed, not when he had such a muscular and perfectly sculpted body.

Was it the scars? Without the high starched collar and cravat, the red splotches on his neck and shoulder blared as brightly as a sun flare. She'd known he had scars, but she hadn't realized they were so pervasive.

An ache radiated in her chest at the hurt he must have suffered. What had happened to him?

"Can I come in?" his father asked.

"Perhaps in the morning."

"I need to talk to you about something now." His father's voice was firm. "Get decent. I can wait."

Sullivan's eyes widened, and he searched the room, clearly trying to decide where to stand or sit.

There really was only one choice. She sat up farther and tossed the covers back on the side closest to him while scooting over. *Here,* she mouthed while patting the spot on the bed beside her.

Sullivan hesitated only a moment longer. In one long step

he was at the bed and sliding in. The mattress sagged beneath his weight, thrusting them together. But she didn't have time to make a fuss, was only in a hurry to ensure his father saw them together.

"You can come in," Sullivan said.

As the door opened a crack, she tossed the cover over Sullivan and at the same time lifted his arm around her.

Sullivan resisted only until the door swung open all the way and his father stepped inside the room. Then he drew her closer into the crook of his body. She quickly slipped a hand over the cover onto his chest, hoping the pose appeared natural.

The Commodore swept his gaze around the room. What was he searching for? Clues that they were pretending to share affection? Did he suspect that Sullivan had intended to sleep on the floor?

If so, she needed to do a better job of playacting, and she needed to do so now.

She slid her hand higher until she reached the v of his neckline. Then she tucked a finger inside and skimmed it across his bare flesh.

Sullivan drew in a sharp breath and immediately lifted a hand to capture her fingers.

She dove her hand deeper to keep him from stopping her, so that before she realized it, she had her arm halfway into his shirt, her palm flat against his chest, almost directly above his heart. His skin was smooth, and the ridges of his muscles were solid.

She'd only felt his chest through the layers of his garments, so to have access in this manner was slightly daring. But she'd never shirked from dares or danger.

Sullivan's arm tightened around her. And as he took in her hand underneath his shirt, his nose flared. Then his eyes lifted to hers, and the dark brown—almost black—wrapped around her like a rich, thick fur coat, engulfing her in heat and luxuriating her in softness at the same time.

"I'm sorry for barging in and disturbing you." The Commodore peeked their way, took in their cozy snuggling, and pulled the watch out of his pocket and began to wind it.

"Do you need something?" Sullivan's voice held a note of irritation. Was he playacting his irritation? Or was it real?

The Commodore fiddled with the watch for another moment before he tucked it away and met Sullivan's gaze directly. "Your mother seems to think Enya is pregnant already."

Sullivan stiffened at the same time she did. It was one thing to pretend to be affectionate with each other. But what should they say now? They couldn't outright lie to the Commodore and his wife, could they?

17

*H*ow had his mother realized Enya was pregnant? Being nauseous from the scent of food wasn't enough of a sign, was it?

Sitting rigidly against the headboard, Sullivan didn't back down from his father's stare. Instead, he held the man's sharp gaze. "It's none of your or mother's concern."

With Enya pressed against him and her hand underneath his shirt, his body was begging him to think about her and how good and right it felt to be in the bed with her. But he couldn't let his thoughts go there tonight. He had to stay focused on what his father was saying. If he hoped to outwit the man, he had to be at his sharpest.

His father cleared his throat, then fiddled with his watch again. "Your mother and I, well . . ."

Enya was growing stiffer with every passing moment. She finally slipped her hand out from his shirt and sat forward, her features tightening with determination. "I have a confession to make—"

"No, Enya." Sullivan knew exactly what she intended to do—tell his father the truth about everything.

But the problem was, his father wasn't very good at keeping secrets. No matter how much they might stress the need to keep the pregnancy private, the Commodore would tell his closest friends, and they would inform their wives. Then their wives would share the news with their friends. Before the week was out, all of New Orleans would know about the pregnancy.

At the very least, most people would speculate that he'd had relations with Enya before they were married. That was better than everyone learning Enya's baby had a different father altogether.

"I feel bad for lying," Enya whispered, her tone filled with remorse.

"My family doesn't need to know our business." He let his father hear his statement. "If we choose not to share our personal life with them, that doesn't mean we're lying."

The Commodore nodded. "If you don't want to say anything that's fine. But we want you to know we're here to support you."

Enya stared at his father intently. "Support?"

"Of course. What's done is done. And we can't change that. All we can do now is support you."

"That's not how my family handles mistakes." A note of bitterness edged Enya's tone, a note Sullivan had heard from time to time when she spoke of her family. Her haste in wanting to leave St. Louis and avoid her mother was telling as well.

"Sometimes we make mistakes." The Commodore met Enya's gaze directly. "When we do, we don't wallow in it.

Instead we ask ourselves what we can learn so that we don't repeat our foolishness."

As overbearing as the Commodore was at times, Sullivan could admit, the man did have a great deal of wisdom. And he'd taught Sullivan a lot over the years of riding together on the river, about more than just steamboats.

"If you're expecting a child," the Commodore continued, "it's something to rejoice over, not hide."

Enya's body was melding into his again.

Sullivan's gaze dropped to Enya's nightgown strap that had slipped off her shoulder, leaving a large patch of exposed skin. What he wouldn't give to eventually have her permission to graze his thumb along her delicate shoulder and down her arm and then back up.

Would they ever reach that point?

"That's all I had to say." His father opened the door behind him, then his lips curved into a crooked grin underneath his long beard. "I would tell you to get busy making a baby, but since you've already taken care of that, I'll just tell you to have fun."

With that obnoxious piece of advice, he winked, stepped out of the room, and closed the door.

Sullivan wanted to sink into the mattress and disappear underneath. Instead he sat frozen to his spot.

Enya didn't move either. She stared at the closed door, her eyes wide.

After the heavy thud of the Commodore's footsteps moved down the hallway, Sullivan began to extricate himself from around Enya.

"Wait," she whispered, reaching for his arm and holding him in place. "He might come back."

"He won't come back tonight." At least Sullivan hoped he wouldn't.

"And what if he barges in and finds you sleeping on the floor?"

Sullivan could feel his brows furrowing. She was right. His father was unpredictable, had almost caught him bedding on the floor. What would happen the next time his father made an unexpected visit?

"I think you'll need to sleep in the bed with me," Enya whispered, and this time her cheeks turned pink.

"That's a terrible idea." The very mention of it made his mind go places that it didn't need to, like back to the loose nightgown strap and the patch of skin he wanted to caress.

"Two people can sleep comfortably in a bed this size. While growing up, my sister and I shared a bed smaller than this. We tickled each other all the time but otherwise were fine."

He pulled his arm away from her and tried to put a couple of inches between them. Unfortunately, the mattress was dipping beneath his bulky frame so much that she remained at his side, with their arms and legs pressed together.

"Let's be clear about two things." He couldn't prevent his voice from turning growly. "One, I won't be like your sister when I sleep with you. And two, I won't be able to sleep comfortably with you anywhere nearby. It's already difficult to sleep with you in the same room, much less in the same bed."

She leaned back and stared at the ceiling.

He wanted to shift and let himself look at her all night long. But he kicked off the covers and sat up. Too late he realized his mistake, that his back was facing her and that she had nearly a full view of all the scars his undershirt didn't cover.

Hurriedly, he tried to swing his legs over the side of the bed.

"Wait." Her hand snaked out and caught his. And in the next moment, she laced her fingers through his so tenderly that the touch immobilized him.

The light in the room wasn't bright, but she couldn't miss seeing his ravaged skin. Wasn't she repulsed by it?

"We can build a wall of pillows between us." Her voice was soft. Did she still want to be with him, even after seeing him at his worst? Why wasn't she running from the room and him as fast as she could?

Every muscle in his body strained to stand up, cross to his wardrobe, and pull out another shirt, one that would cover the burn marks. But she tugged on his hand tightly as though she didn't plan to let go.

A part of him prayed she wouldn't ever reject him because of all his flaws. But another part of him couldn't accept that she'd ever want him—at least not romantically.

"Please, Sullivan?"

With a heavy sigh, he lifted his legs back onto the mattress. Being in bed with her was just asking for trouble. There was no telling what he might do if his thoughts and desires ran away from him. But he couldn't deny that he wanted to be close to her, that the anticipation of lying beside her—even if just for a little while—was better than the anticipation of Christmas morning.

He grabbed one of the decorative pillows and placed it between them. She did the same until a barrier ran from their shoulders down to their feet. Finally, after she snuffed out the light, he settled in on his side of the bed. She seemed to be doing the same, pulling the covers up over both of them and situating herself so that she was facing his direction, using her arm to brace her head.

He was trying to tear down her walls. Why, then, had he built this wall of pillows? Should he toss them all to the floor?

She was still holding his hand, now underneath the pillows. And somehow he sensed she wasn't ready yet for the wall to crumble completely but that she was letting him crack through and disassemble it brick by brick.

For long moments, they didn't speak or move. They just lay there, their breathing filling the silence. Sounds from other parts of the mansion filtered into the quiet—the closing of a door, the Commodore's laughter, the squeak of the floor overhead in the servants' quarters.

He sensed what was coming even before she spoke, and he braced his shoulders.

"Will you tell me about it?" she whispered.

In the darkness broken by the faint moonlight spilling between the cracks in the draperies, he could only see the outline of her face, not more than two handspans away. She was close and yet far enough that hopefully he wouldn't do anything stupid that would send her scurrying like a frightened hare back down into her deep burrow.

He didn't respond to her question. He didn't ever talk about what had happened that day in the war with anyone.

Her thumb grazed the back of his hand. The caress seemed to be her way of reassuring him that she cared enough to listen, the same way he'd listened to her that night at the piano when she'd been heartbroken over her failed marriage.

Even though her pain was more recent than his, she'd been courageous in opening up to him and sharing. Was it time to do the same with her?

He released a sigh. "It happened about two years ago, in March of '47 during the siege of Veracruz."

"During the Mexican War?"

"Yes, I was one of the pilots for the *Spitfire* steamboat." Flames skittered across his skin at just the mention of that tragic day. "The Mexican forces at Veracruz refused to consider a peace treaty. So the Americans laid siege to the city and attacked it with artillery."

"And you were a part of that battle?"

"Yes, after two days with little success, we got word that Santa Anna was marching an army from Mexico City with additional forces."

Her attention was wholly riveted to him, so much so that he could feel her interest and sympathy. But as the memories flared to life, his natural instinct was to stamp each one out. He didn't want to relive that day.

But he forced himself to whisper the words anyway. "General Scott learned of the advance, and even though he dispatched dragoons to intercept Santa Anna, he knew we had to do more or risk defeat."

She grazed his hand again as though she knew the sharing was difficult.

"The *Spitfire* and the *Vixen* offered to get in closer so our cannonballs and Congreve rockets could do more damage."

"But that put you in range of their gunfire and cannons?"

"Yes."

"You were hit?"

He swallowed the revulsion that came from thinking about the damage and loss of lives that night on both sides, even the women and children, because General Scott had refused to allow their evacuation from the city.

"The *Vixen* was hit and exploded. Some of the men were still alive and in need of rescue. Since I know how to swim, I jumped in and saved them."

His explanation was simplified and a much more polite version of the carnage, the burning bodies, the men drowning before their eyes. Even though the *Spitfire* had tried to get closer to the men, the fire covering the debris all along the surface of the bay had been dangerous.

But he hadn't been able to stand back and watch men needlessly die. He'd done what he thought was right. He'd been able to rescue a total of six men and had earned a Certificate of Merit as a result—not that he cared about the accolades.

"You got burned while saving the men?" This time she reached out her other hand and lightly touched the puckered flesh on his neck.

He wanted to recoil, jump up from the bed, and pace to the opposite side of the room. But he held himself motionless, even though he'd turned as rigid as a jack staff.

If she felt his stiffness, it didn't deter her. Her index finger traced the top scar, the one that he tried to keep hidden by his collar but that peeked out. "You must have been in excruciating pain, to be sure."

He'd been in agony for months afterward, agony that not even morphine could entirely take away.

Her finger followed the outline of another scar, this one lower and much bigger. The red splotch was tight and misshapen and a part of him he loathed anyone seeing, much less touching. In fact, he couldn't remember anyone but the doctor and later his mother viewing the wounds as they tended to him.

As Enya's finger moved even lower toward his collarbone, he closed his eyes and fought against the overwhelming urge to pull back and roll away to force her to stop. But again, as before, only one thought stopped him. Her pain. She'd shared it with him. If he wanted her to open up and be honest about all she'd gone through, then he had to be willing to do the same.

He tried to force his tense muscles to relax, but he couldn't, could only picture the flames shooting into the air, the stench of burning flesh, the heat of the flames, the cries of the dying.

Her fingers skimmed from his neck up his cheek and into his hair. She combed back the strands that had fallen over his forehead. Her fingers were soft, even soothing, as she slid them into his hair again. Then again.

He could feel her gaze upon him, and he wished for more light so he could attempt to read her expression. Was she starting to care about him? Or was this more of her offering of friendship?

"Thank you for sharing with me," she whispered.

He nodded.

She stifled a yawn even as she caressed his hair.

He didn't dare move for fear of breaking the beauty of the moment. After a few beats, her fingers slowed until they halted altogether. At the even rhythm of her breathing, he could tell she'd dozed again.

All for the better. He wasn't sure how he would have been able to resist her if she'd continued stroking his hair.

He closed his eyes and forced himself to think on everything but her. The sleeping arrangement was difficult enough. And he didn't want to make things worse.

18

*E*nya awoke to warmth and solidness surrounding her. And the faint scent of bacon in the air.

Her stomach growled, and she started to stretch her legs.

At the pressure of an arm over hers and a hand on her abdomen, she froze.

Her eyes flew open to daylight pushing back the darkness of the night. Her eyes locked in on the masculine blue of the wallpaper and the dark mahogany furniture that graced the bedroom. Sullivan's bedroom.

The events of the previous night returned in full force, especially the Commodore coming to the room to let them know he and his wife wanted to support the pregnancy. She'd expected his censure, disappointment, and frustration. But his chastisement had been mild and his encouragement strong.

If only her own da and mam could accept her mistakes as easily as Sullivan's parents had. But she supposed her da had done the best he could. After all, he'd been the one to pick up all the ruined pieces of her life and try to put them back together.

She glanced down at herself, attired in her nightgown, the covers askew . . . and Sullivan's hand splayed across her stomach.

Her mind sparked into full wakefulness, to the pressure of his body curled against hers from behind, his chest and legs formed to hers. A couple of the pillows still seemed to be wedged between them, forming a flimsy barrier. Because she could certainly feel his presence—the breadth of his chest, the thickness of his arms, the length of one of his l egs.

She didn't dare move. Why was he holding her in such a manner? It was indecent. And they hadn't agreed upon it.

His words from last night came rushing back: *"It's already difficult to sleep with you in the same room, much less in the same bed."* If she wasn't mistaken, he'd basically admitted he was attracted to her.

Even as her thoughts began to spiral with panic, she could feel the even rise and fall of his chest and guessed he hadn't done it on purpose, that somehow during their sleeping, they'd rolled together. Maybe that's why he hadn't wanted to join her in bed, because he'd been afraid of this happening.

She took a deep breath and released the tension. He hadn't taken advantage of her before. And he wouldn't now. She just needed to remind herself of that.

After being so wrong in everything about Bryan, she'd planned to despise all men forever, even her new husband. But she hadn't counted on meeting a man like Sullivan, who put her needs above his own, who was selfless almost to a fault, who respected her enough to give her time to adjust to their marriage.

Even if she couldn't imagine ever anticipating being intimate with him, he made her feel so protected and safe and cherished. She could admit this closeness with him was nice and that she wouldn't be opposed to waking up in his arms every morning.

His fingers on her abdomen shifted slightly, the touch tender, as if he were holding both her and the baby at the same time. She loved that about him. How he was taking responsibility for the baby as if it were his own.

Now that's what his parents believed. That Sullivan had intimate relations with her outside the bounds of marriage, perhaps on a previous trip he'd made to St. Louis. And she hadn't corrected the Commodore and neither had Sullivan.

Would he allow his parents to believe the child was his? Or would he one day tell them the truth?

Sullivan stirred again, and she sensed he was waking—much later than he normally did. Maybe he didn't sleep well on the floor. Or maybe he was troubled by dreams of the war. She would be if she'd experienced what he had.

Either way, she had to insist that he stay in the bed from now on. Hadn't they proven after last night that they could sleep together as a married couple without jeopardizing anything about the relationship they'd begun to build?

He stretched, then stiffened and sucked in a breath.

She didn't move.

He held himself motionless too, the mortification rolling off him in waves. No doubt he was trying to figure out how to extricate himself without waking her. Did he think he could back away to his part of the bed without her being the wiser to the way they'd ended up?

A tiny smile tugged at her lips. Maybe she ought to make his extrication more difficult and have a wee bit of fun with him.

She closed her eyes and tried to make her breathing steady.

He was growing more rigid with every passing second and began to inch his hand away from her stomach. He was reacting as she'd predicted, trying to sneak away from her.

With a pretend yawn, she slid her hand over his on her stomach to prevent him from moving it any further.

He froze again.

She made herself breathe evenly as if she was still slumbering.

After more long heartbeats, he tried to tug his hand out once more, but she let her fingers close around his. As he attempted to slip his arm away, she snuggled in deeper. And when he lifted a leg to move backward, she pretended to let hers fall against his.

He lay immobile behind her, thoroughly trapped, with no way of escape from their indecent predicament.

Her lips curved higher. He was so kind to her that he wouldn't allow himself even the smallest hint that he was taking advantage of her. Captain Sullivan O'Brien was a good, good man.

She tightened her hold on his hand, then realized her mistake too late. Would he recognize she was actually awake and not sleeping?

In the next instant, he relaxed against her, his body pressing into her more fully. His breathing was near, filling her senses with a slow but steady rhythm.

He bent in closer to her ear until his lips were almost

touching her. "I know what you're doing." His voice was gravelly.

The words, maybe the touch of his lips, or the sound of his voice—it all went straight through her with a strange sizzle, one that coursed along her nerve endings.

She pretended to yawn and then murmured, "Hmmm?"

His mouth didn't move from her ear. "I can tell you're awake."

She released a sleepy hum and then tried to roll nonchalantly.

Before she could carry out her charade any further, his fingers dropped away from her abdomen and gently dug into her side.

Was he tickling her?

Her eyes shot open.

He moved higher, near her rib cage, his fingers shifting in a definite tickle.

She couldn't hold back a soft laugh.

"Admit you were pretending to be asleep." His low growl near her ear made her stomach flip.

"Me?" she asked too innocently. "I would never pretend—"

His tickles were gentle, almost careful, but they made her laugh anyway.

She squirmed and wiggled in an effort to get away from him.

But his weight against the mattress and the dip in the middle of the bed caused her to sag against him, preventing her escape. He was relentless and held her captive, tickling her until her laughter rang out.

"Admit it." He paused again, as he had several other times to issue his ultimatum.

He was on top of her, pinning both of her hands above her head, giving her no way to defend herself.

"Fine. I admit it." She could hardly get the words out through her gasping breaths.

His dark eyes were filled with laughter, and he had a gorgeous smile, just as she'd imagined it would be, revealing his even teeth and transforming his face from handsome to irresistible.

Somehow in all the rolling and twisting and playfulness, she ended up underneath him. He was keeping the full weight of his body from crushing her by suspending himself with his straight arms.

"Let me hear you say it." His smile was so content and beautiful; it made her want to spend her life doing whatever it took to make him smile again.

"Say what?"

His mouth and lips were perfect. How had she not noticed them before? And all that dark scruff on his chin and surrounding his mouth only accentuated it.

"Tell me you were pretending."

"And if I don't?"

"I'll have to think of another way to torture you."

"How do you intend to torture me now?"

His gaze slid to her mouth and then quickly away, but in the process, something darkened in his eyes.

Was he thinking about kissing her?

Suddenly she was conscious of the way they were lying together. Her chest continued to rise and fall, her breathing the only sound between them. Even though he was holding himself aloft as best he could, his legs were still tangled with hers. Her nightgown had crept up to her knees, and she could even feel his bare legs against hers. And she wasn't repulsed by it.

In fact, something warm, even delicious, spilled inside her, like a warm fermented drink, sticky and sugary. Her gaze shifted back to his lips. If he tried to kiss her, she wouldn't object. She might even enjoy it. After all, she'd liked kissing Bryan before they'd gotten married. When his kisses had filled her with all kinds of longings she hadn't been able to describe.

Of course, she hadn't liked his hard and demanding kisses later. She'd found them as difficult to tolerate as the rest of his touching.

Would it be the same way with Sullivan?

Her smile faded.

A second later, his smile was gone too, and he was scrambling away from her. He was off the bed and stalking across the room before she could catch her breath.

Clearly he'd sensed her resistance, which was for the best. She didn't want to give him the wrong impression that she enjoyed the physical aspects of marriage. Obviously, if he was ready to have his way with her, she wouldn't resist. He had every right to demand more, especially after delaying as long as he already had.

But was he still waiting for her to do the asking, as he'd said after their wedding? If so, when would he get tired of waiting? Because eventually he'd not only get tired of waiting to have his needs met, but he'd also get tired of her.

He swiped up his trousers almost angrily and stuffed a leg inside. In only his underdrawers and the linen shirt, his muscles rippled with each hasty jerk. Even covered in scars, there was no denying how incredible his body was, with his broad shoulders and thick arms and muscular legs. . . .

She rolled to her side and faced away from him. She didn't want to admire his body. Not now or anytime soon.

For long moments, his shuffling and thudding took up the space in the room, leaving little room for even oxygen. When he finally grew silent, she let out a tense exhale and then tried to breathe normally again.

"Would you like a hot bath this morning?"

Oh aye. What she wouldn't give for a bath after the past few weeks of only sponge bathing. But, once again, he was being considerate to her. Too considerate when she'd just pushed him away.

He cleared his throat. "I can ask one of the maidservants—"

"Maidservants?" Her voice was tight. "Or slaves?"

He didn't respond. He didn't have to. Yesterday during the tour of his home, she'd learned that a large majority of the Black folks who worked for the O'Briens in the city and their plantation were free.

A portion were still enslaved, though. When she'd asked Sullivan about it, he'd indicated that the Commodore wasn't agreeable to slavery, but that he also wasn't willing to come down on the side of being antislavery for fear of alienating business partners.

Sullivan had said that if he were in charge, he'd free the slaves and pay them all a fair wage, even if it did cost them business. He'd also spoken with his father over the years about the issue. But so far, he hadn't been able to change the Commodore's mind.

"I don't want a slave to come attend me."

"Very well. I won't enlist the services of a slave."

"Thank you."

He was silent, and she could sense him watching her,

waiting for her to explain why she was suddenly quiet and abrupt with him. But how could she explain it to him when she couldn't explain it to herself?

He started across the room, his footsteps heavy on the carpet. At the door, he hesitated.

If he hoped she'd turn over and watch him leave, then he was out of luck. She kept her focus on the bedpost.

The door opened, and then a moment later it clicked shut.

As soon as he was gone, she tried to release the tension that had built over the past several minutes. But even as she forced her body to relax, a strange disappointment settled inside. And she wasn't exactly sure why.

She closed her eyes and buried her face in her pillow, wanting to cry, wanting to let out her frustrations the way she normally did—along with all the sadness about Bryan.

But the tears didn't come. Not even one.

Was she finally done grieving over all that had happened? She certainly didn't miss Bryan anymore. In fact, she couldn't remember the last time she'd thought about him. Even the anger that had once burned so hotly inside was now cold, maybe even gone.

Then why was she disappointed? It wasn't aimed at Sullivan. He hadn't done anything wrong. Was it disappointment with herself?

She pushed the pillow aside and rolled to her back.

Aye. She'd disappointed God, her parents, even herself. Not just with how impulsive she'd been with Bryan. But now she was frustrated with herself for how she was treating Sullivan. She hadn't been decent to him by getting upset over a petty issue just now.

No matter her resolve to keep their relationship locked up tightly, she had to do better in treating him with kindness and respect. He, of all people, deserved the same measure of graciousness that he'd offered her.

She'd try harder. It was the least she could do.

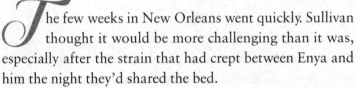

19

*T*he few weeks in New Orleans went quickly. Sullivan thought it would be more challenging than it was, especially after the strain that had crept between Enya and him the night they'd shared the bed.

One moment, they'd been laughing and enjoying each other's company. In the next, she'd been rigid and cold. When she'd brought up the issue of slavery, he'd known that wasn't what was really bothering her. More likely, she'd gotten a good look at his scars in the daylight and had been disgusted by them and hadn't wanted him to see her reaction.

Thankfully, she hadn't been aloof for long. Most of the time, she'd been her usual mix of feisty and playful and talkative. Even so, he'd sensed she'd added a few more invisible bricks to the wall between them in spite of his efforts to break them down.

Regardless, she'd continued to do her part in convincing his father they had a normal marriage. When they'd gone to several parties and dances, she'd been charming and lively and so beautiful he'd ached just watching her, knowing she was too good for him.

During the few days they'd spent on the plantation, she'd been equally social and amiable. Even when they were alone riding or walking in the gardens or in their chamber at night, she kept the polite demeanor in place.

Of course, he'd resumed sleeping on the floor. One night in the bed had been nearly impossible, and he didn't trust himself with any more.

Even though the Commodore had watched them from time to time, he hadn't been able to tell that they'd been play-acting, although the acting hadn't been hard to do. They'd held hands. Once in a while, Sullivan had put his arm around her or squeezed her shoulder.

She'd done more, unafraid to grab on to his arm or rub his hand or brush a strand of his hair back. Her innocent touches only seared him more with each one, so at times he felt like he was a torch covered in tar and set aflame.

He couldn't deny he'd relished the time with her—time that would soon come to an end as he resumed his duties as a steamboat captain during the return voyage to St. Louis. He hadn't exactly plotted how to balance his work and marriage. But he suspected he'd be gone for long periods, at least four weeks at a time, since that's what the round-trip voyage took, give or take a few days.

Would she be relieved to have him gone? She'd likely be busy decorating their new home and preparing for the baby. Whenever he was in St. Louis, how long would she want him to stay? As a captain and part owner, he had some flexibility, but what if she didn't enjoy his visits? What if she didn't ever welcome him completely into her life?

"You'll have to come again soon, Enya." His mother was giving her a hug as the coachman finished loading the last of their bags onto the carriage that would carry them to the *Morning Star*, which was leaving within the hour.

Dawn light had broken, and the sky was awash with patches of pink and orange. He'd already been down to the wharf once to oversee the readiness of the vessel, and now all that needed to be done was to make sure Enya was safely ensconced aboard.

"Thank you for everything." Enya embraced his mother in return. "You've been a delight to get to know."

Enya turned to the Commodore, who was watching her with more than a little awe.

Sullivan couldn't keep a half grin from alighting, as it did whenever he caught his father overwhelmed by Enya's beauty. He understood and empathized with what the man felt, because he was overwhelmed by her most of the time too.

"Good-bye, Commodore." She reached for the older man and hugged him just as warmly.

He patted her back awkwardly, then stepped away. "Come again before it becomes too difficult for you to travel."

The pregnancy had become common knowledge among the family. The news of it also hadn't taken long to spread throughout New Orleans, just as Sullivan had predicted. He'd gotten good-natured teasing from friends, particularly about not being able to stay out of Enya's bed before marriage. Although he'd been tempted to correct them, he let them think what they wanted to keep the focus on himself and not on her.

"I'd love to visit again." She bestowed one of her bright smiles upon both of his parents while taking the offer of Sullivan's hand to assist her up into the carriage.

After he helped to situate her, he hugged his mother, then shook hands with his father.

The Commodore squeezed his hand hard and met his gaze with a level one. "I can tell you love her."

Love her? They'd only been married for about six weeks. That wasn't long enough for love to develop.

Even as the protest rose within him, a strange sense of certainty rolled in and knocked away his resistance. Yes, his father was right. He loved Enya. Somewhere along the way, he'd fallen in love with her.

His father wasn't breaking eye contact, was apparently waiting for him to agree.

"Of course." He just hoped Enya couldn't hear their conversation.

"Good, good." His father smiled with satisfaction.

Sullivan gave him a nod, then started to turn.

The Commodore caught his arm and stopped him. "Don't be so afraid to show her."

"I'm not." Once the words were out, he knew they weren't true. He was afraid. Not of her. But of pushing her away with a wrong move.

"Yes, you are." The Commodore's voice rang with a challenge.

"I'm fine." Or at least he would be once he was beyond the reach of his father's meddling.

"If you're so fine, then show her you love her right now."

"I'll show her later."

The Commodore's brows furrowed, and his expression lost all traces of humor. "Are you defying me, boy?"

Sullivan wanted to tell his father that he was no longer a boy. That he was old enough to make his own decisions and determine when he showed affection to his wife. But he'd never been able to blatantly disrespect his father.

"Go on in there," the Commodore barked, this time for the whole neighborhood to hear, "and give her a kiss that shows her you adore the ground she walks on."

Sullivan almost groaned aloud. He'd been expecting something like this from his father the entire visit. If only he could have gotten away without the last-minute haranguing.

His mother laid a hand on the Commodore's arm, always the levelheaded and calmer of the two. Instead of patting her arm in return, the Commodore slipped one of his hands behind her neck and one behind her back. Then he dipped her backward and at the same time captured her mouth with a kiss, one that was deep and intense and filled with a keen adoration that told Sullivan his father wasn't putting on a show, that he truly did adore the ground his wife walked on, even after all the years they'd been married.

Sullivan had witnessed many such ardent kisses over the years. But somehow this time he was watching it with fresh eyes, as though his father was the master teacher and he the pupil.

As his parents finished their kiss and straightened, his father bent and whispered something in his mother's ear. Her cheeks were already flushed and her eyes bright. But after the whisper, she reached for his hand and then leaned her head against his arm. Clearly being by his side was the only place in the world she wanted to be.

Sullivan exhaled a tight breath. That's what he wanted Enya to feel with him. If he kissed her like that, would she feel the same about him?

He'd been trying to win her heart slowly and steadily, but

he wasn't making much progress. At least that he could see. Maybe it was time to change his tactics.

The Commodore nodded at him, reminding him to have courage.

Sullivan gave his father a nod back, feeling a little silly. Then he climbed up onto the carriage step and poked his head inside.

The dawn light illuminated Enya, attired as usual in one of her lovely gowns. Her eyes were wider than usual, and her expression filled with uncertainty.

He'd told her he'd wait for her to ask him for physical affection. But that didn't apply to kissing, did it?

"You heard my father?" he whispered as he stepped up into the conveyance.

"Yes. He's loud, so he's easy to hear."

Again, Sullivan hoped she hadn't been able to hear his admission that he loved her. That was something he wanted to say to her alone . . . when she was ready to hear it.

"You won't mind if I . . . ?" The words *kiss you* stuck in his throat. Maybe he was much more afraid than he'd realized.

She sat absolutely still, her eyes taking in his face and waiting for him to finish the sentence. Or maybe she was waiting for him to tell her that he didn't plan to go through with it.

But what if he took the chance and showed her how much he adored her in a kiss? And what if that helped alleviate whatever fears were still holding her back?

His large frame filled the carriage interior as he took the seat beside her. Normally, he was careful not to brush up against her, to give her as much space as possible. But this time, when his thigh and knee bumped hers, he didn't pull back.

He could sense his father outside watching and waiting.

Sullivan didn't have to do it. He could tell his father that the matter was a private one between Enya and him, close the door, and call for the coachman to drive away.

But at the happy glow on his mother's face and the way she clung to the Commodore, Sullivan's chest expanded. A burst of energy shot through his blood.

He twisted on his seat and this time forced the whisper out. "May I kiss you?"

Her gaze shot to his parents, his father, before returning to him. "Yes, it's alright," she whispered back. "Of course we need to." For his father's sake. She left that part off. But she probably assumed they were still playacting.

But a kiss wouldn't be playacting for him.

He started to lift his hand to cup her cheek, then hesitated. Should he touch her so intimately too? Or should he just lean in and take a kiss? She was close enough that he could do so easily enough.

She dropped her gaze and tightened her hands in her lap. Was she nervous? Had kissing her previous husband been difficult?

He didn't want to think about her kissing another man. In fact, the very thought sent shards of jealousy piercing him.

Enya was his now. His wife. And maybe he needed to make it clearer to her that he would adore her just as much physically as he did in all the other many ways he tried to show her his love.

This time when he raised his hand, he brought it all the way to her face. He caressed her cheek to her jaw, then glided his fingers over her exquisitely satiny skin to her neck. As he continued to let his fingers trace a path to the back of her neck, he bent in slowly, one inch at a time.

He tried to gauge her reaction, but her eyes remained wide and unreadable.

When he was but a hairsbreadth away, he stalled.

She seemed to be holding her breath.

Without any further thoughts, he closed the gap and touched her lips. At the same moment, his hand at the back of her neck guided her closer. He intended to only press in with a short but tender kiss.

But as his lips brushed over hers, the softness of those curves and their warmth drove need straight through him. The pounding ricocheted through his body, awakening every part of him in every corner of his body.

She seemed to nibble, moving against him just a little, as though she wasn't sure if she dared to give herself permission to return the kiss.

He was already too far gone, like a man inebriated with just one drink and yet thirsty for so much more. He coaxed and tasted, pouring out his reverence for her with each move. Because saints have mercy, he really did adore her. He loved not only her beauty and her body, but he loved her resilient spirit, her caring heart, and her fiery passion.

When she finally rose into him and meshed her lips with his, a surge of satisfaction sifted through him. She wasn't letting him passively kiss her, she was responding with her own awakening desires, wasn't she?

For a moment, there was an equal give and take of pleasure, sweet and keen and delectable, unlike anything he'd ever known. With each stroke, their tempo increased, laced with a note of desperation he didn't understand, almost as if this was their first and last kiss and they had to make the most of it before they were separated forever.

200

"Well, well, well." His father's voice cut into the tidal wave of desire.

Enya broke away first and quickly dipped her head, moving her mouth out of his reach.

Sullivan wanted to chase after those lips—now swollen and even more kissable. But he released a raspy breath and tried to swim to the surface so he didn't drown in all the sensations he was feeling.

"That was perfect," the Commodore said. "Now just make a habit of doing that at least once or twice a day."

Once or twice a day? How about a few hundred times a day? Would anything less than that ever satisfy him?

He doubted it. Now that he'd gotten a taste of her lips, he didn't think he could ever go back to not kissing her.

Somehow he managed to say a proper good-bye to his parents before the carriage rolled away.

His every muscle rippled, and his every nerve vibrated. After that kiss, he felt more alive than he ever had before. Did she feel the same? How had the kiss affected her?

She sat rigidly beside him, unmoving—except for the small tremble of her hands in her lap. She quickly clasped her hands together as if to hide the quaver.

But she was too late. He'd seen it.

He'd never been good at drawing people out, asking them how they felt, or cajoling them into sharing their feelings. But he had to find out what was going through her mind.

"Are you okay?" His voice came out gravelly, and he immediately cleared his throat.

"I'm fine."

"Then you didn't mind . . . ?"

"Of course not."

That wasn't exactly a positive response.

"I'm sure our acting convinced your father." She offered him a quick smile but then peered out the open window.

What about her? Hadn't she been able to tell that he'd intended the kiss to do more than convince his father? Hadn't she been able to tell he'd been trying to convince her too?

He had to say something, had to tell her the truth—that he hadn't been acting. He opened his mouth, but a fist of fear closed around his throat.

Clearly he hadn't convinced her of anything. She'd kissed him as part of their bargain. She'd been polite and diplomatic about it. But it hadn't moved her the same way it had him.

He leaned back and released an inward sigh. Maybe she wasn't attracted to him the same way he was to her. Maybe she tolerated his faults but wouldn't ever be able to truly look past them. If he couldn't, how could he ever expect her to?

20

Enya stretched on the bed, her body tingling with wakefulness. The ever-present rumbling of the steamboat engines greeted her, as did the chill of the air in the cabin.

With her eyes still closed, she groped for the blanket and pulled it up around her closer. The farther north they'd traveled away from New Orleans, the colder the temperatures had grown, especially in the early morning hours before the sun had the chance to make an appearance and warm the river.

She burrowed deeper into the mattress and her pillows, wanting to return to the land of her dreams, the dream where Sullivan was lying beside her on the bed and holding her or the dream where he was pulling her into his arms and kissing her.

It had been close to ten days since his kiss that morning in the carriage as they were readying to leave his parents' home. Ten days since he'd reached for her and tenderly wrapped his hand around her neck. Ten days since he'd acted as if he couldn't get enough of her. Ten days since his lips had meshed with hers.

She could almost feel the strength, the heat, the passion all over again. And the memory swirled a strange warmth low in her belly, a warmth that was slowly building pressure inside her every time she thought of Sullivan.

She hadn't exactly lied to him when he'd asked if she'd minded the kiss. She hadn't told him yes or no. But the truth was, the kiss had been incredible—or at least it had become incredible once she'd swallowed her fear and allowed herself to respond. Every move of his mouth against hers had been filled with an achingly sweet passion and reverence that had torn through her heart.

For several beautiful moments, she'd lost conscious thought, and all that had mattered was being with him and letting him lavish her with adoration—just as the Commodore had instructed him. Sullivan had given her a kiss that left her no doubt that he adored the ground she walked on.

The Commodore had pressured Sullivan into all but admitting that he loved her. Or at least she thought that's what he'd alluded to.

But Sullivan had hardly looked at her since their kiss.

Oh aye, he'd been as polite, respectful, and selfless as always, seeing to her every need. When they'd stopped in Memphis a couple of days ago, he'd taken her shopping to get a new parasol since the wind had destroyed her other one. While there, he'd purchased a beautiful bracelet she'd stopped to admire, one that was much too expensive but that he'd insisted he wanted to give her.

Not only that, but he'd discovered her craving for chocolate and had been surprising her, first with a warm chocolate drink and then with a chocolate cake. Just yesterday, he'd plucked wildflowers during one of their brief stops along the shore and brought them to her in a vase. And last night for their reading time, he'd pulled out another new book.

Even with all his kindnesses, something had changed between them, although she couldn't put her finger on exactly what it was. All she knew was that there was a strange tension, and it was her fault.

She suspected the change had to do with her refusal to acknowledge that their kiss had meant something to her.

Whatever the case, she sensed a barrier between them. And she also sensed, if she wanted to span the distance, she would have to be the one to take the barrier down. That was becoming clearer with each passing day.

But did she want it down? Could she finally accept that he wasn't Bryan?

Week after week and day after day, Sullivan had demonstrated that he was different. Not only that, but she could feel herself beginning to heal and the ache in her chest subsiding. She could even admit there were times when her body craved more of him.

She expelled a sigh.

At a nearby cough, her eyes flew open, and she sat up. Her hair fell in waves around her face, and she swiped them back as she gazed around the cabin. The spot on the floor beside the settee was empty, the blankets folded and put away. Sullivan was gone. Just as she'd expected him to be, just as he was every morning.

This voyage he was serving as the captain, and his duties took him away from her most of the day. He checked on her from time to time, he ate his meals with her in their private dining room, and he made a point of spending a couple of hours with her every evening before she went to bed. But otherwise, the voyage back to St. Louis was different, lonelier.

Sullivan couldn't spend all his time with her. Even if he hadn't been working, why would he want to be around her? She hadn't exactly welcomed him into her life with open arms.

She flopped back down against the mattress and stared up at the ceiling. Now that they'd entered Missouri, the voyage would last only a few more days until they reached St. Louis. Then what?

They hadn't talked about what they would do next. Would he go to their new home and live with her there? Or would he return to the river and be away from her for long weeks at a time? If he did, would she miss him?

Another cough hacked louder. And the sound came from almost directly beneath her.

She bolted up again and this time quieted all her thoughts. Was someone under the bed?

Her gaze flew around the room. She needed a weapon or something she could use to defend herself. Her sights landed upon her new parasol hanging on a hook on the back of the door next to one of her bonnets. It was too far away.

What about the new book on the bedside table? The cover was thick and sturdy. She might be able to hit an intruder with it. Or at least protect herself while she fled from the cabin.

Quietly, carefully, she picked up the book. Then she slid off the bed, pretending to act normally and yawning loudly. Without warning, she tossed aside the bedcovers and bent to peek under the bed.

Other than Sullivan's blankets and pillow folded neatly and stowed away, the space was empty.

With her heart beating at double the speed, she stood and let herself calm down. She must have heard someone from one of the cabins on the deck below, although she hadn't heard anyone before, not on the voyage down to New Orleans or the previous days of the journey back.

She stood beside the bed and listened again, waiting. But at the silence that met her, she tried to shake off the feeling that something wasn't quite right.

She rang her bell, and a moment later, a maidservant arrived to help her groom and dress. All the while the maid tended to her, Enya waited for another cough, wanted the maid to hear it too.

But whoever had coughed had moved on and was no longer there.

As she went about her day, she forgot about it until later, when she lay down on her bed for her afternoon nap. She'd just closed her eyes and almost dozed when she heard the sound again.

It was louder than it had been earlier, almost as if the person was getting sicker. Though the cough was muffled, it was distinct. And it was very close.

She got down from the bed and surveyed underneath it to no avail. She checked the armoire where a number of her dresses had been hung, but no one was inside. And although nobody could fit under the settee, she looked there anyway. She even searched inside Sullivan's trunk sitting at the end of the bed, which was mostly empty, save for a few clothing items.

As she lowered the trunk lid and sat back on her heels in

the middle of the carpet, the cough came again. Directly below her.

She didn't understand how, but someone was there.

Skimming the carpet, she peeled it back just a little. At a large crack in the floor that formed a trapdoor, her heart tapped an uneasy rhythm. What was this? And why was it hidden?

She rose to her feet and unhooked her parasol from the back of the door before she returned to the hatch. Then, gripping the weapon with one hand, she inched the door up. The afternoon sunshine coming in through the cabin window illuminated the interior of closet, likely intended for extra storage for the occupants of the room. But as the sunlight slanted on a petite brown face peering up at her, Enya couldn't hold back a gasp.

A young woman squinted in the brightness, lifting an arm to shield her eyes and revealing red welts where her sleeve fell away. She was attired in a simple cotton skirt and blouse and clutched several blankets around her, likely for warmth and comfort.

One of the china plates from the saloon sat on the floor beside her with the remnants of a meal—chicken bones picked clean.

Someone had delivered a plate of food to this woman. But who? And why?

The woman cowered into the corner of the tiny closet away from the opening, obviously having expected someone else. One of the servants, perhaps?

She had to be a runaway slave. There was no other explanation for it.

"Have no fear," Enya whispered. "You're safe with me."

The woman's gaze darted beyond Enya, almost as if she was considering how she could escape and jump into the Mississippi River. No doubt she would rather take her chances battling the river than be turned over to the slave catchers or her master.

"I promise." Enya glanced over her shoulder now too. She didn't want Sullivan to barge into the room and catch her in the act of speaking to this runaway. He wouldn't stand for a slave being aboard his vessel, not when he'd made it clear how dangerous transporting runaways was to him and his business.

Yet, with the way the woman had begun to cough, Sullivan would hear her sooner or later.

Enya lowered the hatch and replaced the rug. Then she crossed to her toiletries and dug through the cosmetics along with the few tonics and herbal remedies she'd brought along. Would anything help alleviate the runaway's cough?

She shook the stout, clear bottle of laudanum.

From the swishing, she guessed a small amount remained, perhaps enough to calm the woman's nerves and help her rest easier so she coughed less. It would be worth a try, wouldn't it?

With another glance toward the cabin door, Enya returned to the rug, rolled it aside, and lifted the hatch. She thrust the bottle toward the woman, who once again shrank against the wall, as if she expected Enya to point a gun at her head.

"Take a tiny sip of this morning and night."

The woman only eyed it.

"It's for your cough. So no one else hears you."

The woman tentatively took the bottle and then moved back to her corner.

"I'm Enya, by the way." She wanted the woman to know she was safe with her. "What's your name?"

Before the woman could answer, footsteps and voices came from the promenade outside the cabin. Enya lowered the hatch and replaced the rug. As fast as her bell-shaped skirt would allow, she climbed onto the bed, lay down, and closed her eyes.

In the next moment, the door of the cabin squeaked open. She could almost feel Sullivan surveying the room and her. And she prayed she hadn't left anything out of order that would alert him to the runaway's presence.

When the door closed and Sullivan's heavy tread headed away from the cabin, she prayed he'd gone on his way none the wiser to the stowaway.

Instead of napping, Enya's mind was fully awake and alert. If the laudanum didn't work to stop the coughing, she needed to find a way to help the woman remain undiscovered until she reached freedom—wherever that might be.

And she had to protect Sullivan. If anyone found out about the runaway slave, he would get into terrible trouble, even if he wasn't involved. What had he said, that the sentence was seven years in the penitentiary?

She tossed and turned until she landed upon the only solution she could think of.

21

Sullivan leaned against the cabin door and watched Enya with a reverence that bordered on sacrilegious. She was beautiful all the time. But when she sat at the piano and played, she was divine.

Of course, when she'd approached him two days ago and asked him if she could have a piano in their cabin, he'd been more than a little surprised. She hadn't played since the night he'd found her in the dining saloon in the dark. But he hadn't stopped to question what had changed her mind. It hadn't mattered.

Although moving the heavy piano had been no easy feat and required four of his crew, he hadn't been able to tell her no. He could never tell her no. But in this case, he would have carried the piano to their room on his back alone if he'd had to in order to grant her wish.

When the settee had been removed and the piano put in its place, she'd sat and played for only a few minutes before standing up, closing the lid, and pushing in the bench, all the while battling her tears. The next time, she'd played a little longer, still hiding her tears.

Only last night had she played for the first time without crying. And today, throughout the day, she'd finally seemed to give herself permission to find joy in the music.

They'd reached the St. Louis levee a short while ago, but she'd been too distracted at the piano to pay attention.

But he didn't mind. In fact, he wished he'd thought to move the piano to their cabin earlier, even though the pianist they'd hired to play during the evenings had complained several times about no longer having access to the instrument.

Enya's long fingers stroked the keys, creating a whimsical tune that tugged at him, made him want to go stand behind her and wrap his arms around her.

But he'd resolved after their kiss in the carriage, as he had at the beginning of their marriage, that he wouldn't pressure her. He wanted their affection to be mutual and willing or he didn't want her at all.

Well, that wasn't exactly the truth. He did want her. Sometimes very keenly. But it was becoming clearer, with every passing day, that she'd never feel the same level of attraction to him that he did to her.

He supposed he didn't blame her. She deserved someone much more handsome and charming than him. Perhaps Bellamy had meant well in matching them together. He'd been trying to save them both from disaster and hadn't had much time to do it.

But ultimately, Sullivan had known he'd be better off with someone who was more like him, someone who wasn't so perfect like Enya.

Her fingers slowed with the final notes, until they came

to a standstill altogether. The music faded, replaced by the noises of the levee—shouts of the stevedores, the clatter of horses, the booming of other steamboat whistles.

"That was beautiful," he said, alerting her to his presence, guessing she hadn't known he was standing there listening since she seemed to become absorbed in the music whenever she started playing.

She twisted on her bench and offered him a smile. It wasn't exactly a full, radiant one, but it showed off the dimple in her chin. He hadn't seen the dimpled smile in a while. And the sight of it kicked him hard in the gut, making him wish he could walk over and kiss first the dimple and then her lips.

She'd taken extra care with her hair today so that it hung in ringlets, and she was wearing one of her finest gowns, likely because she'd wanted to look her best when they arrived in St. Louis.

The baby wasn't showing yet, but he'd noticed subtle changes in her figure, a slight filling out that hadn't been there when he'd first met her. He wanted to tell her that she always looked her best, no matter what she was wearing, but he didn't want to chance her sensing the heat of his desire.

He shifted his attention to the piano keys. "You're very talented."

She shrugged as if it didn't matter. "When I was younger, I dreamed of being famous and performing in front of crowds of people."

"And now?"

She released a scoffing laugh. "I've grown up and realized my da and mam were right, that such dreams are silly."

"They don't have to be silly."

She seemed about to scoff again but studied his face, as though searching to see if he was being genuine.

"I dreamt of building the fastest steamboat on the Mississippi, one so fast it could almost fly."

"I'm sure you were adorable."

"Maybe I won't build the fastest, but I still love what I do."

She turned quiet, contemplative.

"You might not become a concert pianist, but you can still find ways to use your talents. It would be a shame not to."

"Really?" The one word was loaded with skepticism.

"Really."

"You'd support whatever I choose to do?"

"If it makes you happy, why wouldn't I?"

She didn't answer and instead fingered the keys again.

He peered outside the door to the busy waterfront in the April afternoon. "Most of the passengers have disembarked. We can go too, if you'd like—"

He stopped short at the sight of several men, including a constable and Captain Fitch, striding up the landing stage onto the *Morning Star*. A knot tightened in Sullivan's stomach. What accusations did Captain Fitch plan to level against the New Orleans Steamboat Packet Company today?

"What's wrong?" Enya came to stand beside him, her shoulder brushing his arm. She was situating her bonnet over her head and drawing the velvet ties under her chin. Her sleek, delicate fingers smoothed and wound the ribbons, and he had the sudden wish that he could tie the ribbon just so he had an excuse to graze her neck and chin.

He tore his gaze away from her and settled it back on the visitors. "Wait for me here."

His instructions did no good. As he strode away, she followed behind on the promenade to the stairway. At the top, he placed a hand on her arm. "Stay here, Enya. Captain Fitch is a dangerous man, and I don't trust him."

This time, thankfully, she stopped at the railing while he clambered down the metal staircase to the main deck.

"What's the problem with my boat today, Captain Fitch?" Sullivan nodded at the constable and captain and then sized up the third man. Tall and hefty, with dark hair and sideburns as well as a long, drooping mustache, the fellow looked familiar. In his double-breasted frock coat buttoned all the way up, he held himself with the authority of someone accustomed to unquestioning obedience.

Captain Fitch touched the brim of his flat cap and then offered Sullivan an off-kilter grin beneath his overgrown beard. "You've heard of Roan Whistler, haven't you, Captain O'Brien?"

Sullivan's stomach bottomed out into a sickening chasm. Yes, he knew who Roan Whistler was. Known as the Whistler for the way his whip whistled against the back of slaves. He was a slave catcher, hired by many southern plantation owners to track down and return their slaves.

If he was here on the *Morning Star*, then that could only mean one thing—he was searching for slaves.

Sullivan tipped his hat at Roan Whistler, even though he would have preferred to smash a fist in the man's face. Then he lifted a brow at the constable, a portly man who was one of the captains of the St. Louis police department. Sullivan recognized him but didn't remember his name.

The fellow gave Sullivan a sympathetic shrug, as if to say he was merely doing his duty.

Captain Fitch's smile only grew, as though he relished

any trouble he could bring to Sullivan. "We've heard complaints that the New Orleans Packet has been transporting runaways."

"You've heard wrong." Sullivan didn't back down and didn't let anything show, but the sickening feeling was growing in his gut. The young woman hiding in the closet of his cabin had come down with a cough over the past few days. The fits of coughing came and went. But he never could predict exactly when she'd have one. Her coughing had woken him up twice last night alone.

Roan Whistler was studying Sullivan intently, as if trying to see down to his soul and discover the truth.

Sullivan stared back. Good thing he'd cut off all access to seeing into his soul long ago.

Captain Fitch was glancing now between the two of them. "The Whistler got your name as one of the captains sympathetic to slaves."

Sullivan hated to think about what lengths Whistler had gone to in order to extract that information. But someone, somewhere, had given up his name in an effort to alleviate the torture. He only prayed it had helped.

"If Roan Whistler and the constable want to question my crew, go right on ahead." Sullivan waved a hand toward the stairs. "You'll learn the truth readily enough from them." He prayed his secret was still safe, that none had heard the coughing.

Whistler didn't wait for a second invitation. He marched forward onto the main deck, toward a group of Black deckhands who'd halted their work and now watched his approach with wary eyes.

The constable started to follow but halted, his expression

apologetic. "I'm certainly sorry for this, Captain O'Brien. I told Roan Whistler that your father, the Commodore, has slaves himself and that your steamers have always been reliable. But he and Captain Fitch insisted on searching not only this steamer but all your boats here along the levee."

"I'm sure the Commodore won't be pleased if any of his steamers are damaged or delayed." Damage and delays were the least of Sullivan's concerns, especially if Whistler and Captain Fitch found the runaway he was harboring.

No doubt Whistler would examine every square inch of the vessel. But the compartment in his captain's cabin was hidden enough that the fellow wouldn't think to move the rug and search in the floor. Not unless he heard coughing . . .

Enya hadn't moved from the stairway railing above on the texas deck. From where he stood, he could see her features growing stormy. Should he warn her not to get involved?

With her feistiness combined with her abhorrence of slavery, she might say or do something that would cast greater suspicion on him. And he didn't need that today of all days. Maybe tomorrow. By then the slave would be gone.

But, of course, since Whistler and Captain Fitch suspected him already, they would be on higher alert, would be watching his steamers carefully. They wanted to catch him in the act of stowing a runaway. No doubt Captain Fitch hoped that such a charge would hurt the New Orleans Steamboat Packet Company and in turn send more customers to the Memphis Packet Company.

It would cause a scandal and might decrease business for a time. But eventually, they would recover, and Captain Fitch would be back in the same place, trying unsuccessfully to compete with them.

There was a much bigger problem, one that filled Sullivan with cold dread—the prospect of bringing disgrace to Enya and the baby. She would be supportive of him and wouldn't care about the damage to her reputation. But he would.

Even worse, however, was the thought that he might have to go to prison and be separated from her. He could hardly bear to let an hour pass without checking on her, even from a distance. How could he go years without seeing her, talking to her, or simply basking in her beauty?

With a new sense of urgency charging through him, he could only watch Whistler and Captain Fitch and try not to give away his growing panic.

But it was mounting quickly. He had to figure out a way to distract the search before it was too late.

22

J'll have my clerk take you to the new house." Sullivan finished climbing up the stairs to where Enya stood in the shade of the covered promenade. "Looks like I'll be here for a while."

Enya swallowed the lump that had clogged her throat the longer she'd listened to the newcomers and their mission for coming aboard the *Morning Star*. Upon hearing that they were searching for runaway slaves, she'd frozen to the deck, unable to move, unable to breathe, unable to speak.

Obviously, the men were right about Sullivan's boats carrying runaway slaves. And they would scour Sullivan's personal cabin since they believed he was guilty.

The question was—did Sullivan know about the runaway? Was he even orchestrating the plan to help?

It was also possible one of the Black chambermaids who came in to clean the cabin, press their garments, and attend to other tasks had provided refuge to the runaway.

Though Enya had tried to spy on the woman, tried to catch

her in the act of lifting the rug, she hadn't seen anything unusual.

But just in case the chambermaid wasn't responsible, Enya hadn't called for her assistance as often. After all, she didn't want the maid to hear the coughing and then alert Sullivan or others.

Instead, Enya had fended for herself more often.

And she'd played the piano more frequently. The first day of making herself finish each song had been torturous, and she'd wanted to quit numerous times. But she'd persevered, telling herself she had to be willing to be uncomfortable and even face inner turmoil to do what was right. After all, her discomfort and turmoil couldn't compare to what the slaves experienced.

Each time after that when she sat down to play, it became easier. The haunted sadness had at first been replaced with numbness. The numbness had eventually faded into acceptance. Today, she'd felt twinges of pleasure, giving her hope that someday she might enjoy music again. Maybe at some point, she'd even be able to compose the way she once had.

Sullivan crossed to her and took hold of her elbow. "I'll ask the clerk to make sure the new housekeeper is there before he leaves so you'll have assistance."

"I don't mind waiting in our cabin." She raised her voice enough that Captain Fitch nearby could hear. She had to be in the room and play the piano when the men came in. It was truly the only way to keep the slave safe. "It will give me the chance to play my music longer."

At her declaration, Sullivan hesitated. His dark eyes searched hers. He'd known how difficult playing had been for her. Was he trying to understand her change of heart?

Before he could object, she broke from his hold and started back toward the cabin, forcing herself to walk calmly and confidently, as a lady should. Only after she reached the confines of the cabin and closed the door did she expel a tight breath and press a trembling hand against her racing heart.

Then, before she lost her courage, she rushed over to the hatch and dropped to her knees. Without moving the rug, she spoke in a low voice. "Men are searching the steamer. Try not to cough. And I'll do my best to play the piano as long as possible."

She didn't expect an answer, but a second later, a soft "Thank you" came from the closet.

The young woman had to be terrified. Although Enya had felt a wee bit of what it was like to be mistreated, used, even abused, it couldn't compare with all this woman had gone through.

Even just having to live for nearly two weeks inside a cramped closet was inhumane, not being able to stretch or see sunlight or talk to anyone. Having to crouch in fear every time someone came into the cabin, having to be dependent on someone else for food, having to pretend she didn't exist.

Now that this woman had come this far and was so close to freedom, Enya couldn't let her down. She had to do her small part in helping her reach her destination.

With fresh resolve, Enya went to the piano, pulled out the bench so that two of the legs sat against the hatch, and this time played not for herself, but for all the women enslaved and abused and mistreated, that someday they would be free, free to make their own music in their own way.

She wasn't sure how long she'd played when the door

opened behind her. She guessed she'd look suspicious if she ignored the new arrival entirely, but she could pretend to be engrossed in the song until the ending measure.

Behind her came the heavy tread of boots, the scraping of furniture being moved, the opening and closing of the armoire.

Finally, she let her music taper and shifted on her bench, putting into place what she hoped was her haughtiest demeanor as she took in the broadly built man in the stiff black coat and with the long black mustache who now stood in the center of the room quietly eyeing the walls, the ceiling, and even the floor as though he was searching for a secret compartment.

Was this the slave catcher, the one introduced as Roan Whistler? He didn't have nasty scars on his cheek, a cruel glint to his eyes, or a whip in hand. Except for his unnerving silence, he seemed like an ordinary man, and not one who made a living searching down and returning slaves to their masters.

But she'd learned that appearances weren't always what they seemed. Bryan had taught her that lesson all too well, and she wouldn't soon forget it.

Sullivan stood in the doorway, watching the slave catcher. As usual, Sullivan's eyes were unreadable. If he was worried, he wasn't showing it, not in the least.

Enya lifted her chin toward Roan Whistler. "May I help you, sir?"

His gaze dropped to her fingers.

Were they trembling? She didn't dare to glance down and instead willed herself to remain strong . . . and to figure out a way to continue to play the piano very soon so she could fill the silence. Although the noises of the levee wafted into the cabin, it wasn't enough.

At a flutter of movement low in her abdomen, she drew in a breath. Was that the baby moving?

Sullivan narrowed his sharp eyes on her.

The fluttering happened again, this time more distinctly. She slid her hand over the slight swell and couldn't contain a smile as she met Sullivan's gaze. "The baby moved."

His attention shifted to her stomach, and his eyes rounded. "He did?"

"She did." Enya spread out her hand over the swell, hoping she'd feel the baby again.

"She?" Sullivan's voice didn't challenge her, only contained curiosity.

The slave catcher was watching their interaction without any change in his expression.

Enya wanted to make him believe she didn't care that he was there, wanted to give off the air that she had nothing to hide. So she widened her smile and reached a hand toward Sullivan. "Come. Maybe you can feel her move too."

Sullivan stared at her stomach, took a step into the room, then stopped. "Are you sure?"

She laughed. She wasn't sure if he was pretending for the slave catcher. Whether he was or not, the wide-eyed expression on so big and muscular a man was adorable. She extended her hand farther. "Aye, come here with you."

Sullivan crossed the rest of the distance, lowered himself to the tiny portion of bench beside her. He lifted his hand and hovered it over her stomach before narrowing another glare upon Roan Whistler. "Now that you've disrupted my wife's piano playing and disturbed our quarters, perhaps you'd have the decency to give us a moment alone."

"A moment alone?" The fellow seemed to be calculating their every move.

"Holy Mother Mary," Sullivan said with a snarl as he waved his hand around the room. "You've had your look, now go so I can experience this joyous moment with my wife."

"Very well, Captain O'Brien." Roan Whistler tipped the brim of his hat, spun on his heels, and stalked out of the cabin.

Of course he left the door open. So that he could listen to them? Perhaps even peek back inside? If the runaway started coughing, would he be able to hear the sound outside the door?

Enya needed to start playing the piano again, but now with Sullivan perched on the bench beside her, she had to finish what she'd begun. Sullivan was expecting her to let him feel the baby move. And she truly wanted him to have the amazing experience.

His hand still waited above her stomach. Though his brow was furrowed, the irritation had swiftly dissipated, replaced by uncertainty. "Did the movement hurt?"

His question was so unexpected that she couldn't hold back another laugh. "No. It feels soft and gentle, like a ripple in the water."

He started to lower his hand but halted.

She took hold of it and pressed it to the swell.

He held himself stiffly and waited. "Maybe she's gone back to sleep."

"So you agree the baby is a girl?"

"I hope so." His voice dropped a notch. "I'd be happy with a daughter just like you."

The words were so sweet they nearly brought tears to her eyes. And they nearly made her forget about the mission at hand—to do what she could to protect the runaway.

When he glanced up at her, she caught a rare glimpse of emotion in his eyes, the tenderness that said he meant every word he'd just said. She wished she could say the same in return, that she'd like a son just like him. But she couldn't, not when the baby wasn't really his.

With her hand still on top of his, he cupped her abdomen as if he might crush the baby if he put too much pressure there. His hand was so large, it nearly covered her stomach. His skin was tanned and weathered, while hers was a much lighter shade. His was roughened with small scars and hers was smooth and unblemished. His nails were blunt, and hers were thin and delicately shaped.

They were so different, and yet they fit together well, didn't they?

"I don't feel anything," he whispered.

"She seemed to like when I played the piano. Why don't I try that again?" She released his hand and shifted on the bench.

He politely rose and moved to stand beside her.

She wasted no further time in beginning another melody, Mozart's Piano Concerto no. 20 in D Minor.

After a moment, he grazed her shoulder. "I need to go. But maybe I can feel her move next time." Again his voice was tender, almost timid.

She paused, the music lingering in the air, and she smiled up at him. "Aye. Next time."

He nodded. Although he didn't smile in return, the crinkle lines at the corners of his eyes formed.

As he left, she resumed the song where she'd left off, the notes swelling within her as easily as they swelled from the keyboard. Even though she'd made a disaster of her life, somehow the beauty was beginning to show itself again.

Maybe that's how God ordained it. He didn't prevent the hardships or the difficulties. Instead He pieced the shards together to create something new that wouldn't be perfect and wouldn't be without its blemishes, but the brokenness would be beautiful in its own way.

23

*D*id Enya know about the runaway slave?

Sullivan opened his mouth to ask her but then shut his lips without a sound, just as he'd done several other times since they'd entered the carriage and started toward their new house. If she didn't know, then he couldn't risk bringing it up. And if she did know, wouldn't she have asked him about it by now?

Thankfully Whistler hadn't discovered the secret chamber. The fellow had certainly tried. His search of the *Morning Star* had been thorough and lasted several hours.

Relief now weakened Sullivan, and he let himself recline against the leather seat. After having to keep up the charade for so long, he was both physically and mentally drained.

As the carriage bounced over a rut, Enya's head brushed his shoulder, and she didn't move it or put the usual distance between them.

He dropped his gaze to her face. The lantern at the front

of the carriage provided enough light in the darkness that he could see that her eyes were closed, and she was asleep.

She was clearly exhausted too.

He could admit he was relieved she'd stayed on the steamer. If she hadn't been in the cabin and playing the piano, Whistler might have lingered longer or come back to search again.

As it was, the slave catcher and Captain Fitch had moved to the *Imperial*. They wouldn't find anything there or on any of the other New Orleans Steamboat Packet boats. Not this time.

Sullivan planned to return to the levee after he made sure Enya was settled into the house. He had to be on the *Morning Star* at two o'clock to help with the exchange. He just hoped by then that Whistler and Captain Fitch were gone from the levee and wouldn't linger, hoping to catch him in the act of setting a slave free.

Maybe he needed to wait until another night. He could hold off putting the lantern in the window until the threat of danger had passed. He hated to make the poor woman delay another day. But he'd had to do so in the past when the risk of capture had been too high.

For mid-April, the St. Louis waterfront had been busier than in past years, which might pose a problem as well. Several steamers had pulled up to the levee after the *Morning Star*, and each of them had been loaded with men heading west to seek gold. In fact, the *Grand Turk*'s decks had been lined with at least three or four hundred men, eager to make their way up the Missouri River to St. Joseph and Independence.

Though many of the steamers were filled mostly with

men, there were still those transporting families and weighed down with wagons, mules, and baggage for the trip to California.

The news coming from the West, however, wasn't promising for the prospective travelers. Spring was late in arriving, and snow was still falling in parts of the Missouri River and Platte River valleys.

Such cold weather was preventing the growth and availability of grass for the livestock that would transport the groups the many months overland from the western edge of Missouri to California. One report indicated that upon reaching St. Joseph, the lines of wagons waiting to start their journey stretched for miles.

Yes, between the slave catcher and the busyness, the task of sneaking the runaway off the *Morning Star* and into a waiting boat would be all the more difficult. He'd have to use extra caution.

As Enya's body relaxed more fully into him, he slipped his arm behind her and steadied her against the bouncing of the carriage.

She didn't hesitate to sidle closer, the chill of the night invading the carriage. Spring had been cold in St. Louis as well. One of his clerks that had been in the city for several weeks recuperating from cholera had informed him that the Mississippi River was high, not only with the melting snow from the upper Midwest but also because March and April had been so rainy and stormy.

Newspapers reported that the number of deaths from cholera in the city had remained relatively low, and most of the dying seemed to be new arrivals who had contracted the cholera elsewhere.

Sullivan could admit he was relieved the spread of cholera was mild, that it hadn't overrun the city the same way it had New Orleans. Now, perhaps, he wouldn't have to worry about Enya and the baby being at risk when he left for his next voyage.

As the carriage rolled to a stop, Sullivan peered through the window. They'd arrived at the new home he'd purchased in February. Several windows were alight, which meant the housekeeper was hopefully well prepared for Enya's stay.

She stirred. "We're here?" Her voice was filled with sleep, low and slurred, never failing to stir longings inside him whenever he heard that tone, longings to climb into bed beside her and hold her all night.

The coachman opened the door, and Sullivan ducked out, taking in the quiet well-to-do neighborhood. The homes weren't overly large or grand like the houses in the Garden District where his parents lived in New Orleans. But the place would suffice until he had the chance to build Enya a bigger and better house. There was talk of creating a new neighborhood on the outskirts of the city, Lucas Place, and he had considered purchasing a lot there, only a mile from the waterfront but more secluded and away from the odors and mire of the industries.

Sullivan descended from the carriage, his boots sinking into the muddy street.

Behind him, Enya was already filling the doorway, one foot out on the step and one hand holding her hat in place.

Before she stepped into the muck, he grasped her waist with both hands and halted her descent.

With the carriage's lantern light glowing from the front

side, she was as stunning as always, and her sleep-filled eyes were wide, her lashes fanning around those mesmerizing green eyes.

He didn't give her time to question what he was doing. Instead, he swept her off her feet and cradled her against his chest.

"Sul-li-van." She laughed softly, dragging out his name in chastisement. "You don't have to carry me."

"I don't want you slipping in the mud." He started toward the short set of steps that led to the front door. Maybe it was also an excuse to hold her again. He hadn't done so in a while and relished the opportunity.

"I'm accustomed to battling muddy St. Louis streets." Her weak protest was made weaker as she leaned her head against his shoulder.

His mind traveled back to the last time they'd been at the house, when they'd only been married a short while. Everything had been new and awkward between them. He hadn't been sure what to think of Enya, hadn't known even a fraction of what he knew about her now.

After the past weeks of traveling together, he loved watching her reactions, loved her chatter, loved the brightness of her eyes taking in everything. He loved her.

The love had overtaken him quickly. But he had no reason to deny it. And after the warm way she'd invited him to feel the baby's movements earlier, was she opening herself up to him more? He hoped so.

As he tromped up the steps, the front door opened to reveal a middle-aged woman in a simple black frock covered with a white apron. She had a kindly face surrounded by wisps of grayish hair showing beneath a pleated mobcap.

She introduced herself as Mrs. Christy and smiled at them warmly, easing the tension in Sullivan's chest even more. He'd stressed to his solicitor that he wanted a kind older woman as housekeeper, emphasis on *kind*, so Enya would have a sweet and pleasant companion during the weeks he was gone.

From what he could tell, his solicitor had succeeded in that regard.

Mrs. Christy gave them a short tour through the house to enlighten them regarding the redecorating efforts that had taken place during their absence. With fresh paint in some rooms and new wallpaper in others, the house was beginning to feel warmer and more vibrant—like Enya.

She oohed and aahed over everything, including the new furniture and framed pictures and other decorations that had arrived from eastern cities. When they reached the final room of the second floor, the one Enya had designated to be the nursery, the housekeeper took her leave, letting them know she would have tea and cakes available for them in the front parlor whenever they were ready.

Enya flitted from one piece of baby furniture to the next, exclaiming over each one, until she halted at the window, just as she had the last time. As she peered out, her expression turned serious.

"Will she be safe tonight?" Enya's question was quiet, and as soon as she spoke it, she spun and laid her hands upon her stomach. "The baby, of course. The day has been quite long and eventful."

Although Enya was good at playacting when she set her mind to it, Sullivan could see right past her attempt to cover the question that had slipped out. The one about the runaway slave.

Enya knew. But she clearly didn't know the extent of his involvement.

She rubbed at her stomach, and this time avoided meeting his gaze. "I'm sure everything will be just fine."

He didn't reply. Should he admit his role? He hadn't known if he could trust her with such a dangerous secret. But today she'd proven herself. In fact, she'd more than proven herself. She'd in all likelihood saved that runaway—and him—from discovery.

"Don't mind me." She forced a smile.

Yes, it was time to trust her. And maybe if he showed her that he trusted her with such an important part of his life, she'd take down the last of the barriers standing between them and learn to trust him in return.

He started to cross to her.

"I'm tired. That's all."

At his approach, her eyes widened, and she backed up against the wall next to the window. "Maybe we should go down and take the tea Mrs. Christy is preparing for us."

He didn't stop until he was but inches from her.

She focused on his cravat. "I'm sure the tea will be getting cold before long." She ducked her head and began to slip around him, except he lifted his arms and pressed his palms on the wall on either side of her head, pinning her in.

Worry flashed through her eyes, but then she smiled and masked her concern. Was she anxious about betraying the slave woman or anxious over his proximity?

"Mrs. Christy seems like a very nice lady, wouldn't you agree? I think I'll get along with her splendidly." Enya rushed to speak, her words tumbling over each other. "I like that she's willing to involve me in hiring the maids. Hopefully we can find someone who's also good with babies—"

He cut her off by leaning down to her ear, his cheek brushing against hers. He hadn't meant to touch her in that way. But at the contact of her smooth cheek, he nearly lost his mind, especially as he breathed her in. Her floral perfume filled his nostrils and his head, and he had to close his eyes to keep himself from pressing his body against hers the way every inch of him was now demanding.

Her soft intake told him she was surprised by his nearness. But she wasn't pushing him away or trying to escape from the cage he'd created around her.

He had to say something now. He drew in a fortifying breath, then spoke softly. "Thank you." His lips brushed her ear, and he forced himself to restrain from placing a kiss there.

"To what do I owe such gratitude?" She shifted enough that her cheek grazed against the scruff of his jaw.

"For playing the piano." He took a turn letting the day's worth of bristle brush her smooth skin.

"It's getting easier to play," she whispered. "And I'm starting to enjoy it again."

"Good." He whispered the word against her ear, earning a shiver from her. "Your playing most likely saved her life."

She froze, held herself motionless for long moments. Then finally she flattened herself against the wall so she could see him. She studied his face, as though trying to discover what he was saying, her eyes holding such hope that he wanted to bottle it and save it for those dreary days ahead when they were apart.

He resisted the urge to trail his fingers across her cheek and down her chin. "You're the one who gave her the laudanum, aren't you?"

"I'm not sure what you're talking about," she mumbled, obviously still not certain whether to trust him.

"She was carried onto the steamboat and into my cabin in my large chest."

Enya continued to watch him, warmth now softening her expression.

"Once the chest is in my room, I usually have no trouble concealing the hideaway in the closet for the duration of the trip."

"Then you've done this before?"

"Every single voyage north."

Her chest rose and fell, as if the revelation had taken her breath away. "For how long?"

"Two years."

"Oh, Sullivan." His name falling from her lips was reverent, as though she were whispering a prayer.

"I didn't tell you because—"

"I understand."

"None of my crew knows either. And I need it to stay that way."

She nodded and glanced beyond him to the open door, clearly also understanding that he didn't want Mrs. Christy to hear their conversation. "What happens next?"

He wasn't sure if he should tell her any more details, but at the expectancy in her eyes, he shared with her more than he ever had with anyone else, telling her about the light in the window of his cabin and the rowboat from Illinois and answering her other questions as best he could.

"And that's it. Until I return to New Orleans and start the process over."

"Someday, maybe we can open up our home too." She was still peering up at him, hadn't moved from the spot against the wall. "We could provide refuge to those who need a place to rest or hide on their way to freedom."

He nodded thoughtfully. "I could see that as a possibility."

"Thank you for considering it. No one has ever seriously validated my ideas before." She settled her hands on his arms and squeezed. "You're a good man, Sullivan O'Brien. You know that, don't you?"

He shrugged. "I wish I could do more."

She tugged him closer and slipped her arms around him.

What was she doing? Giving him a hug? For a second, he was too surprised to lift his arms and hug her in return. As she squeezed and began to release him, his body finally got the message that her body was against his.

She took a step back at the same time he leaned down. Her mouth was only inches from his. Close enough to kiss.

Longing swelled within him, but he fought against it. He couldn't kiss her. Wouldn't pressure her.

Before he knew what was happening, she lifted on her toes and touched her lips to his. Softly and sweetly. A friendly kiss, just like her hug.

Except that he didn't want a friendly kiss. He wanted a kiss like the last one they'd shared the day they'd left New Orleans.

As she began to lower herself, he moved swiftly, without giving himself a chance to overthink the situation. He chased after her and captured her mouth.

She didn't resist. Instead, her lips parted to meet his,

and her hands slid up his arms, glided behind his head, and dragged him closer.

Suddenly his body was a dry creek bed in summer, and she was a swiftly moving river sweeping over him. As her lips meshed with his, he soaked her in, eagerly, like parched land greedy for cool water.

A moment later when she pressed her body into his, he nearly combusted with the delectable feel of her and the realization that she was offering herself to him freely. They weren't playacting for his father or their housekeeper or for any of his staff on the boat. No, they were alone, without an audience, and no reason to kiss . . . except that she wanted to connect with him in this way.

For a moment, he let her take charge of the kiss, let her ply his lips, as though she had all the time in the world with no place to go. But as her fingers glided deeper into his hair, he broke the kiss, unable to hold back the groan.

In the next instant, he wrapped his arms around her and hoisted her higher on the wall so that he could feel her wildly beating heart against his. He bent back in, capturing her mouth and devouring her lips, so that everything became heat and taste and wanting.

He wasn't sure how long he kissed her with such abandon, but she broke away, this time her labored breathing a soft moan. "Sullivan . . ."

Was that longing in her voice? Did she want more?

His own breathing was too far gone to come up with a response. Instead, he angled in and kissed her jaw before kissing the soft, beautiful spot he'd always admired on her neck. Then he dropped down farther and let his lips connect with her collarbone.

Now that he'd tasted her, he would never, ever, get enough. Not even if he kissed her every day until the day he died. He would be forever hungering for her each moment he was apart from her.

Was she finally beginning to feel the same for him?

24

The kisses along Enya's collarbone were pushing her to the brink of a place she'd never been before, but one she wanted to come to again and again. Was this paradise?

Wherever it was, Sullivan's kisses had transported her beyond space and time, making the real world disappear completely so that she could hear no sounds except their pounding hearts and labored breathing.

As his open mouth closed in on the pulse point at the base of her throat, she clutched at him, trembling with need and want.

The last time she'd let herself need and want a man, she'd created a disaster of her life. How could she be certain this time would be different?

A deep part of her knew that Sullivan was different than Bryan. She couldn't even begin to compare them anymore. It wasn't fair to Sullivan. But she couldn't shake the uncertainties that always lingered beneath the surface.

His hands at her waist slid higher up her torso, but the strength of his grip was still tender, and the slight quaver in his fingers told her that he wanted more but was using all his effort to restrain himself, that he didn't want to overwhelm her.

What would happen if she let go of everything from her past and gave herself permission to care about this new marriage? Could she really allow herself to be a wife again?

Bryan's words from when he'd been stuffing his clothing angrily in his haversack pushed to the front of her mind. *"No other man will ever want you for a wife, not when you're so selfish and needy."*

Even though she hadn't wanted to think about his statement, it had lingered deep inside and now rose to cut off the air in her lungs. She'd already failed at one marriage. What was to stop her from failing again? Especially in loving Sullivan the way he deserved? And especially since she'd already been selfish and needy the whole trip to New Orleans and back.

She flattened her hands against his chest and pushed.

He paused, his hot breath bathing her neck. He waited. He was giving her permission to put an end to their kissing. Even in this moment of passion, he was in control and wouldn't pressure her to do more than she wanted.

The desire, the connection, the admiration—what she was feeling was even stronger than anything she'd felt for Bryan by far. In fact, what she'd had with Bryan was like a flimsy fake currency compared to solid silver and gold that could possibly be hers with Sullivan.

But she was flimsy too. She wasn't a treasure worth having. And some day Sullivan would realize that.

She pushed against him again, fear rising to choke her.

Gently, he set her down so that her feet rested on the floor.

She plastered herself to the wall.

As if seeing the change in her demeanor, he released her completely and took a step back. "What's wrong?" His voice was gentle.

"I'm okay." She slipped her hands behind her back to keep them from shaking. "I'm just tired."

He cocked his head.

Didn't he believe her?

"It's been a long day." Her voice held a genuine note of weariness. How could he doubt her now?

He jabbed his fingers into his hair, the movement jerky, almost frustrated. "I have to go back to the steamer for the night."

"I understand." And she truly did. He had to ensure the young woman made her way off the boat to freedom. For as much danger as he was in, Enya could take some comfort in knowing he'd done this many other times and had succeeded.

He stuffed his hands in his pockets. "I won't be in St. Louis long before needing to return to New Orleans."

"How long?"

"How long do you want me to stay?"

What could she say? That maybe he should go? That maybe if they were apart from each other, he wouldn't grow tired or resentful of her demands and her neediness?

She gave a casual shrug. "Whatever works for you."

"What do you want me to do?" His expression and dark eyes were unreadable. Even so, she could sense an unrest in him. Was he pushing her to admit if she wanted him?

"You have an important job." She softened her tone, not wanting to hurt him. "I can't stand in the way of what you're doing." Helping the runaways was critical, and surely he would agree with her.

"So that's your answer?"

"I'm sorry, Sullivan."

"Sorry for what?" The question came out low and loaded.

"That I'm unable to give you what you want in our marriage."

"And what is it you think I want?"

If she was completely honest, she knew he wanted more than a bed partner. He'd been wooing and winning her because he wanted her heart. But a heart was harder to give than a body. At least her heart was after having been shattered. And even if God was putting the pieces of it back together, it was too fragile to hand over to another man. "You'd like me to fall in love with you."

"And have you?" His gaze was as direct as his question, demanding the truth. Although he hadn't made an outright declaration of his love for her, she hadn't been able to forget the admission to his father.

Maybe it was easy for him to put aside all the reservations and let himself love someone. But she wasn't ready. "I like you. And I admire you. But no, I haven't fallen in love with you."

He pulled himself up to his full height, a scowl creasing his brow.

She had the strange need to comfort him, to ease the pain that her rejection might have caused him. Because the truth was, she did like and admire him.

He spun away from her and began to cross the room.

"I wish I could give you more, Sullivan. I really do."

"You do this every time." He stopped, and his hard accusation cut through her.

"Do what?"

"Sabotage our relationship."

"Sabotage?"

"Yes, you let me near, but then when I get too close, you push me away, like right now after kissing me."

"That's rather harsh—"

"You get scared and find a way to put an obstacle between us." He stood near the door, his muscular frame radiating tension but entirely too appealing.

She could still feel the heat of his body against hers, the thudding of their heartbeats, the passion of their kisses. Oh aye, she wanted more of him. But it was too daunting to think about what would happen if she allowed herself to love him. Much too daunting.

She shivered and hugged her arms across her chest. "The obstacles are already there."

"They don't have to be." This time his tone dropped. Did it contain a plea? "You don't have to let the scars of your past determine your future."

"Scars? You shouldn't be the one lecturing me about scars, not when you hide behind yours." The words came out before she could censure them.

His expression froze, and his eyes turned almost icy with a fury she'd seen directed at others but never at herself.

For several heartbeats the fate of the future seemed to hover between them. Then, as though her cutting words were severing the threadbare strings holding them together, he spun from the room, clomped through the hallway, and thudded down the stairway. A moment later the house door opened. She could picture him stepping out into the darkness of the night. And then the door rattled closed behind him.

She waited against the wall, unable to move, unable to breathe. Would he go outside for a moment? Temper his anger? And return to discuss the matter civilly?

When the silence of the house prevailed, interrupted only by the distant clang of a fire bell somewhere in the nearby city, her muscles loosened, and she sagged.

She closed her eyes against the image of his icy glare. Aye, they'd had tense moments over their differences since they'd been married. But he'd never been angry and stormed away. Then again, she'd never spoken to him so callously. He'd opened up and shared about his war scars and the difficulty he'd experienced. And she'd just trampled his feelings as if they were completely worthless.

Why had she done it? Certainly not to sabotage their relationship the way he claimed.

Whatever the case, she'd hurt him.

Regret pooled heavily inside, so heavily her knees weakened, and she slid to the floor, her back resting against the wall. If he hadn't already started to realize the mistake he'd made in marrying her, now he finally would.

25

*S*ullivan twisted his mug of ale, his shoulders slumped, his head down. In his corner spot at Oscar's Pub, he wasn't in the mood to talk to anyone. No one except Bellamy McKenna.

But for the past hour since Sullivan had stormed away from Enya, he'd sat alone, and Bellamy remained behind the bar counter, pouring drinks and chatting with the regular patrons who made a home at the pub. Or at least it seemed they'd taken up residence at the counter, especially the red-headed, toothless old fellow everyone called Georgie.

Of course Georgie had noticed his arrival, and he'd called out to Bellamy that the captain was back. Bellamy had given Sullivan a quick nod. But that had been all.

Sullivan threw back a drink of the ale and in the same motion took stock of Bellamy grinning at one of the fellows while he pushed another Guinness toward him. The haze of cigar smoke wafted in the air, as did the scent of whatever had been cooking for supper, something with cabbage and bacon.

Oscar Fingal McKenna, Bellamy's father and a matchmaker for decades, sat at the opposite corner table with his thick matchmaking ledger that had been passed down in the McKenna family for generations. His gray hair was wavy and disorderly, his face and nose were ruddy, and his body was rounded with age. He had an infectious smile and laugh that made him a favorite, and his pub an inviting and popular place.

Maybe that was why Sullivan had frequented the establishment whenever he was in St. Louis, because being there reminded him of his family.

Tonight, though, he hadn't come to be reminded of home. He'd come because he needed to talk to someone about Enya. And Bellamy was the only one he trusted to bare his broken heart to. Was the young matchmaker afraid to talk to Sullivan because he didn't want to accept that one of his matches had ended in failure?

Yes, failure. Sullivan slapped his mug back onto the table, ale sloshing over and adding to the stickiness already coating the polished dark wood.

Enya's parting comment about his scars had stung. And he'd even been angry about her bringing them up. But in the end, what had hurt the most was that she'd pushed him away again, just as she had every other time.

Blast. He'd tried to take up Bellamy's challenge to win Enya: *"You're just the man Enya needs. If anyone can rise to the challenge of helping her, you can."*

Clearly he hadn't been that man. And he hadn't been able to rise to the challenge of helping her.

In that moment at the house in the baby's nursery, she'd kissed him. He'd believed the kiss had been her way of signaling that she finally cared about him, that she accepted him for who he was—or at least was beginning to.

He pushed his drink away, propped his elbows on the table, and buried his face in his hands. Her kiss—their kissing—had been like jumping fully into one of his dreams about her, the dreams where she wanted him the same way he wanted her, where they no longer had any barriers between them, and where they could share everything together.

So what had happened?

If she would have told him that she didn't want to be away from him, he probably would have taken time off from being on the river. Because the truth was, the closer they'd come to St. Louis, the more he'd felt an undercurrent of dread—the dread of having to leave her behind for any length.

He'd contemplated asking her to travel with him on his next voyage. But he didn't want to subject her to living on a steamer in his captain's cabin, especially now that he was under suspicion for transporting runaways.

Yet he hadn't been ready to say good-bye. And he'd hoped she wasn't ready to say good-bye to him either.

Obviously, that hadn't been the case. She'd all but sent him away.

Now what? What else could he do?

The truth was, he'd already done everything he could to win her. But that hadn't been enough. *He* hadn't been enough.

He released another groan, glad for the boisterous conversations at other tables that drowned out his misery. He shoved back from the table and stood. He still had plenty of time before the two-o'clock hour when he'd have to determine whether it was safe enough for his stowaway to make her escape or wait for another night. Even so, he was ready to go.

Without looking around, he wound through the tables. It had been a mistake to come. He could figure out what to do on his own.

As he reached the door and stepped out into the night, he tugged his captain's hat down for protection against the light drizzle. Carriages and horses lined the street. But he intended to walk to the levee. Hopefully, the cool air would help clear his head.

He started down the boardwalk and made it only a few steps before the door behind him burst open.

"Captain, wait." It was Bellamy.

Sullivan didn't slow his stride. He'd already made up his mind. And now he didn't need the matchmaker's advice. Little good it had done him previously anyway.

"The challenge gets hard," Bellamy called after him, "so you give up and run away?"

Frustration ripped through Sullivan's gut, and he couldn't keep from stopping and spinning. "I'm not running. She is."

Bellamy was leaning against the doorframe of the pub, his arms crossed, the light of the nearby street lantern casting a glow over his nonchalance and irritating Sullivan all the more.

"'Tis easy enough to stay and fight for your marriage when you have mostly smooth sailing," Bellamy said. "But it takes a man with courage and stamina to stay and fight when the seas are turbulent."

Other pedestrians were slowing to watch the exchange. But thankfully with the rain and cold, the streets were quieter and fewer people were milling about to witness his humiliation.

Sullivan stalked back until he was only a few feet from Bellamy. "I have been strong." His voice was low. "And I have tried to win her night and day for the past two months. But she sabotages the closeness and pushes me away every time."

"Is that a fact, now?"

Sullivan shook his head. Why had he thought Bellamy would understand? Instead, he was offering platitudes.

"You should have matched me with the type of woman I asked for. Then maybe she'd be satisfied with me."

"From everything I heard tonight about you and Enya, she's satisfied with you."

Sullivan was tempted to ask what Bellamy had heard, but it didn't matter. "She just told me she didn't love me."

"Then keep loving her until she can't help but love you back."

"I've already tried, and there's nothing more I can do."

"Ach, there's always more you can do if you look hard enough."

"Not when I'll never be good enough for her."

Bellamy narrowed his eyes.

Sullivan suddenly wished he could take back his words. Why had he spoken so freely with Bellamy? Sullivan wasn't asking for pity or even compassion. He didn't need either.

The young matchmaker was studying him, as if seeing the truth of the matter. "Sounds like you need to be accepting yourself first, or you'll just keep holding her at arm's length."

She was the one who kept putting up barriers, not him. At least that's the conclusion he'd come to tonight. But what if he *was* letting his insecurities come between them? Maybe he had to examine himself more carefully.

"You're a very fine man, Captain Sullivan. Everyone knows it. Now it's time for you to finally realize it."

Was it? Maybe Bellamy was right that he needed to work on accepting himself, flaws and all, before he could truly break down the barriers between himself and Enya.

"In the meantime, dontcha stop letting her know you care." Bellamy took a step back toward the pub door.

Sullivan breathed out a tight lungful. The darkness of the night fell upon him more heavily, along with the ever-present stench of coal smoke in the air.

Bellamy gave him a nod, pushed open the door, and disappeared inside.

Sullivan stared after the matchmaker, fighting the longing to stalk inside and demand more answers. But even as he did so, he knew he couldn't rush back to Enya without first taking some time to make peace with his own issues.

But he would also keep fighting for their marriage, just as Bellamy had suggested, and he would keep loving her until she couldn't stop herself from loving him back.

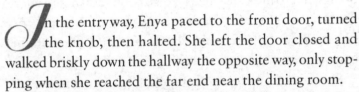

26

*I*n the entryway, Enya paced to the front door, turned the knob, then halted. She left the door closed and walked briskly down the hallway the opposite way, only stopping when she reached the far end near the dining room.

At midday, Mrs. Christy was busy with chores in another portion of the house and wasn't witnessing the complete breakdown of Enya's sanity. Maybe not a complete breakdown, but Enya could admit that after not one word from Sullivan in a day and a half since the night he'd walked out of the house, she was going mad.

Where was he? And why hadn't he returned?

Though she'd expected him to come home that first night, she hadn't been entirely surprised not to see him. She guessed he'd stayed on the steamer to be close at hand to aid the runaway. Or maybe to make sure the slave catcher didn't sneak back on board and search again.

She'd waited expectantly for him all day yesterday, hadn't gone anywhere—not even to visit her family, who was back in St. Louis—because she hadn't wanted to be absent when he arrived.

But as hour after hour slowly passed and he hadn't come, she'd only grown more anxious. Finally, in the afternoon, she'd become so fearful that the slave catcher had found the slave and imprisoned Sullivan that she'd had Mrs. Christy send their newly hired coachman, Mr. Dunlop, to inquire after Sullivan's whereabouts on the levee.

The coachman had come back within the hour to say that Captain O'Brien was on the *Morning Star* and had been overseeing the loading of goods on the main deck. Sullivan hadn't sent back a word to her, not to let her know of his doings, not to indicate when he'd be home, and not to alleviate her concerns. He'd been silent and noncommunicative . . . and it was all her fault. She'd really hurt him with her comment regarding his scars.

She paused and leaned her aching head against the textured wallpaper that covered the front hallway. "I'm sorry, Sullivan." If only he would come home so she could apologize directly to him. Instead, he'd been gone another whole night and then again all morning.

Now, with her coat and hat on, she was ready to summon Mr. Dunlop to take her to the waterfront and go speak to Sullivan for herself.

But what if she arrived at the *Morning Star* and Sullivan ignored her the way he had with the coachman yesterday?

She pushed away from the wall and walked to the mirror that hung beside the front door.

Her face was pale today and her eyes wide, with dark circles under them. Gone was the contented woman she'd become after living with Sullivan for the past two months.

In her place was the frightened and cowering woman she'd been with Bryan—the woman who'd been beaten down and rejected.

Had Sullivan realized he'd made a mistake in marrying her? And was he now rejecting her too? If so, she didn't blame him.

"This is why you weren't supposed to give him your heart," she whispered angrily to her reflection. Maybe she hadn't exactly given it to him. It was more like he'd taken an ice pick to her heart and cracked off all that had been frozen. Then he'd breathed warmth into her with his small acts of kindness every day.

At a firm knocking against the door, she startled and spun away from the mirror. Was that him? Coming back to reconcile, even though she'd hurt him . . . and pushed him away . . . ?

Aye, he'd been right. She was sabotaging their relationship by thrusting him away every time they had a moment of closeness. That hadn't been fair to him. But she didn't know any other way of relating.

Straightening her hat, she placed her hand on the doorknob. It was trembling, but she forced herself to open the door anyway, dragging in a breath to fortify herself as she did so.

At the sight of her older brother standing on the doorstep, she expelled a breath of disappointment.

Kiernan was peering intently down the street, as though watching for someone, his top hat pulled low over his auburn hair, his handsome face shadowed. A cherry red gig was parked on the muddy street, the storm apron pulled up against the cold, spitting drizzle.

"Hello, Enya." Kiernan's keen blue eyes swept over her, slowing at her waistline, clearly gauging whether or not her pregnancy was showing yet. He was likely tasked by both Mam and Da to visit and tell her she needed to conceal any swell until further along in the pregnancy.

"I'm being careful not to show." She might as well get right to the point. "You can take your report back to Mam and Da."

"Good day to you too." Kiernan's gaze didn't miss a single detail as he slipped past her into the hallway, taking in the new wallpaper and carpet and the tall potted plants on pedestals.

She gave the street a hard look both ways, hoping for a glimpse of Sullivan but not seeing his distinctly broad frame anywhere. Then she closed the door. "That's why you're here, isn't it? To give me the usual lecture about how I need to behave now that I'm back in town? So I don't embarrass the family any further?"

Kiernan shrugged. "That's not why I'm here. But 'tis good advice. Please do refrain from any more of your shenanigans."

Enya couldn't keep from pursing her lips. Only a few seconds with her brother and already she was wishing she was someplace else far away.

"Especially now that your husband isn't around to exert his influence."

"Not around?" The question slipped out before she could think of Kiernan's reaction to it.

He tipped up the brim of his hat, and his brow rose. "The *Morning Star* left early this morning for New Orleans."

Her heart snapped loose and plummeted to the bottom

of her chest. The impact was hard and swift and painful, shattering the already delicately repaired organ. Even as the pieces shattered, she forced a casual smile. "Of course. He's off again. As busy as always."

Kiernan, in the process of saying something more, paused and studied her face more carefully. Did he sense the hurt? Did he suspect that something was amiss between Sullivan and her?

"Mam wanted me to offer to have you come stay at the house while he's gone." Kiernan took several steps down the hallway, peeking into the parlor, his eyes widening with interest.

"I intend to live in here." She was relieved more than ever that Sullivan had provided a place for her. "Tell Mam thank you, though, and that I shall visit her soon."

"See that you do." Kiernan gentled his tone. "Everyone would like to hear all about your trip to New Orleans and your visit with your husband's family."

What husband? The question smacked into her so hard that she nearly toppled against the wall, had to grab on to it to keep from wobbling. She certainly didn't need Kiernan figuring out Sullivan had left her without saying good-bye—just like Bryan had. Kiernan probably would assume she'd messed up again and then start working on another solution.

What if Sullivan didn't come back? What if he'd given up on her and their marriage?

A strange despair tightened her throat. Deep down she knew that Sullivan wasn't that sort of man, that he wouldn't run away and leave her forever. But he'd obviously decided he'd had enough.

Kiernan took off his hat and combed his hair's longer front strands back rakishly, then replaced his hat with a cocky tilt of his head. "I heard your housekeeper is seeking to hire a maidservant."

"Aye, she's interviewed a couple of young women." Enya had sat in on the interviews yesterday, but her mind had been occupied with thoughts of Sullivan, and she hadn't been able to focus well. "Two more women are coming today."

"I want you to hire this woman." He lowered his voice and handed Enya a folded slip of paper almost secretively.

Enya took it and flipped it open and made no attempt to whisper. "Alannah Darragh."

"Hush with you now, Enya." He glanced around as though he expected someone to be watching them.

"Who is she?"

"She's in trouble and needs a place to stay."

"One of your women?"

Kiernan had become a womanizer over the past year since ending his longtime relationship with his childhood sweetheart. No matter how much he might deny it, he left a string of broken hearts everywhere he went.

"She's the sister of one of my employees." Kiernan was business savvy like Da, and at twenty-two, he already had his own successful glass-cutting factory.

Enya didn't intend to make the conversation easy for him. "Since when do you concern yourself over sisters of employees?"

Kiernan scowled. "He's one of my best workers but has fallen onto some hard times."

"Where do they live?"

"Does it really matter? Just do as I say and hire her." He

started back toward the door, the arrogant swagger to his steps stirring fresh irritation in Enya.

She followed him. "I'll have to interview her like all the rest."

"No, you won't." Kiernan opened the door and tugged up the collar of his coat against the cool day, the rain having turned to heavy sleet.

"I'll not be hiring someone in order to feed your appetite for dalliances."

At Enya's insinuation, Kiernan stopped in the doorway so suddenly that Enya had to pull herself up short. He held himself stiffly for a moment before he slowly pivoted. "I don't view her that way."

She held his gaze and didn't let him intimidate her into looking away first.

"Hire her." He started to turn, then softened his voice. "Please."

Something about Kiernan was different. Enya couldn't put her finger on it, but his demand suddenly didn't feel so demanding.

She didn't watch him depart. Instead, she closed the door and leaned against it. A sob swelled and began to strangle her.

Sullivan had left St. Louis for New Orleans. He'd be gone for close to a month if there weren't any delays. One whole month. She wouldn't see him until mid-May.

The prospect of the next four weeks without Sullivan in her life only pushed the sobs higher into her throat.

She'd been too stubborn during their last argument. All he'd really wanted was for her to acknowledge that she wanted to be with him, but she'd let her fears keep her from admitting that maybe she was developing stronger feelings for him.

A sob slipped out, and as it did so, she slid down to the hallway floor, her skirt bunching around her. Aye, she had driven a husband away again. But this time she'd done it with a man who was good and honest and true.

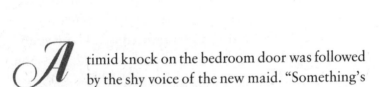

27

A timid knock on the bedroom door was followed by the shy voice of the new maid. "Something's arrived for you, ma'am."

"I don't need anything right now." Enya rolled over to face the wall so that the young woman wouldn't see the tears streaking her cheeks, tears that had been all too frequent during the past week of Sullivan's absence.

Somehow she'd managed a visit to her family's home. She'd also gone to mass. But other than that, she'd closed herself off and spent the majority of time in bed. In fact, most days, she could hardly make herself get up at all.

She'd claimed to Mrs. Christy that she was feeling the effects of the pregnancy, that she was tired and aching and emotional. Though the kindly housekeeper didn't challenge her, Enya knew she wasn't fooling the woman.

The truth was, every day Sullivan was gone, she lost more of the will to go on and fight for happiness. She wanted to lose herself in sleep and never awaken. Once or twice she'd even considered taking laudanum to escape into oblivion and find respite from the constant ache in her chest. But always, she thought of her child, the rounding of her stomach growing more prominent with every passing week.

"Ma'am." The new maid spoke hesitantly. Alannah Darragh had come to the house the same afternoon Kiernan had. Enya had asked Mrs. Christy to hire her, even without the interview.

Alannah was a recent Irish immigrant, and it had quickly become clear she had no domestic experience whatsoever. But with her fair hair, pale blue eyes, and beautiful features, Enya wasn't surprised Kiernan favored her. If the young woman wasn't on his list of women he adored, she soon would be.

Alannah's hesitant steps crossed into the room. "Mrs. Christy said you'd be wanting to see the gift, so she did."

Gift? Enya wiped at the tears on her cheek, then shifted toward the maid.

Alannah stood in the center of the large room, her black uniform and white apron hanging too loosely on her thin frame. Her eyes, though kind, held a frightened wariness to them. Her gaze often darted to the windows, as if she was making sure no one was coming after her.

Thankfully, Mrs. Christy hadn't seemed to mind that she had to train Alannah in almost every task. In fact, Mrs. Christy had said that sometimes she liked training maids with no skills rather than retraining a maid with the wrong skills.

"What gift and from whom?" Enya hadn't received any gifts recently, and curiosity quickly chased away some of her sadness. She pushed up to her elbows.

Though the curtains were drawn at midday, the room was bright, painted a summery green with pale yellow accents. Enya had picked the colors because she'd wanted her room to be cheerful. But so far, she'd only found sorrow here.

"Mrs. Christy told me not to say." Alannah's voice held apology. "But I'm to be helping you get dressed and come down to the parlor."

"Ach, I'm not feeling well enough to do so. Please ask her to have the gift brought up to my room."

"She said she can't be bringing it up to you, that you'll need to be going down."

Enya swiped a thick, tangled strand out of her face.

Alannah didn't meet her gaze. Instead she stood frozen in place, as if she expected Enya's wrath to fall upon her.

Enya sighed and slowly sat up. She should have known Mrs. Christy wouldn't let her lay abed forever, that she'd concoct a scheme to force her to get up.

"She did say you're going to like it, ma'am." Alannah's voice dropped to a whisper, and she glanced past the open door into the hallway, likely gauging whether Mrs. Christy could hear her saying more than she ought.

For the better part of the next hour, Enya allowed Alannah to help her get dressed and brush her hair. Since Alannah wasn't yet trained on the latest ladies' hair fashions, Enya styled her own hair simply.

When she was ready, she sat on the stool at her dressing table a moment longer, extending her hand and examining her wedding ring. The large, circular diamond cluster was as exquisitely beautiful today as when Sullivan had knelt in the bedchamber at her parents' home and slipped it on her finger.

Although she'd assumed he'd expect repayment for the gift, he'd never once demanded anything in return. Not time in bed with him. Not affection. Not even companionship.

He'd been the opposite of Bryan in every way, and still she'd held him at arm's length.

If only she hadn't been so stubborn. If only she'd stopped wallowing in self-pity. If only she hadn't thought just about herself.

Instead, she'd taken Sullivan for granted and hadn't appreciated his steady presence and support. He'd known she was hurting after her failed marriage, and he'd been patient and kind, more than she deserved.

But a man could only be patient and kind for so long. . . .

"I miss him, Alannah." Enya's voice cracked, and she had to blink back rapid tears again.

"Him?" Alannah stood behind her, the reflection of her pretty face in the mirror showing both sincerity and concern. The young woman wasn't pretending interest or merely being polite, like some maids did.

"My husband. I miss him terribly."

Alannah's expression softened. "How long will he be gone?" She appeared not to know all that had transpired, which was another credit to Mrs. Christy for refraining from gossiping with the new maid.

"I don't know. Possibly weeks." Enya hoped he would make the return voyage to St. Louis within the month. But what if he decided to stay in New Orleans for a while? After all, what reason did he have to return to her when she'd spurned him so many times?

"That's a long time, so it is. I'm sure he'll be missing you too, ma'am."

Enya nodded. Of course he wouldn't miss her. Not after the way they'd parted. But she couldn't explain that to Alannah.

Blinking back the tears that had plagued her more frequently during her pregnancy, she rose and glanced at the unmade bed. It beckoned her to flop down, cover herself up, and disappear from the world.

But as Alannah started toward the door, Enya fell into step behind her. Now that she was dressed, she'd make herself useful for a few hours and attend to the remodeling and decorating that still needed to be finished.

A short while ago, she'd heard men's voices along with bumping and banging about in the rooms below. It was likely more of the new furniture she'd purchased, perhaps the dining room set. The least she could do was view the pieces and decide how to arrange them.

As she descended the stairs, Mrs. Christy exited the parlor with a smile, her eyes twinkling with barely restrained excitement.

Nearing the bottom, Enya paused, a strange hitch in her breath. Why was Mrs. Christy excited? Was Sullivan in the room? Had he gotten off at one of the ports south of St. Louis and returned to her on a different steamer?

Oh, if only . . .

She'd run to him, throw herself in his arms, and tell him she was sorry for everything.

She braced her shoulders and then hurried the last of the

distance toward the parlor. Mrs. Christy stepped aside, her smile widening, a knowing look upon her face.

Enya moved into the bright and sunny front room with all the new furniture of dark cherry wood and upholstered in warm cream tones, the blue damask tapestries, and the elegant wall hangings. She searched desperately for the person she wanted to see more than anyone else.

But there was no sign of him. No one was in the room.

Even as disappointment crashed through her, her attention snagged on something standing in the middle of the room.

Her pulse gathered speed, and she crossed to it.

A grand piano.

For a moment, she stood in front of it and could only stare. The dark reddish maple was glossy and polished to perfection. The word *Erard* was written in gold script above the long keyboard. Even the top was open and the stool pulled out, in readiness for being played.

She grazed the ivory keys, then the ebony.

Mrs. Christy stood in the doorway, still beaming.

Enya's throat constricted. Only one person could have given this to her. Sullivan. But how? When? She turned her questioning eyes upon the housekeeper.

"Apparently, Captain O'Brien purchased it on the day before he left St. Louis."

After their argument? After she'd hurt him? He'd still been thinking about her?

"The men who delivered it said that it arrived at the piano store yesterday from Pittsburg."

Erard was one of the best and newest pianos, made in

France, a brand used by famous composers. Sullivan always made sure she had the best of everything.

Her knees began to shake, and she lowered herself to the stool. What did this gift mean? Did he still care? Did he still want to be with her?

Several tears spilled over and trickled down her cheeks.

She wasn't worthy of Sullivan's love. But his continued love toward her made her want to be worthy of him. She wanted to stop being broken, wanted to be less selfish, wanted to be the kind of wife a man wouldn't want to leave behind . . .

But how? How could she become the wife Sullivan deserved, one who would love him unconditionally in return?

His words from their last night sifted through her mind. *"You don't have to let the scars of your past determine your future."*

Was he right? Maybe she didn't have outer scars the same way he did, but what if she had them inside? And what if she'd let those scars keep her from moving on from her past and embracing the future?

She glided her fingers over the keyboard again. Before her mind registered what she was doing, she was already playing a concerto—Vivaldi's *The Four Seasons* arranged for the piano. She started with the first movement, "Spring." When she reached "Summer," her fingers slowed and then stopped.

Was she ready for the next movement? She'd had to push through a great deal of pain in order to learn to play the piano again. But she'd done so, and even now, she was determined to play "Summer," even if it didn't reflect her life yet.

If she'd persevered through the pain to play the piano,

surely she could persevere through the pain to find love with Sullivan. Maybe she wasn't quite there yet, but she wanted to be ready for him, wanted to move past the scars, so when he returned to St. Louis—and if he returned to her—she'd finally be ready to give him her heart.

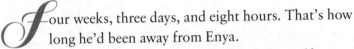

28

*F*our weeks, three days, and eight hours. That's how long he'd been away from Enya.

Yes, he'd been counting. He couldn't help himself.

Sullivan peered eagerly at the St. Louis waterfront as the *Morning Star* churned closer. As with the last time he'd arrived at the harbor in April, it was busier than previous years, likely with steamers still heading to the west side of Missouri filled with more gold seekers. It would be late in the season for the overland travelers to head to California, but no doubt they were too excited to care about the hazards.

The late-afternoon sunshine combined with the warm breeze made the day particularly pleasant. Compared to the gray skies and barren landscape from last month, the warmth of May had brought with it an abundance of color. Though the streets were still muddy, the few trees that hadn't been cut down to make room for warehouses were green and full of leaves. The grassy portions along the waterfront were also vibrant. Here and there, he spotted flowers in bloom.

He expelled a breath of relief that he was back. He hadn't been sure he could last another day away from Enya. The longing had been so keen, his body had ached.

How was it that he'd become so attached to her in such a short time?

Oh, he'd tried hard to get her out of his system over the past month away. He'd done everything he could to stop thinking about her and longing for her. He'd worked himself hard every day until he was utterly exhausted in order not to dream about her. He'd avoided all piano playing because it only reminded him of her. He'd even tried to make himself angry at her by replaying their last exchange a dozen times.

But after plenty of time to think about what had happened, he knew he'd never really been angry. He'd been hurt because he thought she was rejecting him. But he realized now that she wouldn't have kissed him the way she had that night if she were rejecting him.

No, she cared about him. The feelings and passion had been present. Maybe it would continue to grow. But even if it didn't, he would still love her. Because the truth was, he couldn't stop loving her any more than he could stop the Mississippi from flowing.

The shrill blast of the *Morning Star*'s whistle echoed in the air—two shorter, one long, then two shorter—as the pilot guided the steamer into the space between two other vessels—tight enough that a person could climb from one boat to the next without much effort.

He tugged at his cravat, loosening it even more. The

warm breeze soothed his neck and the puckered skin. The mortification of letting the scars show had lessened over the past weeks, but it still wasn't easy to reveal his flaws to the world.

Regardless, he'd wanted to do as Bellamy had encouraged, to accept himself and stop worrying about people rejecting him. He hadn't known any other way to overcome his insecurities except by facing them head-on. And baring his neck and the ugly skin there had been his first step.

Through it all, he'd begun to realize that Enya had always accepted him more than anyone else. When she'd seen his burn marks, she hadn't pitied him, hadn't been bothered by them in the least.

She also hadn't been put off by his quiet, reserved personality or his social awkwardness. In fact, their personalities fit together, almost as if they'd been made to be together.

Even so, he hoped in the process of stretching himself that he'd gained confidence. Especially so that when he visited Enya, he wouldn't give way to the feelings that he wasn't good enough or didn't deserve her. Instead, he wanted to stand before her, knowing that even with all his flaws, he was a man worth having.

The *Morning Star* sidled into the spot and began to shift to allow for the lowering of the landing stage. Dockworkers waited along the bank, and passengers lined the decks, readying themselves to disembark.

Unfortunately, he'd had to stop more than usual during the journey northward to bury people dying of cholera. After the disease had diminished earlier in the year, it was awakening with the warmer weather, like a creature coming out of hibernation, and now fresh graves lined the river-banks.

Everyone was speculating what course the disease would take next, and the latest news Sullivan had heard was that the cases of cholera were surging again in St. Louis. He'd gotten a copy of the *St. Louis Daily New Era* a couple of days ago at a port city, and the top story had been about cholera causing 181 deaths in the past week, which was more than double what it had been a month ago.

If the situation became worse in the city, he'd have to reconsider where to have Enya live. Perhaps she'd be safest residing on his family plantation outside of New Orleans. There she would have plenty of fresh air and good food to eat.

Longing tugged at him—the longing to jump into the river, swim the final distance to the shore, and then run the rest of the way to the house, to her.

But the real question was—would she be happy to see him?

Maybe after the way they'd parted, she'd be less than eager for a visit. Maybe he'd lost the ground he'd gained with her and would have to start over and work hard to make amends.

He released a sigh, one that contained all the worry that had been building.

As much as he wanted to see her this evening, he probably ought to wait until the morning. He'd stop by the bath-house, get a haircut and shave, and then go when he was at his best.

In the meantime, though, he'd send her something to let her know he was back, a way to prepare her for his visit. Or was the delay the coward's way? A tactic for avoiding his fear of more rejection?

He shook his head. No, he had work to do tonight. . . .

He didn't glance behind him at the door of his cabin. Thankfully, Roan Whistler hadn't been able to find any evidence of his helping runaways during his stopover in St. Louis in April.

But now that Sullivan had become a suspect, he'd had to use even more caution for this voyage, especially because he didn't have Enya to play the piano and drown out noises.

Yes, it was for the best if he stayed on the steamer one more night and made sure his cargo was safe.

◆ ◆ ◆ ◆ ◆ ◆ ◆

Enya leaned forward and jotted an A-sharp quarter note onto the sheet music. Then, sticking the pencil between her teeth, she replayed the bar with the change.

The melody crescendoed just the way she'd envisioned, poignant and yet joyful at the same time.

She paused again, took out her pencil, and drew in a series of eighth notes.

"Mrs. O'Brien?"

At the call of her name and Alannah's touch on her shoulder, Enya startled and fumbled with her pencil. She caught it and tucked it behind her ear before she shifted on her stool to find the maidservant standing beside the piano.

Enya splayed a hand over the rising swell of her baby, feeling a fluttering that was becoming more common each day. "I didn't see you there."

"I'm sorry, ma'am. I could tell you were lost in your

composing." Alannah was beginning to fill out and looked healthier than she had when she'd first started her job, even prettier, if that were possible.

Her face had lost the pallor and gained a rosy pink. Her blond hair was more lustrous. Even the fearfulness had dissipated, although the maid never ventured far beyond the yard and always stayed out of sight when visitors came to the house.

"Aye, I'm nearing the end and am too focused." Enya shifted back to the sheet of music, one that she'd been composing for the past two weeks. She'd found solace, even contentment, in creating again. And she'd filled her days—and even some of her nights—with music.

Maybe she'd never be a concert pianist. Maybe she'd never have a career in music. But she appreciated knowing that Sullivan believed in her and that he hadn't tried to control her or stop her from her aspirations, and had instead encouraged her to keep utilizing her musical talent in whatever way she chose to employ it.

That he supported her so completely meant more than he would ever know, and she was looking forward to sharing her composition with him.

With each passing day, her mind filled with more of Sullivan until at times he was all she thought about. She'd relived their weeks together and the many ways he'd shown her that he cared, not for what he could get from her but out of genuine concern for her as a person. Because that's the type of man he was. He had a deeply caring heart and helped others without expecting anything in return.

She should have tried harder to connect with him. . . . She vowed to do so when he returned.

Now that he'd been gone four weeks, she expected him to be back in St. Louis any time. Every day she prayed he would come walking in the door and forgive her for continually pushing him away. But every night she lay in her bed disappointed that another day had gone by without a word from him.

She could admit, her desperation was starting to mount. But she'd done her best to stay busy and not entertain the possibility that he wouldn't want to see her.

Of course, he had sent her the piano. And she wanted to believe it had been his way of letting her know he wasn't giving up on her. Even though she tried to silence the doubts that still lingered, Bryan's voice still whispered in her head that no man would ever want her again.

"What do you need, Alannah?" Enya leaned closer to the sheet and examined the few notes she'd just drawn.

"Something arrived for you, ma'am." The maid's tone held a note of excitement.

Enya swiveled back around, her heart beginning to flutter like a bird trapped in a cage needing freedom. "What is it?" The last time something had arrived for her, it had been the piano. She didn't dare hope Sullivan sent something again, did she?

Alannah smiled, and her blue eyes lit with encouragement.

The wings inside Enya's heart beat harder.

"You'll have to come into the dining room and see." Alannah held out a hand to help her up.

Enya didn't wait for the assistance. She hopped up and raced out of the room, stopping short as she entered the dining room. There at her place was a meal perfectly arranged, the chicken dinner that the *Morning Star* cook made so well, the one Enya had craved often during their travels. Lying on the table next to the plate of food was a bouquet of flowers, one that reminded her of the simple bouquets Sullivan had picked for her from time to time from the flowers along the river.

She cupped a hand over her mouth to catch the half sob and half gasp that escaped.

Alannah was standing in the doorway, gazing at the items on the table too. "The messenger said it was from Captain O'Brien."

"Then he must be back." The ache inside swelled. She needed to see Sullivan now. Right away.

She slipped past Alannah into the hallway. She'd ride down to the levee this very moment and find him. If he'd sent her the dinner, then surely he'd be willing to see her, wouldn't he?

She made it one step toward the coat-tree before halting.

"What's wrong, ma'am?" Alannah had moved to her side, her delicate brows crinkling together with concern.

"Why did he have the meal and flowers delivered? Why didn't he bring me everything himself?"

"Maybe he's busy."

"Maybe." But she'd watched Sullivan enough to know that he didn't let anything stop him when he wanted something. If he'd wanted to see her, he would have made a way to visit, no matter how busy he was.

"You should come eat before it gets any colder." Alannah slid an arm around Enya to draw her back into the dining room.

This time Enya complied and allowed Alannah to guide

her to the table and her chair. But as she sat and took in the meal and the flowers, she couldn't keep worry from mingling with her excitement that Sullivan was in St. Louis.

Maybe he hadn't come because he wasn't sure if she'd welcome him. What if first she had to somehow show him that she was finally ready to open her arms and heart to him?

29

*S*ullivan didn't want to restrain himself from visiting Enya any longer.

Through the blackness of the night, he studied the brightly lit windows of the homes in the general area of their house. Even from as high as he was in the pilothouse, he couldn't distinguish the homes.

Should he have gone to her earlier when he'd had the chance instead of sending her the chicken dinner Cook had made before leaving the steamer for well-deserved time off?

Sullivan's chest squeezed hard, his need for Enya pinching off his airway and slicing into his heart. Maybe he wasn't too late to call back the night watchman for the evening shift. Then he could go see her tonight.

He stepped out of the pilothouse and started toward the stairs.

With a sigh, he halted. What if he went to her and she pushed him away? She might even refuse to see him. After all, when he'd left her that last time, he'd been insensitive and impatient. And he'd gone from St. Louis without a good-bye.

He gripped the railing and held himself in place. "Tomorrow." The whisper came out harsh, the strong, steady wind from the northeast picking up his word and tossing it away.

He had a duty to fulfill to Silas, who was still tucked safely in the closet in the cabin. Even though the night was without cloud cover or mist, Sullivan planned to execute the exchange anyway. He'd already sent the crew away and placed the lantern in his cabin window to alert the next rescuer to row over at two o'clock. He couldn't change the plans now.

A lone man attired in ragged and frayed garments stumbled down the gangplank of the *White Cloud*, one steamer away to the north of the *Morning Star*. The steamer's night watchman rose from his seat on forecastle and called out to the fellow.

Sullivan couldn't hear all that was exchanged, but soon enough the man circled out of sight behind the piles of lumber and bales of dry hemp.

There were always stragglers along the levee . . . and thieves who tried to board the steamers while they were moored so they could steal anything of value left behind. That's why vessels posted a watchman during the night.

Thankfully most watchmen had their eyes on the waterfront and not on the river behind them. Even so, the rowboat coming for the slave tonight would be at greater risk, just as it had been last month.

The danger of harboring the runaway had weighed more heavily upon Sullivan during this voyage. He had so much more at stake now that he had a wife and soon a baby. At the same time, he only had to think about enslaved men his age who had their wives and babies torn away from them.

Sullivan couldn't begin to imagine their pain, and contemplating their plight only strengthened his resolve to do more.

At the waft of smoke in the air, Sullivan straightened and peered over the *Morning Star*, as well as the steamboats moored next to his. Through the darkness, he couldn't distinguish anything unusual. As far as he could tell, there were no flames.

He'd just learned the *Highland Mary* had caught fire two weeks ago as she was moored near the foot of Cherry Street. From the tales the dockworkers told, the fire had spread to every part of the little steamer within five minutes, and the captain had been forced to dive into the river to extinguish the flames from his clothing.

Surely with the story of the disaster so fresh, his mind was playing tricks on him. It wouldn't have been the first time he'd imagined smoke and flames where there were none. He supposed after what he'd experienced during the Battle of Veracruz, he'd always suffer from the vivid memories.

The trouble was that most steamboats were built entirely out of wood, and the wood became drier over the life of the ship, almost dangerously so. Fires were a risk of the business.

The scent of smoke tickled his nose again, and this time he stepped up to the forecastle so he could get a better view of the line of steamers that stretched along the St. Louis waterfront.

Sure enough, a telltale red glow came from the *White Cloud*.

Sullivan's pulse slammed hard and fast. He didn't hesitate before he leapt over the railing to the deck below. He had to get to the steamer and help put out the fire before it spread to the vessels on either side.

To save himself time, he climbed over the railing and jumped onto the *Edward Bates*, the adjacent steamer. He sprinted to the opposite side, and by the time he reached the railing, the flames filled the doorway of one of the *White Cloud*'s passenger cabins.

The night watchman had a bucket in hand already, but he would need assistance if he had any hope of keeping the flames from consuming other parts of the steamer.

Sullivan swiped up several buckets from a supply closet on the *Edward Bates*. At the same time, the *White Cloud*'s fire alarm bell rang out into the silence of the night.

Sullivan wasted no time climbing the railing and leaping onto the *White Cloud*. As his feet slammed onto the deck, the watchman gave a start, but at the sight of Sullivan's buckets, he nodded toward the barrel of rainwater down the passageway.

The heat and the intensity of the flames reached out as though to grasp Sullivan in their dangerous tentacles, but he raced along with the night watchman to wrestle the fire under control.

Even with the two of them throwing water upon the fire, it continued to spread, and he prayed that the nearest fire department had heard the alarm bell and would respond soon. The Franklin Fire Company No. 8 was the closest, only three blocks from the levee. But the Missouri Fire Company No. 5 was also fairly close.

Would they be able to reach the waterfront in time to save the *White Cloud*?

After what felt like an hour later but was really only minutes, the shouts of firemen on the levee broke through the crackle of the flames and the pounding of Sullivan's heart.

From his periphery he could see men dragging hoses to the nearest fireplug attached to the foundry at the corner of Main and Cherry Streets.

Sullivan and the night watchman continued to douse as much of the fire as they could, but the wind was fanning the flames, and it was moving to the pantry beside it.

"We've gotta keep it from reaching the *Edward*," the watchman called above the roar of burning wood.

Sullivan nodded. But as he turned to take stock of the distance of the flames from the *White Cloud* to the steamer beside it, his heart plummeted. A faint reddish glow from the *Morning Star* illuminated the darkness. And he didn't need to examine it closely to know that now his steamer was on fire too.

Sullivan cocked his head toward his vessel. "Looks like I've got trouble."

He didn't wait for the night watchman's response. Instead he leapt from steamer to steamer until he reached the *Morning Star*. He quickly grabbed more buckets and then followed the trail of red glow until he found the passenger cabin that was ablaze. The fire was almost identical in nature to the one on the *White Cloud*.

Did that mean someone had purposefully set both fires, maybe waited until he'd left his steamer before sneaking on board and starting it? Perhaps the same raggedy-looking fellow?

Thankfully the fire was a deck below and farthest away from his cabin and from the closet where Silas was hiding.

As Sullivan dipped his buckets into the rain cistern on the prow, he threw a glance toward the levee, hoping to catch sight of the culprit. Someone had to identify him and hold him accountable.

In that single glance he noticed two things. The first was that amidst the growing chaos on the levee with firemen and others rushing to the emergency, one man stood absolutely still, his eyes fixed upon Sullivan. With the tight black coat, stocky build, and stiff posture, Sullivan recognized him right away.

Roan Whistler, the slave catcher.

The second was that the *Morning Star*'s landing stage was gone. And that couldn't happen unless someone had purposefully tossed it into the river.

Sullivan didn't have time to stop and demand an explanation. He sprinted back to the cabin that was ablaze and threw first one bucket of water, then another onto the flames, hardly touching the extent of the fire.

As sweat ran down his forehead and cheeks, he tried to make sense of everything. He and Silas were trapped on the steamer. If the blaze fanned out of control—which was very possible with the strength of the wind—then the entire vessel would become a death trap. Without the landing stage, he wouldn't be able to disembark, and no one would be able to come aboard to help.

Sullivan would have no choice but to jump overboard with Silas to save both their lives. And the moment he did, Whistler would be watching and waiting for him to swim ashore with the runaway slave in tow, ready to capture them both.

30

*S*he hadn't been able to play any music all evening.

With a sigh, Enya lowered her head to the keyboard, letting the discordant notes fill the parlor since they already filled her heart.

No matter how much she'd tried to distract herself with various songs and even her latest composition, her mind always wandered back to Sullivan, to his sweet gesture with the flowers and the meal.

As much as she liked them, she knew deep inside she wanted something else even more. She wanted him. Aye, she wanted to hold him, talk with him, and spend every day with him.

But how could she show him that?

As the final strains of music faded to silence, another distant clang took its place.

She sat up and strained to listen. The fire bells near the river were ringing. And that meant only one thing.

Another steamboat was on fire.

Her heart gave an unsteady lurch. Of course fires happened along the levee because of the steamboats. In fact, she'd heard the fire bells on the waterfront only a couple of weeks ago. The steamboat had been set adrift and burned down to the hull. But no lives had been lost.

Even so, Sullivan was there tonight. What if the fire was near one of his steamers?

She pushed up from her stool. The window in the nursery. She'd be able to see something from the window. She had during the last fire.

With her footsteps thumping hard, she hurried out of the parlor, up the stairs, and into the nursery. As she crossed to the window, she breathed in rapidly through her mouth to push down a swell of nausea. She hadn't experienced nausea in weeks. But tonight, with Sullivan possibly in danger, her stomach was rolling.

Sweeping aside the draperies, she peered out toward the waterfront. At the sight of the leaping red blazes lighting up the sky, she sucked in another breath. But in the next instant, she bent over and wretched, only managing to grasp the closest basin just in time.

As she heaved for a few more seconds, Mrs. Christy's gentle touch upon her back let her know she wasn't alone.

As Enya straightened, she grabbed on to the older woman. "I need to get down to the waterfront now."

Mrs. Christy's gaze darted out the window too. She'd likely already heard the fire bells, and now her eyes widened at the conflagration in the distance. "I think Captain O'Brien would want you to stay here where you're safe."

"But I need to go see him—"

"It's after ten o'clock. And you'd just be in the way, dear."

Enya started back toward the stairway. "Please tell Mr. Dunlop to be ready as soon as possible."

"Mrs. O'Brien, the captain won't be happy with me if I let you go." Mrs. Christy rarely contradicted her, but this time her voice held distress.

Near the top of the stairs in the dimly lit hallway, Enya paused and clutched the older woman's hands. "I love him."

"Of course you do." Mrs. Christy squeezed back, her face wreathed with worry.

"I really, really love him." Each word drove the certainty of her love for Sullivan deeper. Somewhere and at some point, she'd fallen in love with him. She'd waited long enough to see him—weeks, days, hours. And now her love was relentlessly urging her to go be with him. She couldn't delay another moment.

Mrs. Christy studied her face, then released a sigh. "You promise you won't get too close to the fire?"

"I promise."

With each step down the stairway and through the hallway, Enya's heart thudded with painful need. As she reached the coat-tree and began to tug on her cloak, she could hear Mrs. Christy calling out the back door across to the carriage house where the coachman lived in the second-floor apartment.

A moment later, Alannah hurried down the stairs in a robe, her hair plaited in a long braid, likely already having been abed.

Enya didn't owe either of her servants an explanation, but over the past weeks they'd become more like family than hired help. "I have to see him tonight."

"Of course you do." Alannah lifted Enya's bonnet from a hook and settled it on her head.

"I should have gone earlier. Should have told him I loved him then."

"You'll tell him now, that you will."

Enya's fingers were trembling, and she fumbled with the velvet tie of her cloak. "What if I'm too late?"

"You'll be hurrying there, and we'll be praying you find him straightaway, that we will." Alannah finished tying the bonnet and then nudged Enya's hand out of the way before working on the cloak. "Even though I haven't met him, 'tis obvious he adores you."

"I hope you're right." He still cared about her, enough to send the meal and the flowers. But that didn't mean he could so easily forgive her for how she'd hurt him.

Within minutes, she was in the carriage and hurtling toward the waterfront at top speed. The closer they drew, the more people they had to dodge, until at last they turned onto the levee and slowed to a crawl. Enya peered out the window, glimpsing the waterfront and the steamboats and the dark sky reflecting the blaze.

So far, from what she could tell, the fire was mostly contained to just a few steamers on the north end of the levee.

She released a tight breath. Maybe she was worrying for nothing. And maybe Mrs. Christy had been right, that she should have stayed home away from the busyness and the danger.

The *Morning Star* seemed to be the steamer Sullivan commanded the most often, and in the glow of the firelight, she searched for the familiar luxurious vessel with its high side wheel and the name painted in fancy gold lettering.

She impatiently skimmed her gaze over the boats as the carriage drew closer. And then, in the light of the steamer that was blazing the highest, she caught sight of the word *Star*. It took only another moment to comprehend what she was seeing—the *Morning Star* was one boat away from the fire, and already the flames had spread to the steamer next to it as well as engulfing a portion of Sullivan's steamer.

"Mary, Joseph, and Jesus have mercy." Her whispered plea slipped out even as her chest constricted with fear.

If the *Morning Star* was ablaze, then no doubt Sullivan was on board doing everything he could to douse the flames. He was right in the middle of the disaster and the danger.

And what about the runaway slave? Sullivan wouldn't have had time yet to help the slave leave the closet and get to freedom, would he? Was the slave in danger too?

The carriage rolled to a stop near a grouping of barrels whose staves were marked with bold print: *Bacon* and *Lard*.

She was far enough back from the waterfront to remain safe from the fire, along with any sparks and embers, and she needed to stay in the carriage, just as Mrs. Christy had instructed. But her heart had ceased to beat, and it wouldn't resume functioning again until she had the chance to see for herself that Sullivan was safe.

Tossing aside caution, she threw open the carriage door, stepped down onto the causeway, and called to Mr. Dunlop, "I'll be back in a moment."

She didn't wait for his response, guessing he'd been tasked by Mrs. Christy to make sure she stayed well away from the danger. Although Enya was sorry she had to break the promise she'd made to Mrs. Christy, she wasn't sorry enough to hold back.

Sure enough the coachman called out, "Mrs. O'Brien, please stop! You need to remain with the carriage."

She only lengthened her pace, skirting past the piles of goods and making a direct line to the *Morning Star*.

"Mrs. O'Brien!" Mr. Dunlop's voice turned frantic. "Come back!"

Her feet picked up the pace as if they had a will of their own, and all she could do was bunch up her skirt and let fear and passion drive her toward the man she loved.

Billows of smoke rose into the night sky above the flaming steamboats, and the wind was pushing it over the levee now as well. The pungent scent filled her nostrils and stung her eyes.

At least a dozen firemen—if not more—were working at trying to douse the flames, having carried a hose aboard the steamboat between Sullivan's and the one engulfed in fire. They were spraying what appeared to be gallons of water onto the first steamboat, and though they seemed to have made some progress on the bow, the stern was blazing fiercely.

A gust picked up the flames, cinders, and sparks and sent them flying up into the air and onto the pilothouse of the middle steamer where the firemen had taken position.

Meanwhile, the *Morning Star* continued to burn, the flames slithering up the rails now and creeping toward the texas deck.

She pushed her way through the melee of onlookers and those trying to offer assistance. Why wasn't anyone boarding the *Morning Star* to help? If no one else would, then she'd assist Sullivan. Someone had to.

She pushed forward until at last she neared the water's edge. Stopping short, she had to pull back abruptly. The landing stage had been raised. Or maybe it was gone altogether. In the darkness she couldn't tell.

But the firelight provided enough illumination for her to search for Sullivan. She scanned the decks and the flames spreading much too quickly. In just the short time she'd been here, the fire had spread to at least double of what it had been.

There, among the flames on the hurricane deck, Sullivan was slapping what appeared to be a wet blanket against a wall of flames already flickering against the stairs. But he was only one man against an enormous hungry beast. How would he be able to stop it?

Should he get off now before he was hurt or before it was too late? Yet he wouldn't abandon the runaway, at least not willingly. The only way he would leave the steamer was if he had the runaway with him. But how could he do so without anyone being the wiser?

She glanced around the levee again. Another fire company was charging toward the fires, dragging their engine behind them. She guessed by the time they hooked up their hose to a fireplug and positioned themselves, it would be too late for the *Morning Star*.

Sullivan continued to beat against the flames, desperation in every strong blow.

"Sullivan!" Maybe he would be able to instruct her on how to help.

Among the clanging of bells and shouts of men, her call seemed to get lost.

"Sullivan!" She called his name louder, but still he didn't hear her, didn't turn.

A timid hand touched her arm, startling her.

She jerked back to find her coachman in his fine suit and top hat, standing beside her wringing his gloved hands. "Please, Mrs. O'Brien, come back to the carriage."

"Help me call to my husband. I must get his attention." She faced Sullivan and then shouted his name again.

After a moment, Mr. Dunlop joined her. Together their voices wafted over the river to the steamer.

Somehow, their calling penetrated through the noise. Sullivan halted and spun, scanning the shoreline.

Her heart jumping into her throat, she waved an arm. "Here! I'm here!"

He approached the railing of the hurricane deck, the light of the blazing flames behind him shining on him and revealing his face streaked with both sweat and soot, his dark hair plastered to his forehead. He'd either lost or discarded his hat, coat, and cravat. His white shirt beneath his vest was singed and blackened in places.

But he'd never looked better.

"Enya?" His eyes widened, and his voice held both surprise and dismay. "What are you doing here?"

She cupped her hands around the sides of her mouth, hoping to project her voice. "Tell me what I can be doing to help you!"

He glanced first to the steamer next to his and the firemen now attempting to extinguish the flames that were spreading. Then he shifted his gaze to the vessel opposite of his that hadn't yet been touched by the fire.

His expression remained grim.

She had no doubt he was frustrated about the loss of the *Morning Star*. At one point during their voyage, he'd explained to her just how costly every steamboat was, and the *Morning Star* had been even more so because of her size and all the luxuries she offered.

But she also knew Sullivan was trying to figure out how to save the life of the runaway more than he was wanting to save his steamer.

As he turned his attention to the shore, his jaw hardened. "Help me cut the moorings!"

She scanned the ropes that ran from the main deck to the riverbank. If she severed the lines, the *Morning Star* would float away from the riverbank, be caught in the swift current, and hopefully take the flames away from all the other boats nearby.

In doing so, Sullivan's steamer would burn up and sink. Most likely it would take him and the slave down with it. Even if he managed to jump overboard before being burned alive, the current was dangerous to navigate for even the best of swimmers.

She wanted to shout at him no, that she refused cut the moorings, that she would do anything but that.

"It's the only way!" he shouted.

Something in his tone told her what he couldn't say aloud, that even though it was risky, it might save the runaway from being discovered . . . and might keep him from being caught for helping the runaway.

Already, he was hopping over the rail and down to a lower deck, his agility and ease showcasing his experience. He reached the main deck within seconds and raced toward the stern, toward the mooring rope.

It was clear he intended to cut the *Morning Star* free whether she helped or not. She didn't want to, but the sooner the boat moved out into the middle of the river, the more time he'd have to try to escape the burning vessel before he and the runaway were consumed by the flames.

With a burst of determination, she turned to her coachman. "We need to find knives and cut the moorings." Even as she moved to begin asking fellows standing nearby, her gaze snagged upon a large man with a long black mustache wearing a stiff black coat buttoned all the way up.

She froze.

Roan Whistler stood only a dozen feet away, his expression as stoic as the last time she'd seen him on board the *Morning Star* the day he'd searched for runaways.

What was he doing here on the levee at this hour? Was he hoping to catch Sullivan and the slave trying to make an escape from the burning ship?

Of course he was.

He wanted the *Morning Star* to incinerate here near the shore so that he could prove to the world that Sullivan O'Brien was helping to free slaves. In doing so, he'd put Sullivan in prison and return the runaway to slavery.

He started toward her, his mouth set in a firm line.

Did he intend to stop her from intervening? Perhaps even restrain her?

She backed away from him and then darted toward the newest group of firemen who were rushing around with their hose.

"Help! Over here!" she called to them. "We need to cut the *Morning Star* loose from her moorings!"

Several stopped to watch her.

Behind her, Roan Whistler's footsteps crunched against the levee.

She picked up her pace, knowing she couldn't let him get

ahold of her, and he wouldn't dare touch her if she was near the firemen. "The captain of the *Morning Star* wants us to set her free so she can drift away from the other steamers and prevent the fire from spreading!"

As the men took her in, she could see the frank appreciation in their eyes.

"Aye, miss!" one of the younger men said, already unsheathing his knife.

Several others followed suit and jogged toward the *Morning Star*. She kept on their heels, praying Roan Whistler wouldn't try to stop the firemen from their heroic act of trying to save the rest of the steamers lined up on the levee.

She huddled close to them as they sawed at the ropes, and the next time she glanced around, Whistler wasn't in sight.

She guessed he hadn't gone too far, that he'd be watching the *Morning Star* until it sank.

As the firemen cut the moorings and the *Morning Star* began to float away from the levee, the flames flickered onto the texas deck. Sullivan was climbing back up, and now the firemen were calling for him to jump, to save himself before the inferno took him down with the boat.

But Sullivan didn't stop climbing until he reached the pilothouse. He disappeared inside the small glass-enclosed room. Was he planning to try to steer the steamer to keep the burning inferno from inadvertently floating in the wrong direction and causing more havoc?

Whatever the case, the *Morning Star* was soon moving farther into the middle of the river and at the same time was floating downstream. Enya stood with the firemen silently watching, even as she inwardly screamed and prayed and ranted.

As the flames shot up and lapped at the pilothouse, she held her breath and waited for Sullivan to come out and make an effort to enter the captain's cabin to free the runaway.

With the ticking of the seconds, and no sight of him, her muscles tensed.

The fire was spreading with each gust of the wind, leaping and twirling and setting fire to every inch of the boat. Within only minutes the entire vessel was engulfed. And still there was no sign of Sullivan.

The weakened beams began to crack, and pieces fell into the river. A moment later, a whole side broke free and disappeared under water.

The fireman beside her made the sign of the cross, clearly counting Sullivan a casualty. Then he spoke to her gently as he sheathed his knife. "You shouldn't be down here, miss. This is no place for a pretty lady like yourself."

Another flaming section of the *Morning Star* toppled and crashed into the water. Even if Sullivan made it off, how could he get away with the debris burning all around? What if he was on fire like he had been during the battle that had given him his scars?

At the thought of the horror and suffering he might even now be experiencing, she couldn't hold back a small cry. Her body swayed.

In the next instant, the young fireman was bracing her up, and Mr. Dunlop was directing him toward the carriage still parked near the barrels of bacon and lard.

As they reached the carriage and the fireman helped her

inside, she couldn't take her eyes off the *Morning Star* completely ablaze.

When the carriage began to roll forward, she craned her neck to watch the burning boat until she could no longer see it. Even then, the image stayed in her mind. It was seared there forever.

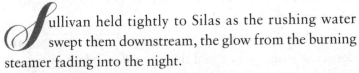

31

$\mathcal{S}$ullivan held tightly to Silas as the rushing water swept them downstream, the glow from the burning steamer fading into the night.

"That's right," he called above the river. "Lie on your back. Don't fight the current."

The runaway had fought him when they'd first jumped off the texas deck into the river. But Sullivan had expected it. Most people who thought they were drowning struggled hard. But thankfully, the young man had remembered Sullivan's warning in time and had cooperated enough that Sullivan had been able to drag them both up to the surface, far enough from the flaming pieces that they hadn't needed to worry about the debris.

For mid-May the water was still icy, and Silas was shaking uncontrollably now. They had to get out soon before their bodies went into shock.

Sullivan kicked his legs and stroked with his free arm, guiding them closer to the bank. Although he couldn't distinguish the riverbank well, he could see enough to know that if he tried to bring them to shore along this particular stretch, they'd risk hitting rocks and logs. Instead, he was aiming for a section of grassy and sandy bank down farther.

If they could withstand the cold long enough to get there . . .

What he wouldn't give for just a little bit of the heat he'd just experienced in the conflagration. As he'd crawled out of the pilothouse window on the starboard side facing away from the St. Louis waterfront, he'd kept low. And as he'd snaked down the railing to the texas deck, he'd smashed open the window to his cabin with his boots to find the flames burning the bed.

Silas had already exited the closet and was cowering in a corner, staying in the room the way Sullivan had instructed him when the fire had first started. Sullivan had given him only the briefest of directions as they'd climbed out the window facing the Illinois side of the river. Then they'd jumped.

Moments after they'd hit the water and gone under, he'd heard the crashing of the steamboat collapsing upon itself. All he'd been able to do was offer silent prayers of gratefulness that they'd made it off in time.

The river wasn't running as fast as it had been in April. He was thankful for that too. He at least had some control of where he was swimming, even if it was difficult to navigate while trying to keep Silas from going under.

"There!" he called, cocking his head toward the shore. They were getting close to the grassy, sandy area, and now was the time to break out of the current. If he couldn't do it at this juncture, he didn't know where the next safe landing spot would be. Maybe another mile. The trouble was, their bodies might not last another mile.

"Kick your legs and veer to the right." He shoved hard against the water, attempting to propel them east to the bank ahead.

Silas did likewise with quick strokes. His eyes were wide and white in the darkness, but his face held a determination that Sullivan drew strength from. The young man wasn't more than fourteen, small enough to fit into the trunk he brought on board with every voyage. But even at so young an age, he'd likely been weathered and shaped by all that he'd gone through so that now he was able to face this new challenge without flinching.

"Harder!" Sullivan pushed toward the shore, but with only one arm to use in propelling them, he wasn't gaining the traction they needed.

Silas kicked more furiously. But the current seemed determined to keep them within its deathlike grip.

Was this it, then? Was this how he would die? Freezing to death and drowning in the Mississippi?

Enya's beautiful face flashed to the front of his thoughts. To say he'd been surprised to see her at the waterfront was an understatement. Had she viewed the fire from their upstairs window and come to investigate whether he was safe? It was possible.

Although he hadn't liked that she'd been so close to the danger, he couldn't deny he'd relished seeing her. And now he *needed* to make it back to her.

"Let's go!" he called to Silas. "We have to push together."

"Now?"

"Now." At the same time, they both kicked and shoved

against the water, fighting their way with forceful strokes closer to dry land.

Sullivan could hardly feel his frozen legs and feet. But a moment later, the pull of the water broke away and their momentum slowed. They'd reached the shallower and slower water near the shore.

After only a dozen more strokes, he grabbed on to the grassy bank. Beside him, Silas latched on to the tall new growth hanging over the river. For several seconds, they clung to the earth, trying to catch their breath. Then the young man clawed his way up the grassy bank until he pulled himself out of the water.

He turned around and reached a hand for Sullivan. With the cold numbing his limbs, he could hardly grasp on, but somehow between Silas's efforts and the desire to see Enya again, Sullivan managed to climb out of the river's clasp.

As soon as he dragged himself to solid ground, he collapsed into the grass.

He'd survived. Though he'd felt like he was walking through the gates of hades, the same way he had when he'd been among the burning debris that day at Veracruz, he'd made it out alive.

God had spared him, had given him another day to live. Maybe it was past time to make peace with his frustrations with God. He'd been blaming God for rejecting him, but in reality Sullivan had let his insecurities push him away from God, the same way he'd let his insecurities push him away from others.

Now all he wanted to do was go home to his wife and be with her. Whether she ever reciprocated his love the same way or not, he wanted to spend every day that he had with her. Because the next time he faced death, he might not walk away. God might not give him any more chances.

It was a morbid thought. But his brush with death made him realize he wasn't infallible, that life was fragile, and that he needed to cherish every day with the people he loved because he didn't know how many he had left.

32

he fire will soon be here!" The frantic call from down the street sent chills up Enya's spine as she stood on the front stoop outside her home.

An eerie orange glow hovered over the rooftops to the east in the direction of the river, growing brighter with each passing hour. The night sky that had been clear earlier was now covered in a haze of smoke and black billows.

At least four hours had passed since she'd ridden away from the waterfront and the *Morning Star* dying a blazing death in the middle of the Mississippi. After arriving home, she'd been unable to do anything but huddle on the settee beside Alannah, too shocked by the turn of events at the levee to speak or even cry.

When shouts of dismay had begun to echo in the nearby streets, Mr. Dunlop and Mrs. Christy had gone out to find out what was happening. Mrs. Christy had returned with a pale face along with the news that the fire among the steamboats had spread, with at least twenty or more blazing like torches in the night.

What was worse, with the wind fanning the flames, the sparks had set fire to the lumber and hemp stacked on the levee. The casks of bacon and lard had exploded. It hadn't taken long after that for the blowing flames to spread to the warehouses on Front Street and then to cross over to Locust.

Over the past hours of watching and waiting, they'd continued to receive news that Main Street had turned into a roaring furnace, that houses and businesses on both sides were burning to the ground. The surrounding streets were filled with storekeepers and merchants attempting to cart away as much as they could out of the path of the inferno.

Now, it appeared that the fire was moving into the residential areas.

Enya shivered and hugged her arms to her chest.

Mrs. Christy was there in an instant, draping a cloak about her.

"Thank you." Enya reached for the older woman's hand. The world around them was coming to an end, and they needed each other now more than ever.

Though it was well past two o'clock in the morning, nobody was sleeping. The lights in every home were lit, and families and servants were scurrying about filling carriages with valises and trunks and even pieces of furniture. In a frantic effort to leave the city ahead of the spreading inferno, people were trying to save important items.

Not Enya. She didn't care about anything in her home. Not even the grand piano that Sullivan had given her. The only thing that mattered was him. And he was gone.

She wanted to hang on to the slim chance that he'd found a way to survive. She'd inquired of every passerby whether there was any word about the *Morning Star*, and the dismal news was always the same—the blackened hull had drifted into a sandbar and no survivors had been found.

Alannah hadn't ventured outside and was busy packing so they could leave at a moment's notice if the flames truly did spread to their street.

The only reason Enya would go was because she didn't want to bring harm to Alannah, Mrs. Christy, and Mr. Dunlop. And, of course, she didn't want to endanger the baby.

Even though the child hadn't been conceived in love, she already loved the baby more than she'd ever believed possible. A mother's love . . .

She'd never understood her own mam, had never felt as though her mam understood her. But now that she was growing to love her baby, a part of her wished she'd tried harder to connect with Mam. Maybe she still could.

"The fire is already burning up Second Street!" The call came from down the street again. "And it's moving fast!"

The air was growing heavier with smoke, and bits of charred debris had begun to rain down on them.

"Should we go?" Mrs. Christy asked.

Mr. Dunlop was standing on the small patch of grass at the front of the house, speaking with several other men who, from their humble attire, appeared to be servants from the neighboring homes. At Mrs. Christy's question, he nodded gravely. "We're discussing whether we should make attempts at saving the houses by putting wet blankets on the roofs."

"Would it work?" Enya tried to muster the energy to think and plan and decide what to do. But the emptiness inside was deafening.

"We have to try something." One of the other men in the

cluster on the yard spoke. "We can't just let the fire continue to spread without making an effort to stop it."

Another of the fellows nodded. "If we don't, it's gonna burn down the whole city."

Enya pushed through her emptiness. Sullivan had sacrificed himself tonight to save that runaway. If he could make such hard sacrifices, surely she could set aside her own grief for a short while and work to save lives and homes. Instead of focusing so much on herself, as she'd been doing since all that had happened with Bryan, perhaps it was time to start thinking more about others.

She squeezed Mrs. Christy's hand before she released it. She could do this. She had people around her who cared about her. It was time to show them that she cared about them too.

"Let's get to work," she called.

Her coachman and the others paused in their conversation and gave her their attention.

"Several of us will visit the homes closest to the fire to let them know we'll put the blankets on their houses first." As she issued the instruction, her voice rang out, drawing attention from those nearby. "I need the rest of you to find blankets and drench them in water."

The coachman and the other men regarded her with wide eyes, as if uncertain of her intentions. She moved down the steps and began striding down the street. "Mrs. Christy, you'll be in charge of gathering blankets. And Mr. Dunlop and I will go door to door."

She didn't wait to see if anyone followed her instructions. Instead, she forced herself to move one foot in front of the other, praying for strength to do what was right and good for others without thinking of herself. It's what Sullivan would have done if he'd been here. And now she would do it too.

Within the hour, they'd rallied everyone who hadn't already left the neighborhood. Every available blanket and sheet had been brought out. And every woman and child hurried to soak the linens in cisterns and wells, while the men climbed onto the tops of the homes, spreading the wet items over as much of the roofs as possible.

"It's almost here, Mrs. O'Brien." Disheveled and damp, Mrs. Christy pointed to the bright light drawing ever closer. "I think it's time to get you to safety."

Enya paused at the base of the ladder and followed the woman's gaze. Were those flames sparking into the air or only the glow from afar? She shook her head. "I think we still have a little more time—"

"Enya?" A shout from down the street cut her off, and she drew in a sudden and sharp breath at the familiar voice.

Two horses and riders had turned the corner.

"Enya?" This shout was different and belonged to Kiernan. His proud bearing was easy to spot atop one of the horses.

But it was the other rider who drew her attention and whose powerful build, broad shoulders, and intense posture made her tremble. Was it really Sullivan? Or was the smoke distorting her vision and mind?

As the horses thundered forward, the flurry of activity ceased, and people moved out of the way to make room for the two to pass. Through the glow of the night sky and the lanterns set about to aid their work, Enya locked her gaze onto the face she hadn't been sure she'd ever see again. She eagerly took in the hard lines of his jaw, the firm set of his mouth, and the furrows in his forehead.

He was still hatless and his dark hair mussed, as though he'd hastily combed it off his forehead with his fingers. His trousers and shirt appeared damp and dingy with smoke or mud or perhaps both.

But he was alive. And that's all that mattered.

The relief swelled inside her so swiftly that her knees gave way, and she sank to the grass of the neighboring house.

He was scanning their home, the front stoop, the yard, the road, until at last his gaze landed upon her. He reined in his horse abruptly and didn't wait for a complete halt before he dismounted and strode toward her, his footsteps heavy and purposeful.

When he reached her, she grabbed on to the ladder to try to hoist herself to her feet. But in the next instant, he was slipping his large hands underneath her and lifting her off her feet so that she was cradled against his chest the way he always held her.

His muscles were tense, his body rigid, his expression fierce. She loved every detail about him, every single one. And she had to tell him while she still could before anything else happened to rip them apart.

"I love you." She didn't care that the words fell so easily from her lips and that everyone around could hear her declaration. All that mattered was making certain he knew that she'd fallen in love with him.

His eyes were as inky as the smoke in the sky. Cloudy and unreadable. What did he think of her declaration? Did he still love her?

She opened her mouth to say more, to convince him that

she really meant it, but before she could speak, he swiftly and decisively bent in and captured her lips with his.

She rose into the kiss, wrapping her arms around his neck tightly and falling into the kiss with abandon. Each stroke of his mouth was desperate and powerful and hungry all at once, leaving her breathless and completely undone.

She wanted to arch into him, crush her body to his, feel his hands on her. She needed to be closer to him, wanted him to know that she was finished putting obstacles between them.

He pressed in as though telling her that he knew who she was and what she was communicating and that he would take whatever she was willing to give him.

She dug her fingers into his hair and let her kiss delve deeper, hoping he could read the message that she was giving him everything. She didn't want to hold anything back. She was all his and would be forever.

But before she could find a way to convey her feelings, he broke the kiss just as quickly as he'd started it. He pivoted and glared at Mr. Dunlop and Mrs. Christy, who had dropped whatever they were doing and were watching and waiting.

"You should have taken my wife out of the city earlier." His voice was harsh.

Behind them, Enya glimpsed Kiernan dashing up the stairs into her home. He was in a hurry, his movements intense too. Where was he going? To warn Alannah?

"We were just about to leave, sir." The coachman bowed his head at Sullivan.

"Get the carriage now!" Sullivan practically roared, sending the poor man and Mrs. Christy scurrying away.

"I'm the one who decided to stay," Enya called out. "Mr.

Dunlop and Mrs. Christy wanted me to leave the city hours ago."

"They shouldn't have listened to you," he growled, already stalking after Mr. Dunlop and still carrying her as if she weighed no more than a piece of luggage.

"Oh, Sullivan." She couldn't hold back laughter, her heart suddenly full and happy. "You know they didn't have a choice. I'm too stubborn and do what I please."

"I'm firing Mr. Dunlop for bringing you down to the levee earlier." Sullivan's tone was still hard and unrelenting, as was his stride.

She laughed again, this time more softly. "I love you so much." She lifted a hand to his cheek and skimmed his jaw and the thick layer of scruff there.

He dropped a glance to her face, to her lips, one that made her body flush with need, the kind that urged her to go right up to their bedroom, slam the door closed, and kiss him the rest of the night through.

"I thought you died, so I did," she whispered.

"I'm stubborn too," he whispered back. "Too stubborn to die without seeing you again."

His words sent need spiraling through her again, this time even more keenly. She breathed him in, mentally mapping every part of him—the hard ripples of his body against hers, the warmth of his flesh, the possessiveness of his hold.

He'd come back to her. Now she never wanted to be away from him again.

He turned the corner of their house, where Mr. Dunlop was already with the team which he'd had ready for the past couple of hours. As Sullivan stopped in front of the carriage, Mrs. Christy was waiting to open the door.

Sullivan stepped up and deposited Enya on the seat, the interior crowded with bags of all shapes and sizes. He was as gentle with her now as he'd been that first night after they'd been married in the cathedral.

She clung to him. "You must come with me, Sullivan."

"I'm staying in the city."

His words didn't surprise her. She had no doubt that every man in St. Louis was needed now to fight the fire alongside the firemen if they had any hope of stopping it.

There was so much yet she wanted to say to him, so much left unfinished. And she wanted to hear all about how he'd made it off the steamer and what had happened to the runaway. But now wasn't the time or place for any of that. It would have to wait until they were reunited again.

If they were reunited . . .

He started to retreat, but with a tremble deep inside, she clutched his shirt to hold him in place. "Kiss me again."

Without hesitating, he leaned in and took possession of her mouth just as explosively as he always did. Like kegs of gunpower touched by cinders, she let her lips combust with his, taking and giving with unrestrained passion.

One of his fingers traced the line of her jaw down her neck to her collarbone, burning her into a smoldering heap. She started to groan and wrap her arms around his neck.

But he pulled back, breaking their kiss. Then in the next instant, he was shutting the carriage door and barking commands at Mr. Dunlop. "Get her out of the city as fast as you can and take her to her parents' home in the country."

Before the carriage could start rolling, the opposite door opened, and Kiernan was carrying Alannah and thrust her inside all the while she was protesting. She slid onto the seat across from Enya, and Mrs. Christy followed a moment later.

When the door closed on the three of them, the carriage jolted forward.

Enya peered out the window, wanting more of Sullivan. But all she saw was his broad back next to Kiernan's as they jogged to their horses.

Soon enough, he was out of her view, and she sagged against the seat, her heart already beating with the need to see him again.

33

*S*ullivan stood back from the wreckage and wiped a hand across his stinging eyes. The light of dawn was breaking through the haze of smoke that hung low around him, revealing the extent of the damage.

"Holy thundering mother." Kiernan's gaze swept over the decimated block. As far as they could see, building after building lay in ruins, blackened and smoldering as if bombed by cannons.

Smaller fires still burned here and there among the ruins, but the worst was finally over . . . at least they hoped so.

With more than a thousand men joining the fire departments to battle the fire, they'd done the best they could to extinguish flames. But at some point during the long hours, the city's water system gave out, so the fireplugs ran dry, likely having been overextended by all the fire departments tapping into the system.

Everyone had been left without water. Those departments closest to the river had been able to run their hoses down to the water and pump directly from the Mississippi onto the flames.

But Sullivan and Kiernan hadn't been among those groups. Instead, they'd joined Fire Captain Targee and the Missouri Company in getting barrels of gunpowder from the St. Louis Arsenal where the stores were kept.

They'd realized along with everyone else that the only way to stop the fire from consuming more of the city was to make a physical barrier to slow the progression. And to create that barrier, they'd needed to blow up a block of businesses, essentially eliminating the fire's fuel.

For a couple of hours, they'd hauled the barrels of gunpowder, covering them with wet tarps to protect them from any flying cinders. Since one spark could ignite the gunpowder and cause a deadly explosion, they'd operated meticulously, blowing up one building after another, finally bringing the conflagration to a halt.

They'd all faced death again and again through the harrowing hours. And they'd survived, except for Captain Targee, who'd been killed when one of the kegs exploded too early. Every one of the men had been devastated at the death of the captain, but he'd died a hero for his plan.

Sullivan's whole body ached with weariness from the long night, including his battle on the steamboat and the hours afterward. After walking for many miles with Silas, Sullivan had connected him with the rowboat that had still been waiting in the shadows of the eastern bank. Then, after borrowing a horse, Sullivan had crossed over the bridge to St. Louis.

All the while he'd traveled, he'd watched the fire spreading and wreaking more devastation, and his thoughts had turned to Enya and the need to make sure she was safe. He'd bypassed the fire district and had been nearing the street where his house was located when Kiernan had ridden up, also intending to visit the house to check on Enya.

Sullivan had been angry to see her still there so close to the danger, but his relief had made him weak with a need so pervasive that he hadn't been able to stop from kissing her in front of everyone, especially when she'd looked at him the way she had, with adoration brimming from her eyes, and told him that she loved him.

He still couldn't believe that she'd told him that she loved him not once but twice. *"I love you so much."* Her declaration had played through his head dozens of times as he'd battled death again. It had kept him going with the need to see her and be with her. And even now, he longed for her more than anything else.

"It seems like everything is under control here." With another glance to the eastern sky and the sunlight glinting through the haze, Sullivan rubbed a hand over the scruff on his chin and jaw, more than ready for a bath. "I'm heading out to see my wife."

With his face nearly blackened with soot, Kiernan nodded, his attention fixed upon the men, women, and even children still in their nightclothes wandering about, their sooty faces haunted and stricken. They poked through the remnants and ash heaps, searching for possessions that might have survived the heat.

"I'll stay," Kiernan said quietly. "I need to ride over and see if the family home is left standing."

They'd already walked past Sullivan's home to find that most of the neighborhood had remained unscathed. He wasn't sure if the wet blankets on the rooftops had helped keep sparks from landing or if the wind had blown the flames a different direction. Either way, he was relieved the home had survived. "Do you need my help?"

Kiernan gave him a ghost of a smile. "No. You go on. I can tell you're dying to be with Enya. And she needs you too."

Sullivan didn't care that he'd made it plain to everyone how much he craved Enya. He didn't even care that she knew. He supposed that was progress in developing more confidence.

Within minutes, he was mounted and riding west through the city, Kiernan's directions to Oakland at the forefront of his mind. As the outer edges of the city soon turned into woodland and pastures, he pushed his horse faster.

All the while he rode, he plotted out the different possibilities for how he could be with Enya more often and yet still maintain his work as a steamboat captain. Could he do shorter trips? One thing was certain, he didn't want to be away from her for so long ever again.

Finally the two-storied Italianate-style home that belonged to the Shanahans came into view. Just as Kiernan had described, it was a sprawling L-shape with a square tower and a bracketed cornice rising from the roof. Painted white with black trim, the home sat back from the road among towering oak trees.

Even though Sullivan had left the smoke behind, he still reeked of it—and of the Mississippi mud that had dried in every crevice of his body. He didn't want to go to Enya in such a state, so he detoured to a nearby pond, stripped out of his garments and washed up, then changed into the clean garments he'd packed before leaving the city.

With the sun now fully risen in the morning sky, he started

down the lane, hoping the sound of his approach would bring Enya running out the front door. But only James Shanahan and two of his youngest sons stepped outside to greet him and get the latest news of the fire.

Of course, when Enya had arrived in the early hours of the morning, she'd shared with them all that she'd known at the time about the devastation throughout St. Louis. But they hadn't heard the final harrowing details and were relieved to learn the fire was over.

Sullivan was afraid that James would keep him occupied for overlong, but as they entered into the front hallway, James confided that he planned to leave for the city shortly to see what had become of not only his house but also the ironworks.

Sullivan was relieved when Mrs. Christy came down the stairs and assured him that Enya was doing well, that she was still sleeping since she'd been awake until only a little while ago.

He followed Mrs. Christy up to the second floor and down a long corridor. As she stopped in front of a closed door, he almost hung back. Past doubts crowded into his thoughts to tell him he couldn't go to her, that he ought to wait, that maybe he'd only imagined her love and kisses earlier in the night. Or what if she'd only made her declaration of love in the hysteria of the moment? What if now that the danger was passed, she pulled away from him again?

Even as all the uncertainties crashed through his mind and threatened to swamp him, he forced himself to remain rooted to the spot outside the door instead of striding away. And as Mrs. Christy placed a hand on the knob, he didn't turn away when she paused and smiled at him. "She'll be happy to see you, Captain. She missed you terribly while you were away these past weeks."

She'd missed him? Terribly?

Mrs. Christy opened the door and waved him through into the bedroom. With the draperies drawn, allowing in only a sliver of sunlight, the room was mostly dark. He expected Mrs. Christy to trail him inside and attend to Enya. But at the click of the door behind him, leaving him alone, Sullivan's muscles tensed.

What would Enya say when she saw him standing there?

He swept his gaze over the room—one tastefully decorated. As he reached the bed and caught sight of her on top of the covers, wearing the same clothes as the previous night but covered with a blanket, his pulse slowed, and he expelled a breath.

Her eyes were closed in slumber, her long lashes resting against her cheeks, the dimple in her chin a delicate dip, her lips rosy and full. Even in sleep, she was the most beautiful woman in the world, her red hair cascading loosely around her. Why would she care about a man like him?

He reached to tug up his collar but stopped. No, he wouldn't disparage himself, not anymore. He intended to climb into bed with his wife, and he didn't plan to let anything stop him.

He started quietly toward the bed, not wanting to wake her. He bypassed the chair that called out to him to sit by her side and simply wait for her to awaken. Instead, he walked around to the opposite side of the bed, carefully lowered himself to the mattress, and then held himself still for a heartbeat.

When she didn't move, he inched closer and situated himself behind her. Resting his head on the pillow beside hers, he leaned in and brushed his nose into her hair. The silky strands soothed him, and her warm body seemed to welcome him closer.

He moved in until his chest brushed against her back. Gently, he draped his arm across hers. Then he closed his eyes as pure contentment flowed through him. This was where he wanted to be. Nestled by her side, holding her. No other place could ever compare.

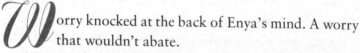

34

*W*orry knocked at the back of Enya's mind. A worry that wouldn't abate.

Shooting flames and black smoke filled her dreams along with the fear she'd lose Sullivan. And she couldn't bear the prospect that she'd only get two brief kisses with him on her way out of town then never see him again.

She started to shake her head in protest, but at a nuzzle against her neck she halted. Warm breath and lips brushed against her skin where her hair had been pushed aside.

Full wakefulness surged through her, and she was aware of not only the soft mouth near her neck, but the hard length of a body behind her and a bulky arm holding her.

She rolled over as quickly as she could in the tangle of her skirt and covers. As she faced Sullivan, his eyes remained closed.

"You're back." She didn't care if he was sleeping and she woke him up.

His lids raised halfway. But he didn't speak.

"Thank heavens." She threw herself against him, wrapping her arms around him and burrowing into him. Her joy at seeing him was too hard to contain.

His arms slipped around her in return, and he pulled her closer.

Her whole body trembled, and tears stung at the backs of her eyes. They'd made it here. They were both safe. And maybe now they could be reunited for good.

But first . . . she had to apologize.

She pushed against him.

He didn't budge.

"Sullivan, let me go." She wiggled to free herself.

"No." He pressed a hard kiss into her hair. "I won't let you go ever again."

At the possessiveness in his tone and in his hold, she couldn't hold back a smile. How was it possible it had taken her so long to fall in love with this man? Or maybe she had loved him earlier but had just been too scared to admit it?

Regardless, she had to make things right with him. "I promise I won't go anywhere. I just wanted to see your face when I apologize."

He stilled.

This time when she tugged away, he allowed it. In fact, he rolled to his back, crossed his arms behind his head, and watched her through half-lidded eyes.

With his muscles straining against his shirtsleeves and his vest, she was tempted to run her fingers up and down his arms. But she propped herself up on one elbow and then placed the other hand on his chest, at his heart. "I'm sorry I pushed you away for so long. You were right about how I sabotaged our relationship."

He continued to watch her, his eyes dark and intense—or at least the small slit that she could see.

"I was putting obstacles between us, though to be fair, I didn't realize it."

He removed one hand from behind his head and trailed a finger through her hair hanging around her in disarray.

"And I was letting my scars from my past determine my future."

His finger moved languidly. So sensually. So enticingly.

A flare ignited within her. "I can't promise that my scars won't affect us ever again. Because they might."

He dropped his hand to her neck and drew a trail down to the base of her throat, to the pulse that was starting to pound harder there.

"But I do promise that when I'm hurting, I'll try not to push you away again."

"I can live with that."

At the rumble in his voice, the spark inside flamed hotter. "Good." After the kisses she'd shared with him last night, she had the feeling that if she kissed him again right now, she'd incinerate. Maybe they'd even incinerate together.

But that was okay, wasn't it? After all that had happened, she'd never believed it possible that she would have a beautiful and loving marriage. But God had given her this man and this opportunity. How could she do anything less than fully give Sullivan her heart and hold nothing back?

The prospect didn't terrify her as much as it had a month ago. Aye, it was still frightening to trust another man so completely. But hadn't she just promised not to push him away?

Without letting herself think about what she was doing, she lifted up so that she was lying on top of him.

At her bold move, his eyes flew open, revealing the dark brown that she could lose herself in every time. She tried to bite back a smile, but her lips quirked.

His gaze locked in on the quirk.

She was surprised at how good he felt beneath her, how right it felt to press into every inch of him and know that he was hers. "I forgot to thank you for all your gifts." It was her turn to lift a hand to his hair and let her fingers linger there lazily.

His eyes were still riveted to her mouth, and from the slight flare of his nostrils, she could tell he was thinking about kissing her.

She bit her lip to tease and entice him.

His hand snaked around her and splayed at the small of her back. Hard.

Oh, she loved him, loved this. "Since you gave me so many lovely gifts"—she dropped her voice to a whisper—"I wanted to give you one in return."

"There's no need." His voice was a whisper too. "I don't expect anything in return. I hope you know that."

"I do." She bent in lower so that her lips hovered above his. "But this is something I want to give you."

"What?" The brown of his eyes had lightened, revealing the flecks of amber she liked so much.

"My heart. I'm giving you my heart, Sullivan." With that, she lowered her lips the rest of the way, fusing her mouth to his in a slow meshing, then pulling back, lightly teasing, before pressing in to start it over again.

He only played her game for a few seconds before growling and chasing after her.

This time she sat up and placed a hand on his chest to stop him.

Head off his pillow, he paused, but the look in his eyes said he was coming after her again in a second whether she was ready for him or not.

"Not only am I giving you my heart Sullivan, but I'm giving you all of me." As the words spilled out, she flushed at her brazenness.

His gaze met hers, wide, questioning, as if testing her sincerity.

She nodded. "You told me you'd make sure that this would be something I wanted."

"And is it?"

"Aye. Very much." Then she bent down once again, letting her lips meet his with all the passion and love swirling within her.

The rhythm of his mouth accelerated quickly, but then he broke away abruptly and framed both sides of her face with his hands. "I love you now, and I always will." His breath was already labored, and his eyes were dark with desire.

He hadn't needed to say it. But she liked hearing it anyway.

She smiled. "I love you now, and I always will too." Then she aimed for his lips again. And this time she had no intention of stopping.

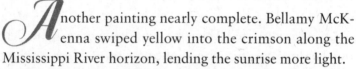

35

*A*nother painting nearly complete. Bellamy McKenna swiped yellow into the crimson along the Mississippi River horizon, lending the sunrise more light.

Then he stood back, tilted his head, and examined the landscape, narrowing his eyes critically and taking in every detail.

The river needed another shadow.

He stuck the paintbrush he'd been using for the sun behind his ear and pulled out the one resting behind his other ear that he'd used for the darker paints. He dipped it in the sapphire on the palette and added a stroke below one of the sycamores that leaned out over the riverbank.

The lantern hanging above him from the rafter of the shed gave a flicker, as if to remind him that the oil was burning low and the night would soon be over, leaving him little time for sleeping.

"Who needs sleep anyway?" He set the palette down on the tall, wobbly table that held his paint box. Of course, after the past few hours of working, his paint box was mostly empty, and his supplies were now scattered across the table—brushes, rags, paint tubes, lids, bottles of varnish and turpentine, stubs of chalk, and the other items he used to create his artwork.

The artwork he created in his studio.

He snorted and glanced around the shed.

Floor-to-ceiling shelves lined one wall and were filled with crates of all the various spirits sold in the pub. The wall closest to the door was crowded with casks of beer, ale, and, of course, Guinness.

A large trunk sat on the other side of his worktable and was where he locked away his easel and everything during the daylight hours—everything except for the paintings that were drying, which he laid on the top shelves on crates that no one ever disturbed.

Now that he'd actually started selling his work, he'd been painting longer hours, sometimes until the wee hours of the morn.

He wasn't complaining. Not at all. It had taken him years to reach this point, years of practicing and perfecting his skills, years before finally selling anything and making a name for himself.

Ach, he wasn't making a name for the Irishman Bellamy McKenna. No, he was making a name for the good American man William Moore.

He crossed his arms and studied the scrawled initials at the bottom of the painting. W. B. M. If only he could tell everyone the initials stood for William Bellamy McKenna instead of William Bennett Moore. If only people weren't so set against Irish immigrants.

With a tired sigh, Bellamy swiped up the closest rag, already saturated with turpentine, and began to clean the paint from his fingers as meticulously as always. His chest burned with an indignation that was getting harder to ignore with every painting he sold under his false name.

But what choice did he have? None of the curators, patrons, or shopkeepers had taken him seriously when he'd tried to sell his realistic landscapes as himself. But as a courier and servant for an eccentric and reclusive and entirely made-up St. Louis artist named William Moore, he'd garnered interest.

Finally last autumn he'd made his first sale, and he'd had a steady stream of requests ever since. In early May, there had been a span of a week or so when the interest in William Moore's paintings had gotten almost too serious. One of the patrons had wanted to meet William, had insisted on it, actually.

But with the resurgence of cholera and then the devastating fire that had swept through the city several weeks ago, the interest in William Moore and his paintings had dwindled, and rightly so. Many had lost everything in the fire. Those who hadn't had their livelihoods destroyed by the raging flames were busy trying to escape the deadly grip of cholera.

Even so, Bellamy had several orders to finish. And when those were delivered, he'd keep painting just as he always had, whether he sold anything or not, because he loved it. Painting was in his blood every bit as much as the matchmaking, if not more.

A soft tap on the door broke through the quiet of the night.

The windowless shack didn't afford natural light, but through the crack in the back wall, it was easy to see that darkness hadn't yet been broken by dawn.

It was still too early for Jenny to be up and puttering about. But maybe his sister had had a bout of sleeplessness as she did from time to time and was coming to watch him paint. She was the only one he ever allowed in while he was working, the only one who knew about his painting besides her husband, Galvin.

Of course, Oscar also knew, but he acted like he didn't, was too embarrassed to have a son who painted to admit it to anyone. Whenever any of the customers asked about the paintings on the pub walls, Oscar refused to acknowledge that Bellamy had painted them. He claimed he'd gotten them from someone when he'd first opened the pub.

Maybe once upon a time, it had mattered that Oscar was ashamed of him. But now the secrecy was working to his advantage. Or was it?

Another rap came against the door, this time louder.

"Mind you, I'm coming." He wiped at the last streaks of paint on his hands, tossed the paintbrushes to the table, and then crossed to the door. He lifted the latch he'd installed long ago to keep anyone from barging in on him. As he started to swing open the door, he halted at the sight of a man, leaving only a crack to peer through instead.

"Bellamy McKenna?" The fellow's voice held a strong Irish brogue, one with a County Kerry accent. A recent immigrant, no doubt.

"Oh aye, I'm he." From the sliver of soft light coming from inside the shed, Bellamy got a glimpse of the man's face—lean but hardened, young but aged beyond his time like so many of the immigrants.

Beneath his cap, his hair was fair and overlong, covering a scar on his forehead. He wore spectacles that shadowed his eyes but couldn't hide the worry there. "Are you the match-maker?"

Bellamy always believed a person's eyes could tell a great deal about them. And in this case, this fellow's eyes were calling out for help.

Bellamy slipped out of the shed and closed the door behind him. "Right enough. I'm the matchmaker." After forming two matches for the Shanahans, he had every right to call himself the matchmaker, didn't he? It didn't matter that he hadn't matched anyone else since Shrove Tuesday. "Who is wanting to know?"

The man glanced around the alley behind the pub as though to make sure they were alone. The pub windows were all dark, including those on the second floor where he made his home with Oscar, Jenny, and Galvin. The buildings on either side of the pub—a grocery and a barbershop—were both equally as dark. The sheds and privies and stables that lined the alley were also quiet. As far as Bellamy could tell, even the rats were asleep.

"The name is Torin," the fellow whispered. "Torin Darragh."

Torin Darragh. Bellamy sifted the name through his mind. It was familiar. Where had he heard it?

Torin again glanced around, shifting nervously. "Can you help me with a match?"

Did the fellow suspect he was being watched, perhaps followed? This time as Bellamy cast about the alley he spotted two other men, both on each end of the street, as though standing guard.

What were these fellows doing out at this time of night? And why was Torin visiting him so secretly? Something wasn't right. Usually only gangs or thieves were out in the wee dark hours.

Gangs. Aye, that's how he knew the name. Torin Darragh was one of the leaders of Saints Alley. Although not as dangerous or violent as some of the other gangs, Saints Alley was still a gang, and Bellamy didn't want to have anything to do with the lot of them.

He'd managed so far to stay uninvolved and neutral for the ten years he'd lived in St. Louis, and he had no intention of being dragged in now.

He gave a curt shake of his head. "Sorry. I can't—"

"The match isn't for me." Torin spoke in a rush, his voice still low. "'Tis for my sister, Alannah."

"Is it now?"

"Aye, so it is."

Bellamy's mind set to work again. Who was Torin's sister? From the little he knew about Torin Darragh, the fellow had arrived last summer without any family. That wasn't necessarily unusual for a young man like Torin. Maybe he'd been sent ahead by his family to work and earn passage for the rest of them. Or maybe he'd lost most of his family during the Great Hunger.

Whatever the case, 'twas difficult for a penniless man to make his way in St. Louis, and gangs offered the promise of safety and help and family for those newly arrived fellows who had no one else. The trouble was, the gangs not only fought amongst each other, but the fighting was spilling over to the nativists, the Protestant and native-born who resented the Irish Catholics.

Apparently sometime recently, Torin's sister had arrived in St. Louis. He'd likely put her in danger because of his involvement in his gang. Or maybe she was falling prey to the debauchery of the Kerry Patch slums. Being the good brother that he was, now Torin was trying to find Alannah a match, hoping to save her.

No one could fault the man for caring for his sister. In fact, Bellamy liked him because of it. But still, he wasn't willing to risk his own family's safety and livelihood. "Ach, I'd like to help you, that I would. But it just wouldn't work."

Torin pushed up his glasses, even though they weren't sliding down his nose, likely a nervous habit. "I heard you made matches for the Shanahans."

"Aye, so I did."

"I work for Kiernan Shanahan, at his glass-cutting factory."

Kiernan was a good man, and Bellamy liked him. Did Torin expect that the connection with Kiernan would help his cause? Because it wouldn't.

As if sensing another refusal, Torin lowered his voice another decibel. "Kiernan's been helping me keep Alannah safe, got her a job. But now her mistress is going away, and she'll be without work."

Bellamy needed no other information to piece together the puzzle. Alannah was likely working for Enya in the house that Sullivan had bought for her. But now with the rapid spread of cholera, Sullivan was moving his wife down to New Orleans. Bellamy had learned of the plans just yesterday.

"If I can find Alannah a nice fellow, that'll solve all the problems."

What kind of danger was she in? Bellamy was tempted to ask. But it wasn't his place since he had no intention of getting involved.

"Please," Torin whispered, as if seeing Bellamy's resolve. "I'm sure you'll be finding someone for her soon enough on your own."

"I don't want anyone from the Patch." His tone turned hard. "I want someone better for her."

Better? Really? What did Torin expect, that Bellamy would be able to waltz into a family like the Shanahans and set up a match for Alannah with a wealthy man like Kiernan?

The Shanahans would never—not in a hundred years—consider such a match, especially not Kiernan. As decent as the fellow was, he was too ambitious to marry beneath him.

Final words of denial crowded to the tip of Bellamy's tongue. But at the desperation etched into Torin's face, he expelled a sigh. How could he refuse? But how could he possibly help Torin—and Alannah—when doing so would be inviting a whole load of problems upon himself that he didn't want?

The only way such an arrangement would work was if Torin didn't say a word about it to anyone. Was that why he'd come so secretly? Did he realize the same?

Torin didn't move, didn't blink, just watched him hopefully.

"Fine," Bellamy whispered. "I'll see what I can do."

Torin nodded. "That would be grand—"

"Dontcha be getting your hopes up, now," Bellamy said in a rush. "And you'll not be telling nobody."

"I won't."

"It'll stay right here between you and me?"

"Aye, so it will. You have my word." Torin gave a final nod, then pivoted and began to jog away.

Bellamy watched until the fellow disappeared around the corner, taking his lookout men with him. Then Bellamy leaned against the shed door and peered up at the sky, the few remaining stars winking at him.

Whatever had he gotten himself into now?

If you enjoyed
Saved by the Matchmaker,
read on for an excerpt from

$\mathcal{A}$ $\mathcal{C}$OWBOY FOR

$\mathcal{K}$EEPS

Available now wherever books are sold.

CHAPTER

1

COLORADO TERRITORY

AUGUST 1862

"Stop or we'll shoot!" A dozen feet up Kenosha Pass, three robbers with flour sacks over their heads blocked the way, their revolvers outstretched.

Walking alongside the stagecoach, Greta Nilsson didn't have to be told twice. She froze—all except her pulse, which sped to a thundering gallop.

Next to her, the Concord jerked to a halt.

"Come out and put your hands up where we can see 'em," called the lanky robber at the center, peering through unevenly cut holes in his mask.

Greta raised her gloved hands and hoped they weren't trembling. Likewise, the two gentlemen hiking near her wasted no time in obeying.

Before she'd left Illinois, everyone had warned her of the

trouble she might encounter on the route to the west, including the growing problem of stagecoach robberies. Over the past eight weeks of traveling, she'd braced herself for the possibility, had mentally rehearsed such an encounter and what she'd do.

But today, on the last day of the journey, she'd finally allowed herself to relax and believe that for once things might work out in her favor, that she hadn't made a big mistake in moving to Colorado.

Apparently, she'd assumed too much too soon.

At the rear of the stagecoach, several men had been pushing it the final distance to the top of the pass, and they now eased out into the open, their arms up. The driver sitting on his bench atop the stagecoach set the brake, then released the reins controlling the two teams of horses that had been straining to pull them up the mountain. He, too, cautiously lifted his hands.

She guessed, like her, the other passengers were well aware of the tales of murder and mayhem along the wilderness trails. And they weren't taking any chances either.

At least Astrid was inside the coach. After trekking uphill for the first hour, the little girl's poor lungs hadn't been able to handle the exertion. As much as Astrid had loathed returning to the bumpy conveyance, she'd been able to have a seat to herself since everyone else had gotten out to lighten the load.

Last time Greta had peeked through the open windows, her sister had been sprawled out asleep, and now Greta prayed the precocious child would stay that way.

The middle robber inched toward them, his revolver swinging in a wide arc. His leathery hands and dirt-encrusted fingernails contrasted with the ivory handle of his revolver. "Nobody move."

Morning sunlight filtered through the aspens, their white bark and green-gold leaves making the trail feel more open and airy than other parts of the mountainous road. A cool, dry breeze rattled the leaves, swishing like ladies' skirts brushing against grass.

Just minutes ago, Greta had been marveling at how different the dry and cooler climate was from northern Illinois, where oppressive humidity plagued the summers and made every chore feel like a burden. What she wouldn't give at this moment to be back there shucking corn or snapping beans, even if she was dripping with perspiration.

"Anyone left inside?" one of the other robbers asked.

"No," Greta said quickly. "Everyone's out."

Just then the stagecoach door inched open.

The lanky robber with the uneven eye slits swung his revolver toward the door and clicked the hammer.

"No!" Greta threw herself between the robber and the stagecoach, shoving against Astrid's strong push.

A short distance away beyond the trees, the mountainside overlooked the sprawling grasslands of South Park, nestled between the Front Range in the east and the Mosquito Range in the west. Their destination was within eyesight. If only it was also within shouting distance so they could call for help.

The bandit shifted the barrel's aim to Greta, his arm stiff, his fingers taut. "Woman, unless you want to find yourself eating a bullet, you'd best step aside and let that person out."

Inside, Astrid cried out in protest and once again attempted to open the door. But Greta flattened the full length of her body against it.

"Move on outta the way, woman," the robber said, louder and more irritably.

"It's her little sister." One of the other passengers moved to stand beside Greta, a middle-aged man who'd introduced himself as Landry Steele yesterday morning when they boarded the stagecoach in Denver. He'd spent the majority of the journey conversing with the other gentlemen. However, during the few brief interactions she'd had with him, he'd always been considerate.

"The girl is ill and is of no concern to you." Beneath the brim of Mr. Steele's bowler, he shot Greta an apologetic look, as though realizing she'd wanted to keep Astrid hidden away and out of the conflict.

"That so?" The gunman's revolver didn't waver. "If she's of no concern, then let her on out."

Greta pressed against the door harder. She hadn't brought Astrid all this distance to have her die at the hand of a robber. "She's only eight years old—"

"I'm nine," came Astrid's indignant voice.

"Allow her to come out," Mr. Steele said with a quiet urgency. "You don't want her to end up an orphan, do you?"

Astrid an orphan? Never in Greta's plans had she counted on dying before Astrid. The truth was, Astrid's days were numbered, and Greta hoped to lengthen and make them as pain-free as possible. But she couldn't do that if she let the robber kill her.

Swallowing hard, Greta stepped away from the stagecoach. The door flew open with a *bang*, and Astrid tumbled out. She landed with an *oomph* onto the grassy road but then bounded up as nimbly as a barn cat. Though the consumption had emaciated the girl so that she was thin and petite for her age, somehow she still retained a fresh and vibrant spirit that made up for her physical frailty.

Her big silver blue eyes, so much like Greta's, took in the scene—the robbers, their guns, and all the passengers standing motionless with hands in the air. Astrid's hair was also the same color as Greta's, a golden brown now sun-streaked from so many days of neglecting her bonnet. Astrid had refused to allow Greta to plait her hair when they'd arisen at half past four in the morning for a hasty departure from the stagecoach station, and now it hung in tangled waves.

Even so, Astrid was the picture of perfection. She had dainty porcelain but beautiful features that drew attention everywhere she went. Greta had never considered herself to be a beauty, not like some of the other young women back home and certainly not like Astrid.

But too many people to recall during the journey west had exclaimed how much she and Astrid looked alike. The admiring glances and flattery had been strange but not un-welcome. At times, she wondered if maybe she was prettier than she'd realized, if maybe she'd been hasty in accepting the first mail-order bride proposal that came along.

Astrid took several steps in the direction of the closest robber. "Why are you wearing a sack over your head?"

"Astrid, come here this instant," Greta whispered in her sternest tone.

The thief's gaze darted over to the passengers, revealing a crooked, lazy eye that didn't focus. "It's what robbers do, kid."

"W-e-l-l." Astrid drew the word out and cocked her head. "It makes you look kinda silly, like a scarecrow."

Greta lunged for Astrid, but the girl dodged away and skipped toward the robber.

His gun wavered, as though he was considering turning the weapon on Astrid.

"Astrid!" Horror rose in Greta's throat, threatening to strangle her. "Don't you dare go a step closer."

Astrid halted and held out her hand. "Here's some money, Mister. It's mine, but you can have it since you need it more than me."

The man's lazy eye shifted to Astrid again. "Drop it on the ground."

Astrid released a crumpled wad and a few coins. They bounced in the grass near the robber's feet. "My sister has more—"

"No!" Greta couldn't let these bandits discover her secret stash since she'd taken pains to sew the cash into the lining of her coat after the passengers had been warned not to carry valuables.

It was her jam money. Her earnings from picking and preserving the wild berries that grew on the farm. The accumulation of two years of working every spare minute.

Astrid turned her pretty eyes upon Greta. "They have to wear flour sacks instead of hats. Guess that means they need the money more than we do. Right, Mister?"

"Right, kid." This time the robber's voice hinted at amusement.

The thieves made quick work of emptying the locked box next to the driver and then divested each of the passengers of anything of value. Within a few minutes they ran off into the woods with their loot.

Greta stood with the others, surveying their belongings

strewn over the grass surrounding the stagecoach. Astrid had lost interest in the robbers and was intent on picking a bouquet of wildflowers.

"We got lucky." The driver broke the silence, his voice shaky as he closed the now-empty box next to him. "Last time the Crooked-Eye Gang struck, they killed three men—"

Mr. Steele cut off the driver with a glare and a curt nod toward Astrid.

The driver clamped his mouth closed, and everyone set to work repacking their bags and trunks.

Greta fingered the frayed coat hem. Although Phineas Hallock, her intended, had informed her he had plenty of money since he was part owner of a gold mine, she couldn't keep dismay from weighing upon her.

She'd corresponded with Phineas by letter on several occasions last year, and she sensed in him genuine kindness, especially since he'd so readily agreed to take care of Astrid. He also made all the arrangements for the trip, including paying for their fare.

Though the small daguerreotype he'd sent in his last letter the previous autumn had shown him to be a plain-looking and somewhat older man, his face held a look of integrity as well as honesty. Maybe he wasn't handsome or young, but that didn't matter. What she needed was a husband who was reliable, dependable, and able to provide for her and Astrid.

Besides, after making up her mind, Greta had wanted to move as quickly as possible to get Astrid to the healing air of the Rockies. Why waste time corresponding with other men when Phineas had been so eager and ready to help her?

Maybe she'd acted rashly. But what was done, was done.

She was on her way to marry Phineas. She would, in fact, wed him by the day's end.

Still, she blinked back tears. All of her savings was gone. If only Astrid knew how to obey better. If only the little girl had a real mother and father to raise her. Instead, she was stuck with a mere half sister who clearly didn't know how to keep her in line.

Greta sat back on her heels and watched the young girl with a mixture of frustration and helplessness.

"Don't be too hard on her." Mr. Steele bent next to Greta and retrieved a shiny leather shoe.

"She's a handful."

"She saved us from meeting our Maker today."

"She did?"

The gentleman removed his bowler and smoothed back his dark hair, which had hints of gray at his temples and streaking his long sideburns and mustache. "The gang leader liked her and showed mercy on us as a result."

Mercy? Each of the passengers had lost everything of value. But she supposed that was better than losing their lives.

"I have a son about Astrid's age." Mr. Steele replaced his hat, watching Astrid wistfully.

"You must be looking forward to seeing him when we arrive in Fairplay."

He focused on the child a moment longer, his expression filled with sadness. "Unfortunately, I won't be seeing him anytime soon. He lives in New York with his mother."

"I'm sorry." Greta didn't know what else to say.

Mr. Steele shook his head, as if by doing so he could shake away his morose thoughts. "Tell me again why you're moving to Fairplay."

Greta hadn't told him anything yet, since he hadn't asked. But she wouldn't be so impolite as to say so. Instead, she gave him the rehearsed line she'd spouted to everyone else who'd wanted to know. "My fiancé lives in Fairplay, and I'm traveling there to marry him."

"Your fiancé? Is that so?" Mr. Steele's eyes lit with interest. "May I ask who the lucky fellow is? I'm mayor and have gotten to know many men in the area."

All the misgivings she'd had since agreeing to marry Phineas soared. What if she'd made a mistake in coming west and agreeing to marry a stranger? What if he wasn't who he had claimed to be? What if he mistreated Astrid?

Just as quickly as the doubts assailed her, she tossed them aside. If Phineas wasn't the man he'd portrayed in his letters, then she'd have no obligation to stay with him. In fact, perhaps Mr. Steele would be able to advise her regarding the true nature of Phineas's character. Then if her fiancé had any glaring faults, she'd be well aware of them before arriving in Fairplay.

She cast a sideways glance at the other passengers, who were in the finishing stages of stowing their belongings and were thankfully heedless of the conversation. "I haven't actually met my intended."

Mr. Steele, in the process of picking up another shoe, paused.

"We've written to each other."

He straightened and gave her his full attention. "You wouldn't happen to be Phineas Hallock's mail-order bride, would you?"

Something in his tone made the skin at the back of her neck prickle with unease. "Yes, Mr. Hallock is my fiancé. Do you know him?"

The gentleman shook his head, his features creasing. "I knew him well. He was a good man."

Her heart began to patter fast and hard. "Knew?"

"I'm sorry, Miss Nilsson. Phineas Hallock is dead."

"The mine owner Phineas Hallock, originally from Connecticut?"

"Yes, he left for California last October. Said he was traveling there to purchase supplies for his new bride and that he planned to be back by late spring. When the thawing came and he didn't return, we all thought he was delayed. Until a body was discovered on Hoosier Pass."

"His body?"

"As far as we can tell, after so many months of being exposed to the elements . . ."

She stared at Mr. Steele, but somehow he faded from her vision. All she could see was the black-and-white photograph of Phineas.

In his last letter, he'd mentioned his trip to California and his excitement over picking out additional furniture and items for their home. He expressed his desire to have the newly built house well-stocked and ready for her arrival. She hadn't heard from him since and assumed he hadn't had the opportunity to send further correspondence. Even if he had, mail delivery via the Pony Express and stagecoach wasn't reliable. Letters were sometimes lost or stolen.

Besides, she'd been busy preparing for the trip, sewing clothes for Astrid and her, packing their belongings, and saying good-byes. She'd never in her wildest imagination believed Phineas Hallock hadn't written again because he was dead.

He was dead.

She swayed, her vision growing fuzzy.

Mr. Steele's grip on her elbow steadied her. "I'm truly sorry, Miss Nilsson."

With a deep breath, she tried to bring the world back into focus. The sunlight streaming through the aspen branches above splashed across her face as though to wake her from a nightmare.

The man she'd come west to marry was dead. Every penny of her savings had just been stolen. What would she do now? How could she, a lone woman with a sick child, survive in the wilderness knowing no one and having nothing?

Jody Hedlund is the bestselling author of over fifty novels and is the winner of numerous awards. Jody lives in Michigan with her husband, busy family, and five spoiled cats. She writes sweet historical romances with plenty of sizzle. Visit her at JodyHedlund.com

Sign Up for Jody's Newsletter

Keep up to date with Jody's latest news on book releases and events by signing up for her email list at the link below.

JodyHedlund.com

FOLLOW JODY ON SOCIAL MEDIA

Author Jody Hedlund   @JodyHedlund   @JodyHedlund

More from Jody Hedlund

When a St. Louis Irish matchmaker pairs a shy young woman who spends her time caring for immigrants with a wealthy, flirtatious man whose father wants him to settle down, they can't imagine a more opposite pairing. But as they work together to protect the neighborhood from an epidemic, all they know about love and sacrifice is tested.

Calling on the Matchmaker
A SHANAHAN MATCH #1

When midwife Catherine Remington is accused of a murder she didn't commit, she flees to Colorado to honor a patient's dying wish to deliver a newborn to his father. But what she doesn't bargain for is how easily she'll fall for the charming sheriff, or how quickly her past will catch up with her and put their love and lives in danger.

The Last Chance Cowboy
COLORADO COWBOYS #5

Ivy McQuaid has been saving up for a home of her own with the winnings from the cowhand competitions she sneaks into—but everything changes when a man from her past returns. Undercover Pinkerton agent Jericho Bliss is on the hunt for a war criminal, but when Ivy becomes involved in his dangerous life, his worst fears come true.

Falling for the Cowgirl
COLORADO COWBOYS #4

BETHANYHOUSE

 Bethany House Fiction

 @BethanyHouseFiction

 @Bethany_House

 @BethanyHouseFiction

 Free exclusive resources for your book group at BethanyHouseOpenBook.com

 Sign up for our fiction newsletter today at BethanyHouse.com